DEATH UNDER THE DELUGE

A SPIRIT ROAD MYSTERY

Also by C. M. Wendelboe

Bitter Wind Mysteries
Hunting the Five Point Killer
Hunting the Saturday Night Strangler
Hunting the VA Slayer
Hunting the Mail Order Murderer

Spirit Road Mysteries
Death Along the Spirit Road
Death Where the Bad Rocks Live
Death on the Greasy Grass
Death Etched in Stone
Death through Destiny's Door
Death Under the Deluge

Tucker Ashley Western Adventures
Backed to the Wall
Seeking Justice
When the Gold Dust Died in Deadwood
Fork in the False Trail

Nelson Lane Frontier Mysteries
The Marshal and the Moonshiner
The Marshal and the Sinister Still
The Marshal and the Mystical Mountain
The Marshal and the Fatal Foreclosure

~ Other Novels ~
The Man Who Hated Hickok
An Extralegal Affair

DEATH UNDER THE DELUGE

A SPIRIT ROAD MYSTERY

C. M. Wendelboe

Encircle Publications
Farmington, Maine, U.S.A.

Death Under the Deluge Copyright © 2023 C. M. Wendelboe

Paperback ISBN 13: 978-1-64599-480-0
Hardcover ISBN 13: 978-1-64599-482-4
E-book ISBN 13: 978-1-64599-481-7

Library of Congress Control Number: 2023944253

ALL RIGHTS RESERVED. In accordance with the U.S. Copyright Act of 1976, no part of this publication may be reproduced, distributed, or transmitted in any form or by any means, or stored in a database or retrieval system, without prior written permission of the publisher, Encircle Publications, Farmington, ME.

This book is a work of fiction. All names, characters, places and events are either products of the author's imagination or are used fictitiously.

Editor: Cynthia Brackett-Vincent
Cover design by Deirdre Wait

Cover photographs and author photograph by Heather M. Wendelboe

Published by:

Encircle Publications
P.O. Box 187
Farmington, ME 04938

info@encirclepub.com
http://encirclepub.com

To the Code Talkers of the various Indian Nations who served in perilous conditions during the Second World War to ensure we all maintained our freedom we often take for granted.

Chapter 1

Mel Peel brought the binoculars down from his eyes and handed them to Deputy Sam Christian. "I'm only a lonely diver hired by you guys now and again and who flunked anatomy class in school, but I suspect those five fingers are attached to a wrist down there somewhere."

Sam adjusted the focus as he glassed the middle of the river. He had flunked anatomy in school as well, but he knew enough to identify skeletal remains. In this case, a bony hand jutting out of the water, one finger pointing upwards as if invoking the god of the river himself. Or was it herself? He'd flunked local superstition class, too. "Think that floater got snagged on something under water?"

"Be my guess," Mel said as he stretched the wet suit over his legs. "Give me a hand."

Sam helped Mel into his wet suit, and he jumped up and down, seating it.

"'Member that last fisherman that popped up down by the old bridge pylons last summer?"

Sam 'membered. The victim had been in the water near a year, but his hand still didn't look like that one. "Kinda fleshed out I'd say."

"Maybe this guy was just a bit tastier to the fish and snapping turtles than the other guy," Mel said. "You sure you don't want to go down there with me?"

"I can't scuba dive."

"I have a snorkel."

"I'll pass," Sam said. "It's going to be bad enough hauling him up out of the river as it is."

"It is. Ready?" Mel grabbed his tank and face mask and flippers and walked to the small boat that would take them to that area locals know as American Island. An island Louis and Clark first discovered. An island that hadn't been seen for more than seventy years hidden under the waters of the Missouri River. An island that—even now—appeared to be giving up some secrets.

Chapter 2

"I can't believe you talked me into taking this beater," Willie With Horn said as he fidgeted in the seat, his long legs butting against the dash of the old '55 sedan. "We could have taken my truck instead of this… what the hell'd you call it again?"

"I call it a Mercury. They quit producing cars about the time you were in high school," Manny Tanno answered.

"I can see why. We had a hell of a time getting another tire in Ft. Thompson. Now we're stuck with a 'may-pop' on one wheel." He forced a laugh. "May-pop, hell. It's a *will*-pop—it's just a matter of time before it blows."

"Can I help it if it came with fourteen-inch tires that are just a little hard to come by nowadays?"

"The least you could have had is a spare to put on before we left," Willie said. "You'd think the FBI would pay more so you can afford something nice to drive. Don't you just beat all."

Manny patted the metal dash. "Now, how can it get nicer than this beauty?"

When he thought about Willie's argument, Manny could only conclude that he was right. When it came time for Manny and Willie to go on their road trip, Manny had suggested they take the old '55 Montclair he'd picked up at the Kool Deadwood Nites car auction last year. "Our *Nostalgia Vacation*," Manny had said. He'd never thought about making sure it had a spare tire. But when he ran over that piece of angle iron entering Crow Creek Reservation and trashed the tire, he found out real quick that the '55 had none. "We were lucky that wrecker driver had a tire to fit."

"That tire," Willie said, "isn't worth the ten bucks you shelled out for it. You saw where that dude got it from—he took it off a grain wagon crapped out beside his wrecking yard."

"Can I help it if it's hard to find fourteen-inch tires nowadays? The bottom line is we're in business once again. You had a nice visit with your aunt in Ft. Thompson while I was getting the tire mounted and now we're Mitchell-bound."

"That's if the tire holds."

Manny patted the cracked steering wheel. "Colette will make it."

"Colette?"

"Colette."

"Where'd you come up with that name?"

"I had a dog named Colette when I was a younger," Manny answered.

"And what, this... *thing* looks like your dog?"

Manny laughed. "Heavens no. Colette got waffled by a semi when she broke loose of her leash. No, this baby," he patted the dash again, "is *exactly* the shade of brown Colette was."

"Can we at least stop in Woonsocket and see if we can find a tire for this heap that's at least a decade newer and hasn't been patched a dozen times?"

"We can," Manny said, "but don't call Colette a heap." He massaged the steering lovingly. "She's got feelings."

* * * * *

They walked out of the Archedome at the Prehistoric Indian Village on the banks of Lake Mitchell, drying their hands with their bandanas. They had stopped at the archaeological site where students from Augustana College and from Exeter, England excavated some seventy earthen lodges once inhabited by mound dwellers. The dig and the museum was Manny's concession to Willie for visiting the Corn Palace. "Now wasn't that worth the stop?" Willie asked.

Manny had to admit it was worth the slight detour to see where indigenous people had lived a thousand years ago. Where they had butchered and processed huge numbers of buffalo on a ridge overlooking a creek that was flooded in the late 1920s to form Lake Mitchell. People weren't allowed to dig at the site unless they were students, but the public was allowed to clean and wash the artifacts in the laboratory. Willie had insisted they do just that, much of the dirt and mud finding its way on to Manny's trousers and shirt. "It was all right."

Willie stopped and looked down at Manny. "You *know* that was cool whether or not you're trying to come to grips with your Lakota roots."

"I am not coming to grips..." Manny trailed off, knowing Willie was right once again. Since being reassigned to the Rapid City Field Office from his instructor slot at Quantico some years ago, Manny had been the *de facto* FBI agent assigned to Pine Ridge and Rosebud Reservations, Standing Rock and Cheyenne River Reservations as well, whether Manny wanted it or not. And since coming back to his home, visions popped into his consciousness now and again, ghosts of Manny's roots nudging him toward acknowledgment of his Indian heritage.

"Come on," Willie prodded, "admit it was way cool."

Manny nodded. "That Boehnen Museum did have a nice diorama and I'd never seen a whole buffalo skeleton actually put together and displayed like that."

They headed out of the parking lot and drove the few miles south. When they pulled onto Main Street in Mitchell, the small town seemed... *happy,* if a town could have emotions. But then, Manny reasoned, a town can have emotions if Colette the car could have *feelings.*

"I'm still at a loss as to why you wanted to make this detour," Willie said, "just to see the Corn Palace."

Manny parked at the curb across from the Corn Palace. He ground the gear shift into *reverse* and shut the old car off. "Tell me, when was the last time you visited here?"

Willie shrugged. "Couple years ago when Doreen insisted we stop here on the way to that Vikings game in Minneapolis. Why?"

Manny turned in the seat and looked out the window at the *World's Only Corn Palace*. "Because the last time I saw it was when Unc took me in 1971. Dragged me along 'cause he heard Andy Griffith and Jerry Van Dyke were to perform and he just loved watching Andy on that TV show."

"At least you got some culture that year."

Manny chuckled. "I never saw the show. That was during Corn Palace week, and they always have an awesome midway set up on Main Street. Unc let me beg out of going with him to the show if I promised to stay on the midway."

"As I recall," Willie said while he extricated himself from the car, "Mitchell always had the best carnival rides so you must have had a blast."

Manny closed the car door after he got out and batted dirt off his trousers. "We didn't have money to spend on carnival rides."

"Then what did you do, stare at the kids who had lucky bucks to ride the Tilt-A-Whirl and the Ferris Wheel?"

"Unc gave me two dollars he'd been stashing away for our trip to spend how I wished, and I wasn't about to spend it on a two-minute ride."

"That would get you about four rides in 1971, I imagine," Willie said, looking up at the side of the Corn Palace.

"I said, I never wasted the money on rides."

"Then what did you do while your Uncle Marion was watching ol' Andy?"

"I played the games."

"Carnival games?" Willie said. "The kind that fleeces you out of your money and are next to impossible to win."

"Unless you have the time to study them while you're waiting for your uncle to leave the Corn Palace show." Manny looked down the street, with cars coming and going, recalling how the street had been blocked off for the midway that week. He could see in his mind's eye the carnival rides and the kids screaming in delight. He could see the people playing various games of chance. He could see their disappointment when they lost. And they almost certainly lost every time.

"Before I gave those vultures one dime as a kid, I sat back and watched the games. I saw how people were losing their money so easily. I saw the balloon pop was rigged with under-inflated balloons and dull darts, so I threw like I was aiming all the way home. I noticed the basketball toss had the baskets a little off like they were oval or something and picked the one basket that was most round and aimed for the rim." He snapped his fingers. "And just like that, I had a lovable little teddy bear I could give to Emily."

"Emily?"

Manny nodded. "She was my crush when I was in the fifth grade. But," Manny smiled wide, recalling the fleecing the carnival barker took at the time, "it was shooting the star on the paper with that BB gun that got me the *real* prize. A teddy bear near as big as me."

"Didn't know you were a shooter except for your yearly qual for the Bureau."

"Back then I was. Had to be. Unc would send me out with my .22 and tell me to bag supper, so I had to learn how to shoot a rifle if I wanted to bring home a rabbit or squirrel. But that carnival game is more than just knocking the star out with some BBs. It was rigged all right, and it took me a while watching the shooters losing their shirts until I figured out how to win."

Willie guffawed. "A ten-year-old beating that game? I don't

think so. As good a shot as I am, I've never shot the star out, much to Doreen's chagrin."

"Do this next time, my doubting friend—look at all the BB guns laid out on the counter and pick the one that has the least bend to the sights. The carnies purposely bend the front sights so they don't shoot to point of aim. Then use one dime and pick out a spot on the star. Figure on losing that round as all you're doing is finding out where that BB gun shoots to. Then use the same gun for the next round. And the next. Like I did."

"For one thing," Willie said, "it costs a buck for each play nowadays. And I've tried so many times to shoot the center of that star out—"

"But have you concentrated on shooting *around* the star?"

"How's that?"

"Don't shoot for the middle. Shoot the outside of the circle. Walk the BBs around now that you know where that particular gun shoots."

"That's how you beat it? That's how you won the big prize to give Emily?"

"That's how I *should* have won the big prize. Each time I won, I traded my small teddy bear in for a larger one. But when it came to the carnie giving me the giant Panda, he refused. 'You're a ringer,' he said. 'Get the hell outta here, kid.'"

"That's a shame you never got the big one—"

"But I did."

"How?"

"Unc," Manny answered. "About the time the carnie was giving me the bum's rush, Unc was walking the midway looking for me and he spotted me arguing with the guy." Manny laughed. "It didn't take long for Unc to… persuade the man to give me the panda, big as my Uncle Marion was."

"You said he was a pretty big man… big as me, you said a time or two."

"And he could be intimidating," Manny said. *Were his eyes damp because of the corn chaff coming off the Corn Palace or because he thought once again of his Uncle Marion who had raised him after his folks died?* "Once Unc threatened to lean over and rip the guy's nose ring off, he finally gave me the panda. I was so happy I didn't even mind sitting in that big ol' tent they had set up for their Bingo game. Unc would set there putting his kernels of corn on the Bingo card—"

"You mean he grabbed his dauber to mark the spots?"

Manny shook his head. "Back then, people used kernels of corn to cover the numbers being called. Remember, this was during *Corn Palace Week*. I'm here to tell you it was a real donnybrook when someone nudged another player and the kernels spilled all over the ground. Anyways, that was the last time I was here."

Manny took off his Stetson and craned his neck up as he looked at the building across the street that took up much of one block. "I recall those domes were wooden or something."

"They were trashed and replaced with those metal ones a few years ago," Willie said. "Doreen got the whole lowdown when we were here last time. The first Corn Palace was built in 1892 and they take all the corn down every year and replace it according to what the mural designers gave the workers. That's why it looks kinda ratty now—they're stripping murals and tacking corn back up."

Manny looked up at the enormous domes overlooking the street below and at the two murals that had already been put up that appeared to be a circus theme. As he stood in front of the grill across the side street across from a building, he marveled at this year's theme being *painted* with just split corn cobs of various natural colors and of the native grasses tacked to the side of the murals. Just like he had marveled at it as a boy. "Lordy, it must take a pile of corn to decorate a building that big?"

"Doreen read somewhere that a dozen different colors of corn are used and takes a month to strip and split the ears and nail them up for the murals," Willie said.

Manny felt lightheaded and he looked down at the ground. "Oscar Howe... that name sticks in my mind for some reason."

"He used to design the murals," Willie said. "I remember him when I was a kid on Crow Creek before we moved to Pine Ridge. His paintings were displayed all over the rez."

Manny leaned against the fender of the car, his vision coming to him as if he were looking through a fishbowl and he pointed to a mural. "Oscar Howe designed that one—"

"No, he hasn't designed any since about the time you and your uncle were here. Dakota Wesleyan students create them now. Looks like they're tacking up some scene," Willie said, "of a guy hunting pheasants—"

"No... that one," Manny pointed. "That one that shows an Indian squatting beside a flowing river—"

"I don't know what you're looking at," Willie said, "but there's no mural like that up there."

Manny felt his legs buckle and he put his head between his legs for a moment, his hands resting on shaky knees.

For just a moment.

When he looked back up at the side of the building, Oscar Howe's mural was still there. Taunting him, when Manny heard the sound of water approaching. Louder than anything he'd ever heard. He clamped his hands over his ears and slumped to his knees, screams overriding the sounds of the deluge. "Get... get out of there!" he screamed. "Run!" and the last thing he saw was the mural undulating as if alive.

As if it were telling him something that he could not decipher.

Chapter 3

Willie's massive arm encircled Manny's waist, holding him up, ushering him through the crowd that had stopped and watched them like they were contestants in a three-legged race. The chime above the door of the Corner Stone Coffee House across the street dinged as they entered, and a girl half Willie's age walked around the counter. "He don't look so hot, mister. Maybe you ought to take him to the ER."

"He'll be fine," Willie said, "soon's he gets some coffee in him. He just gets a little lightheaded now and again. Can you bring two cups of the strongest you got?"

The girl rubbed her bare leg sticking through her fashionably-tattered jeans and nodded. "Just make sure he don't puke on the floor 'cause I'm the one who cleans it up."

Willie helped Manny to a corner booth away from others sitting and staring and eased him down.

"Don't take me to the ER—"

"I'm not," Willie answered. "I suspect the doctor you need ain't one you'll find at any hospital."

Manny took deep, calming breaths while he rubbed his forehead. "I suspect you'd be right."

"Another vision?"

Manny nodded. One of his unwelcomed visions had engulfed him just now, one of many visions he'd had ever since returning to work the reservations five years ago. And although visions were a private thing that he usually told only to brother Reuben, Willie was a *Wicasa Wakan*, a sacred man, in training and would keep Manny's vision to himself. "Oscar Howe."

"What about him?" Willie asked.

"He designed that mural."

"What mural?"

"That one showing… a lake. Maybe a river."

"There is no mural like that up the side of the Corn Palace—"

"There was in 1952. I'm sure of it." The waitress set two cups on the table. "Indian motif that year," the waitress said. "I heard you guys talking."

"No offense," Willie said, "but you're just a bit young to know that."

"Mister," she said, "when all you got to do all day at work is stare at that Corn Palace, you get to learn things about it. Call it me not going crazy looking at it every day."

Manny grabbed a napkin from the table dispenser and wiped sweat from his forehead. "I told you I saw some guy. Maybe an Indian by a river up there."

The waitress turned and said over her shoulder, "and Oscar Howe did design it. They have photos of past murals inside."

Willie sipped his coffee and stared out the window at the side of the Corn Palace. "If they have murals of past years, maybe the one you saw in your vision will be up there on the wall."

Manny downed half his cup of coffee and slid out of the booth. "Then let's get across the street and look at them."

"Sure you're up to it?"

"Nobody else is gonna see what I just saw."

Manny stood on wobbly legs with Willie close beside him. They walked out of the coffee shop and stood on the sidewalk. Manny looked up at the murals, many picked over by the birds feeding on the corn, awaiting complete dismantling in preparation for this year's theme to be depicted with various colors of corn. *The world's biggest bird feeder*, the locals referred to it. "It was right there," Manny said and pointed to the side of the Corn Palace.

"I'm sure in your mind it was," Willie said.

"There were two like… giant black-and-white barber poles on either side of the entrance to the building going all the way up. Smaller ones right over the marquis. They weren't there when Unc brought me here as a kid."

"And they're not there now," Willie said and started across the street. "Let's see if we can find a 1952 mural."

Cars stopped to let them cross and they entered the building. Photos of murals past lined the walls, and they started walking the halls when a man pushing a wide broom stopped them. "You fellers look lost."

Manny looked around. "I'm trying to find murals from 1952," Manny said.

"I know just where they are," he said and offered his hand. "Denny Geidel."

Willie gave the man a second look and shook hands. "You sure you know—"

"Been working here for years. Lived in Mitchell most my life, so I figure I know something of the Corn Palace." Denny leaned his broom against the wall. "Follow me."

Willie and Manny followed him down the hallway. Each time they passed a photograph of a mural from previous years, Denny began with a mini-history lesson about the theme that particular year. He explained the prominent features that the artist wanted depicted in corn.

When they had walked down one long hall and started into another Denny stopped in front of photograph. *1952* had been spelled out in corn, large white and black pillars like barber poles guarding the entrance to the building. Just like Manny remembered. "Take as long as you like," Denny said and headed back the way they came. "I'm going to finish up for the day and head out to the bowling alley."

Manny stood staring at the mural for long moments before Willie asked, "Is that what you saw?"

"It... might be. Already things are fading. But what I vaguely remember is a lost soul crying out for my help." He rubbed his temples as he started at the photograph. "I need to get right in the head."

"What you need is to sweat," Willie said, "and have help with your vision. That, and a meal at some place other than Micky D's."

* * * * *

Manny pushed his plate away and did the obligatory tummy pat. "I don't think I can eat another bite."

Willie laughed and eyed what meat was left on Manny's plate. "You ate more 'n me so it must have been good."

"Even *bad* chislic is *good* chislic," Manny said. "You should have ordered a plate."

Willie eyed his chef's salad and said, "Doreen's got me on a diet. She insists us *Injuns* are prone to diabetes about my age and wanted to nip it in the bud." He nodded at Manny's plate. "The last thing I needed was to stuff myself with deep fried mutton."

"I am sure I'll catch heck with Clara when I get home. But it was... patriotic for me to order it."

"Patriotic how?"

"Ordering this," Manny nudged a piece of *chislic* with his fork, "is practically the South Dakota state food you won't get it anywhere else." Manny had first tasted the dish when he'd went to live with his Uncle Marion after Manny's folks had died in a car wreck in '66. One of the first things Unc whipped up for supper was deep fried chislic made from deer meat instead of lamb, dusted ever lightly with garlic.

The waitress came to the table with refills of iced tea, but Manny waved his away. "I think," he told Willie, picking his words carefully, "that this vision was the most realistic I have ever had." He leaned forward and lowered his voice. "Even now I know that it was frightening, even if I can't recall much about it."

Willie looked around as if Doreen were there monitoring his meal and grabbed a toothpick before jabbing into a cube of chislic left on Manny's plate. Willie put it in his mouth, closed his eyes and hummed softly. "Damn, that's good."

Manny slid his plate toward Willie, but he set it aside. "This better be my only cheating on my diet or Doreen will know." He wiped his mouth before saying, "You were rambling on about some dude hanging around a river or a lake. You remember that?"

Manny rubbed his forehead, a rising headache making his face throb. "Vaguely. It was much like what I thought I felt for the briefest of moments when we crossed the Missouri River on the Crow Creek Reservation."

"Well, it appears as if it's gone now," Willie said before nodding to the plates. "The Bureau getting this?"

Manny guffawed. "Buying their agents meals while they're on vacation is not part of the benefits package. But if you grab this, I'll spring for the motel room."

Chapter 4

Manny hung up the motel phone as he sat on the edge of the bed shaking his head.

"I've seen that shake before," Willie said while he put on his socks, "and it's usually not good."

"My vacation's been cut short."

Willie groaned. "Not again."

"'Fraid so." Manny recalled a few years back when he and Willie had been on vacation on the Crow Agency in Montana. They had enjoyed the reenactment of the Little Big Horn battle when the Billings regional office called about a death on the Crow Reservation, FBI jurisdiction. As the *de facto* reservation agent, Manny had his vacation cut short then, too.

Willie sat on the edge of the bed and grabbed his mule ears to tug on his cowboy boots. "Let's hear it."

"How does the Bureau even know where I am—"

"You always said they know most everything," Willie said. "Now tell me what they want you to do."

"Some kids fishing the Missouri River saw an arm that happened to be attached to the rest of a body sticking up out of the water. The locals might need some assistance with the investigation."

Willie wrestled his other boot on and stood, stomping the floor to seat his feet. "Last I knew, drownings were usually accidental. Besides, it's not a federal issue—it's one for the local law enforcement."

"That's why I said they *might* need help. Unless the body drifted from somewhere up stream, then it's federal."

"I don't understand—"

"The victim appears to have popped up at Chamberlain, but it's not known if he drowned a few miles north on the reservation side and floated down or not. If the victim drowned on the reservation part of the river, it would be in the Bureau's bailiwick. And mine unfortunately."

"I just don't understand how a drowning victim—regardless of where he went into the river—is federal jurisdiction," Willie said. "Chamberlain gets two or three fishermen drownings every year. When they open the dam, it creates powerful undercurrents. Men in small boats in the wrong area get sucked under. It's accidental—"

"Unless the victim had an obvious hole in his chest. Which, it sounds like is just what the victim has."

Willie stuffed his dirty clothes into a pillowcase he'd brought for the trip and stood waiting for Manny to finish packing. "You going to need me?"

"If I did, the Bureau couldn't pay you."

Manny zipped his suitcase shut and patted Willie on the back. "I know you'd help even without pay—wouldn't be the first time. No, this seems pretty straightforward. Floaters usually don't make it that far south of the reservation without getting snagged on something on the riverbank. Or a submerged tree. My guess is I'll be home within a few days."

"Then I might as well head back to the rez," Willie said. "Doreen's due to come back from her mother's with the baby tomorrow anyway."

"You need the Mercury?"

"How would you get home?" Willie asked.

Manny shrugged. "Hop a puddle jumper to Rapid City."

"That was my plan," Willie said, "except I'm not going to foot the bill for an expensive plane ticket."

"I'm not following you."

"I'll rent a plane at the airport here and fly my big butt to Rapid. Catch a ride to Pine Ridge from there."

Manny took a final look around the room before heading out the door to checkout. "I thought the FAA took your pilot's license after that last wreck?"

"The FAA's a federal agency."

"Your point?"

"You're not going to rat me off to another federal agency if I did something… illegal?"

"Not unless you plan on flying with explosives in your pocket. Why, what did you do?"

"Nothing," Willie said, "yet. I still have my license to show to rent a plane."

"Like I said, I thought the FAA took it."

"They asked for it," Willie said. "But I told them it was in my wallet when I accidentally dropped it into Oglala Lake one day when I was fishing."

"So you lied to them?"

Willie shrugged. "Call it a little red lie. All I need is a ride to the Mitchell airport."

"I'm not so sure I want to be a part of this," Manny said, then added, "just don't fly as crappy as I drive."

* * * * *

Manny left the rest area on Interstate 90 and started down the steep hill towards the Missouri. The fifty-foot-high stainless metal statute of a Lakota woman holding a star quilt in the bright morning light overlooked the rest area above the Missouri River. *Dignity* had been erected there twelve years ago, and each time Manny stopped at the rest area he stood in awe at the sculpture. A vision had overcome him when he was here last time. Not one of his frightening visions but a vision of unity, where the past injustices to Indians were being addressed by the current population of the state. Manny prayed now, as he had then, that the rift would heal in his lifetime.

He got back on the interstate and took the off ramp that passed by the South Dakota Hall of Fame Museum where stories of heroes of the state were told. Manny made a mental note to stop by this time after he finished with the investigation into the drowning victim.

Manny followed the instruction of his Garmin navigator, though 'she' often gave Manny confusing and contradictory directions. *Marge*, as Manny dubbed her, had that soothing voice that caused stirrings within him just listening to her talk. He often wondered if the thing would make any more sense if it had a man's voice, but then, the directions would be less pleasant to listen to and he might end up in places where he didn't want to be.

He turned onto a side street and pulled into the Sheriff's Office and jail, a two story beige-bricked structure with a side garage. He parked beside a Dodge truck bristling with antennas and emergency lights and a shotgun secured to a dash rack. Even before he climbed out of his car, a stout young deputy burst from the building and approached Manny. Standing several inches taller and forty pounds heavier than Manny, he *swaggered* up to the car and said, "Move that heap. I need the space for an FBI agent who's coming this morning."

"Kind of stereotyping, aren't you?"

"What's that?" the deputy asked.

"You're assuming I am not said FBI agent and that this car is one a federal officer wouldn't be caught dead driving."

The deputy put his hands on his duty belt and eyed Manny.

"You a wise ass or something?"

"Or something." Manny dug his badge and ID wallet out of his pocket. He flipped it open and showed it to the deputy, whose face instantly turned red. He stepped back and stammered, "didn't mean… didn't mean anything by it. I just thought—"

"You just thought an FBI agent might be driving something a bit newer and fancier and you weren't expecting an Indian to show up with FBI credentials?"

"Well," the deputy said, "you gotta admit it is a beater."

"It is," Manny said, "but it drives like a champ."

"Besides, I never seen an Indian FBI agent before…" he snapped his fingers. "You're that feller from Rapid who works all the reservation cases."

"Not by choice," Manny said and pocketed his wallet.

"Start over?" The deputy asked.

"I'd like that." Manny introduced himself.

The deputy offered his hand. "Sam Christian." Standing several inches taller than Manny, he filled out in his chest and shoulders. The young officer looked as if he would be capable in a bar fight or a domestic call, which were their normal calls here in Brule County. *Let's see how you handle a drowning and possible homicide.*

"Sam," Manny said, "let's get right down to it—tell me about your floater."

"Maybe it'd be better to show you." He checked his watch. "The Medical Examiner from Sioux Falls pulled in an hour ago and wanted to start the autopsy at noon so's he could get home before dark. Dude's a tad on the old side and doesn't want to drive at night if he can help it."

"Then I got just enough time to stop at Micky D's and grab a quick bite. Want to come?"

Sam shook his head. "With an autopsy following lunch? Not on your life."

"Suit yourself," Manny said as he climbed back into his car. "Where's the autopsy to be performed?"

"Hickey Funeral Chapel on Main Street. Can't miss it."

"Not with Marge telling me where to go."

"Marge?"

"My navigator. See ya there."

Chapter 5

All the while inside McDonald's, Manny watched people stopping to look at the old Mercury in the parking lot in all her unrestored glory before coming inside the café. Manny was sure it was because she appeared as if the tow truck had just dropped her off at McDonald's doorstep. When Manny bought the car, he made a decision not to restore it, but to just make it reliable. So he had turned his car over to Reuben, who had gone through it carefully making sure it was as dependable as a new vehicle. A couple coats of clear coat paint to enshrine the patina and Manny had been happy with it since.

When he left Micky D's, people rubber-necked staring at the Indian driving the pathetic-looking old sedan, and Manny was certain all those old stereotypes were working overtime. He cringed as Marge instructed him where to go and he pulled into Hickey's parking lot a block south.

Manny tripped a soothing chime above the door and entered to funeral music sounding like other funeral music he'd heard as if death were a pleasant thing. A small man emerged from somewhere behind a curtain and stopped, wringing his hand, a mournful look on his thin face. "We usually show our… products by appointment only, but I can make an exception in your case, sir."

"By products you mean—"

"Yes." He lowered his voice and said, "caskets. We have an excellent selection."

"When the time is closer," Manny said, "I'll keep you in mind."

"When the time is closer?"

Manny looked around the office and said to the man, "Yes. I am not ready to keel over just yet, and none of my loved ones are either."

"Then why—"

"I am here to witness an autopsy."

The man's demeanor faded into pure business mode when he said, "Oh, the floater that popped up in the river. Doctor Death is just about done now. Follow me."

Manny followed the man through a door into an embalming room. A body—if one could call it that with only a few bones encased in what was left of clothing—lay on a porcelain table. Drainage tubes ran into a floor drain beside a row of chemicals. *Forever juice.* Sam stood looking over the shoulder of a large man, his long gray ponytail tucked out of the way by a bone hair clasp. "Agent Tanno, I presume," the pathologist said without looking up from the corpse resting on the table. "Grab a beer from the fridge if you're needing one."

"I'll pass." Manny stepped around Sam and Doctor Darden and peered down at the corpse. Little more than a skeleton with few shards of clothing and little flesh remaining, the victim was missing the lower jaw and some long bones. The doctor told his scribe standing next to him, "Note this strand of rope was attached to his wrist and we'll bag him."

Doctor Darden stepped back and took off his examination gloves, placing them into a body bag that would soon contain the victim, all thirty pounds that was left of him.

Darden walked to the fridge and grabbed a beer, once again offering Manny and Sam one. "I don't drink," Manny said, "and I'm sure Deputy Christian here is on-duty."

"I am," Sam said, eying the beer, "but let me tell you, even some nasty stuff like that *Blatz* would taste good about now."

"Nasty?" Doctor Darden popped the top and took a long pull before saying, "When I was the ME in Milwaukee not long out of med school everyone drank *Blatz*. It was about all you could buy there, and I developed a… taste for it." He downed the beer and opened the fridge for another one. He sat on a stool and looked up at Manny. Though the doctor's face was as wrinkled as most drowning victims' skin, his blue eyes sparkled with mischief. "So now, you want to know about this floater?"

Manny sat on a stool opposite him and grabbed his pocket notebook. Sam stood poised with pen and pad ready for some insightful revelation. "While I was examining this man—for the skeleton barely contained inside this tattered clothing is a *man*—I thought we three could have a real CSI moment here." He swiveled around on the stool and lobbed the empty can into the trash. He watched his scribe grab a bag to hold the remains before turning back to face Manny and Sam. "But I know very little about this guy."

"Anything would help," Sam said, "such as where do you think he drowned? The reservation maybe?"

Doctor Darden smirked. "You'd like that, then you could turn the whole thing over to this poor schmuck working for the FBI. But it's not that simple. For starters, all I can speculate is what might have happened to him."

"We're all ears and notebooks, doc," Manny-the-*schmuck* said.

Doctor Darden stood and paced the table where his assistant prepped the body for transport to the doctor's morgue. "I'm calling this John Doe John Spitz—kind of like Mark Spitz except this one didn't know how to swim 'cause he's been in the water for years."

"How many years would you think?" Sam asked.

Doctor Darden shrugged. "I would speculate nigh onto seventy years."

"Seventy?" Manny clarified. "You're saying this man has been under water for seventy years?"

"That's my professional opinion. Want a beer?"

Sam and Manny declined once again, and Darden sat back down with another can.

"Just what the hell caused him to be in the river that long?" Sam asked.

"Didn't you say some kids fishing spotted him?"

Sam nodded. "We've had a drought the last few years. The Corps of Engineers have struggled to keep the river as high as it is, but water's been down. The kids saw a hand sticking out of the river and reported it to the police who passed it to the Sheriff's Office. I grabbed the diver we usually use to look for floaters and we motored out to the middle of the Missouri to retrieve this victim. Seems like he had rope around his wrists that somehow got snagged on an old cabin down there."

Doctor Darden polished off another beer and sat looking at the fridge. He burped and said, "All right then. I'm thinking he drowned—"

"But he has a hole in his brisket," Sam said. "We spotted that right off, and you think he's a drowning victim and not a victim of homicide?"

"I'm getting to that," Doctor Death said, his speech slurring slightly. "The hole in his chest would have caused a great deal of… discomfort, no doubt, but it wouldn't have been fatal. Doesn't appear by the trajectory it did anything but go through-and-through ol' John Spitz here. It would have taken him a while to die, and I'm thinking the water got him first."

"Doctor," Manny interrupted, "why do you think he's been under that long?"

"Usually when a body drowns, they sink. Then they are under for two or three days unless people dragging the water find him. Like that drowning we had last month," Darden said to Sam, "that fisherman from Sioux City. A classic drowning."

"We dragged the river for two days," Sam said, "and never did hook into him."

"They tend to sink," Darden continued. "Decomposition starts immediately and within a few days gas causes the body to bloat and eventually pop goes the floater as they rise to the surface. They bob around until someone spots them, like those goofy little plastic chicks at carnivals." The pathologist said. "I just loved those things when I was a younger. Anyways, the body pops up then unless they've gotten snagged under water. I know there are a lot of old buried trees in the Missouri and parts of the old concrete bridge that's still down there that could have snagged him. And that cabin that Sam's diver saw that's still submerged."

"With the water flowing whenever the Corps opens the dam up by Ft. Thompson he would have popped up," Sam said, "if it hadn't been for that piece of hemp around his waist anchoring him to what's left of one of the old cabins."

"I was wondering what the rope was doing on the John Spitz's wrist," Doctor Darden said. "That would explain why he's been in the water so long and why he hadn't went pop goes the weasel after a few days like most drownings."

"Tell me about the cabin where you and your diver recovered the body," Manny said to the deputy.

"The sheriff and me figure it was one of the cabins on American Island—"

"The island Lewis and Clark wrote about?" Manny asked.

Sam nodded. "There used to be cabins and an amusement park and things to do before the Corps put it under water back in the fifties. That's when they flooded the area to make Lake Francis Case."

Manny jotted what he needed to research later before asking the doctor, "You seem pretty sure that the victim's been under water for seventy years. I still don't know why you think he's been in the water that long?"

Darden motioned for Manny to follow him across the room to another table where shards of clothing were laid out beside plastic and paper bags waiting to be labeled. "What do you see, Agent Tanno?"

Manny walked around the table as he looked at a pile of rags. "Looks like the victim was wearing denims. What's left of them."

"Good." Darden popped the top of another *Blatz*. "Did you notice the back pocket rivets are still there."

"Meaning?"

"Meaning that Levi Strauss and Company removed the rivets from their jeans in the 1950s."

"He could have just worn old denims," Sam said.

"I thought about that," Darden said, using the edge of the table for support.

About one more Blatz, Manny thought, *and you'll be too Blatzed to even stand, let alone drive back home.*

Darden motioned to the shredded and rotted piece of denim. "This victim rolled the cuffs of his jeans up."

"Like they did in the fifties," Manny said. "Good eye. Now all we gotta do is figure out who this feller is and start there."

Darden sloshed the last of his beer around in the can before polishing it off. "Already know that."

"What," Sam said, "did you tap into some whiz bang DNA data base already?"

Darden smiled and crushed the can before lobbing it towards the trash can. It bounced off the rim and landed on the floor, but he made no move to grab it. "I wish. No, I just know this man was Robert Bear Paw."

Sam sucked in a quick gasp of air.

"Know him?" Manny asked.

"I knew a Robbie Bear Paw… can't be the same guy though. The Robbie Bear Paw I knew was a fascinating guy. Used to come to the schools when I was a kid and talk about his experiences as a Lakota Code Talker during World War Two. He hasn't been here in Chamberlain for years." He turned to Doctor Darden. "But this can't be the same man I knew growing up, not if he's been swimming with the walleyes that long."

"I could be off on my estimation," the pathologist said. "River drownings aren't exact, especially since victims are usually snacked on by fish. Turtles. You get the picture."

"How the hell did you figure out this was Robbie Bear Paw?" Sam asked.

Doctor Death tapped the side of his head. "I'm just smart. And I can read."

He opened a manila evidence envelope and withdrew a set of military dog tags. The small chain threaded through the hole in the tags still glistened in the light of the embalming room. Doctor Darden laid them and the chain carefully on the table and said, "they're stainless steel. The only reason they haven't rusted away all this time."

"Can I?" Manny asked.

"Go ahead," Darden answered. "They're about the only thing on the victim that's not been totally destroyed by the river."

Manny donned examination gloves and reading glasses while he held the dog tags to the light. *Robert Bear Paw* was stamped, along with his serial number and blood type *O* along with a *T* to indicate he'd had his tetanus shot. Manny handed the tags to Sam who looked at them for a brief moment before slipping them back into the evidence envelope.

"The letters and numbers are *debossed.*" Doctor Darden hiccupped. "Sunken *in* as it were into the metal. The military started using an *embossing* machine in the 60s which caused the letters to be *raised*, so we know they date from before that time."

"You seem to know a lot about dog tags," Sam said.

"In my previous life I was career Army and saw a lot of soldiers come across my table, sorry to say. Everyone had a set of dog tags of some sort."

Sam took out a can of *Copenhagen* from his back pocket and stuffed a pinch of the tobacco into his lower lip. He offered Manny and the doctor some but they both waved it away. "We didn't see the tags when we were taking him out of the river."

"You wouldn't have," Darden said. "The tags had that long chain attached to the victim's neck and over time—with the water flowing over him and the decaying and the fish snacking on him—ol' Robert here had the dog tags down into what was left of his chest cavity. You didn't see it because the collar of his shirt—what was left of it—covered the chain."

Sam looked down at the pile of rags and over at the disarticulated skeleton missing one arm and both legs, probably resting downriver in the Missouri someplace. "A shame, too, if it had been him. He was a nice guy."

"We're pretty sure this is not the Robbie Bear Paw who used to come to your school, but to tickle my curiosity, tell me about him," Manny asked.

"Not much to tell," Sam said. "He would come to the school and give us kids talks about his days as a Lakota Code Talker. Sure hope it's not him slabbed up over there," Sam nodded to the autopsy table set with the bones laid out.

"How old are you, Sam?"

"Turned thirty-three on April Fool's Day this year. Why?"

"And when did Robbie come to your school to give his presentations?"

Sam thought for a moment as he counted on his hands. "I'm thinking the last time was when I was twelve, maybe."

"We're talking 2000-ish," Manny said." Manny walked around the corpse once more, trying to figure out how a man rotting in the river since the nineteen fifties wound up giving talks to children years later. "We have a live Robbie Bear Paw talking to your elementary class long after this man's been murdered."

"Whoa!" Darden said as he backed up and put his hands up as if in surrender. "I never positively said anything about murder."

"No?" Manny asked, motioning to the skeleton. "You said yourself that hole in his sternum was probably from a gunshot."

"I said *probably*." Darden blurted out, then added, "you're just making extra work for me?"

More work, indeed, Manny thought. If the victim was a drowning and not a homicide, the good doctor could motor back to Sioux Falls and be tipping more *Blatz* just in time to catch the *Keloland Evening News*. "I know the water has smoothed the edges of the entry wound," Manny said, "but it looks like a gunshot to me, too."

"You *might* be right. I'll have to look more at the sternum when I get him back to the cooler."

"Then there's the problem of the rope." Manny faced Sam. "You said that piece of rope still held him to what was left of an old cabin, did you not?"

"The water deteriorated most of the rope, I'm thinking, " Sam said. "But his wrist still had thin tendrils around it attached to the corner of the cabin when we looked at it in the water like it had got stuck there."

Manny picked up the piece of rope. He tugged on it lightly, yet it didn't come apart. "How positive are you that this body has been in the water for that many years?"

Darden shrugged. "Nothing is positive when you're talking water deaths. I could be off by as much as twenty years. Maybe thirty years. But those dog tags are that old."

Manny bent to the bones, the odor long lost to the mighty Missouri. "How big a man was Robbie?"

"Not big," Sam said. "Five-and-a-half feet perhaps."

"Doctor Darden," Manny said, "how tall would this man have been in life?"

Darden burped again and Manny moved up wind. "Very

difficult to say without the long bones to measure. I can't make even an educated guess."

"But I bet in your travels you've met pathologists who are subject matter experts in determining size from other than the long bones," Manny said. "And in that wager, I bet you could contact them—"

"All right," Doctor Darden said. "All right. It looks like I'll have to lay over here in Chamberlain for the night and dig into my contacts list."

Manny smiled. "That is all I can ask, doctor."

Chapter 6

"That was a good idea picking up that order of rocky mountain oysters," Manny said as he propped his feet up on an open desk drawer in the Sheriff's Office. "Figured take-out would be greasy by the time you brought it here, but these aren't." Manny did not feel like talking with anyone after the autopsy, and wanted just to bounce things off Sam. Besides, autopsies often made him hungry, and he'd suggested Sam call someplace for an order of *oysters*.

"The Silver Dollar Bar has the best bull nuts in the county." Sam leaned back in his chair, a satisfied look on his face as he picked his teeth with his pocketknife. "What's the chance that Doctor Death is going to be able to give us a general description of the victim?"

"I would bet pretty good," Manny said. "I suspect the good doctor had gotten a bit lazy in his old age—passing off things like drownings when the victim could have died of something violent. I bet Doctor Darden has colleagues he can call to send the victim's measurements to so they can determine the victim's height and age."

Sam stood and dug his can of snuff from his back pocket as he walked to a picture hanging on the wall. He tapped it and said, "that picture of Robbie was taken at the 4th of July parade here in Chamberlain that year, so you can get an idea how short he was. Just glad it wasn't him we pulled out of the water."

Manny stood and donned his reading glasses as he looked at the row of photos chronically showcasing each year of the town's annual parade. The photo showed a float pulled by a shiny Ford truck, both decorated in red, white, and blue crepe paper. Two men rode the float but only one waved and smiled at the crowd, the other one scowling at the photographer. *Fourth of July 1952* was noted on the picture.

"The sheriff says Robbie was always given center stage on the float, him being a Lakota Code Talker and all."

Manny stepped to one side and looked closer. "Which one's Robbie, the happy guy or the guy who looks like he had just sucked on a lemon."

"That grouchy-looking little guy is Robbie, though he was always so happy to talk with us kids."

"You certain?"

"I'm not that old that I'd forget what he looked like."

"Then if that's Robbie Bear Paw," Manny said, "that proves he can't be the floater those kids came across. Not if Doctor Darden is correct that the victim was in the water for seventy years."

"Those were my thoughts" Sam said. "We got ourselves a real conundrum here."

"What's this *we*, white man? By the looks of it, the victim was still found in your jurisdiction."

Sam exaggerated a frown. "You said yourself he could have floated down from the reservation part of the river. And your office did assign you to help as I recall."

"I can't say as I can be *any* help. This whole mess doesn't add up—Robbie's dog tags around the victim's neck who drowned probably in the fifties—or at least thirty or forty years ago. Like the good doctor said, water deaths are hard to age. All I can wonder is that—whoever this floater is, and it's not Robbie Bear Paw—somehow got hold of his dog tags."

Sam grabbed a Perrier from a small fridge beside his desk

and unscrewed the top to wash the nuts down. "What if Doctor Death is right—that he's way off on his estimation about the length of time the corpse has been in the water?"

"Still helps us little until we ID the victim. If we found anyone who hung around with Robbie. Any idea who the other feller riding the float is?"

"None. I asked the sheriff one time and he said he was just some friend of Robbie's who stopped in Ft. Thompson on Crow Creek Reservation where Robbie visited now and again and hung out here for a few days before moving on."

"Does the Sheriff's Office have any record on Robbie?"

Sam brushed Copenhagen off onto his jeans and turned to an olive drab filing cabinet. He flipped through files and came away with a faded-manila envelope which he opened on the desk. "The last contact we had was about the time I was in the Army. Before I was even hired at Brule County. A deputy was assigned to act as an official witness when Robbie turned the business over to his daughter," he turned the faded form to the light, "in nineteen-seventy-two."

"What business?"

"Bear Paw Trucking. Antionette—Annie we call her—took over the business and runs it. Tough lady, too. Not easy ramrodding a trucking business with a bunch of Neanderthals behind the wheels."

"Ever see Robbie since you were discharged?"

Sam shook his head. "Man left town by the time I mustered out and moved back here."

"Up to paying Annie a visit tomorrow?"

"If you want to go in the afternoon," Sam said. "The morning I'm tied up with a funeral escort to Pukwana cemetery."

"I'll see what time I'm up and around," Manny said. "Or I should say, I'll see what time these bull nuts settle in my gullet enough so I can get some work done."

DEATH UNDER THE DELUGE

* * * * *

Manny checked his text message and found out he'd been booked at a Best Western Motel along old highway 16 in Chamberlain and drove the few blocks from the courthouse to the motel. As he was filling out the motel's registration form, the clerk seemed to look around Manny with his one roving eye while he nodded to Manny's car. "We don't cotton to no junkers sitting in our lot," the clerk said, holding a cigarillo between his yellowed fingers. "Gives the place a bad name."

"With luck, I won't be here long enough to cast aspersions on your little *Shangri La*," Manny said.

He lugged his suitcase up to the second floor and entered his room that he'd have here until the investigation was completed. Which he prayed would be soon. Tomorrow wouldn't be too soon. He had packed for an extended vacation with Willie, intending to hit pools and hot tubs and immerse himself in the whole touristy thing while on their road trip. Manny had packed shorts and Hawaiian shirts and all manner of clothes that a sightseer would wear. What he hadn't packed was a decent set of clothing befitting an FBI agent doing an investigation. He made a mental note to find a clothier here in town if for some un-Godly reason the investigation took longer than a couple days.

After he unpacked, he opened his laptop and logged into the motel WiFi. He sent a message to FBI records in Quantico, giving what information he had read on the dog tags and asking for any information available before checking his watch. It was two hours later back on the east coast and the request would not even be read until morning. But that was alright—he had swim trunks and the motel had a pool and damned if he wasn't going to take at least one dip on this little trip.

When Manny walked through the doors of the pool building, two ladies only slightly smaller than Willie splashed around displacing as much water as a small boat, while a family looked up from lounging on the side of the pool. Six Indian kids gathered around the mother and dad, all screaming at one another. All *Eastern Indian*, and the man glared up at Manny as if he were an intruder. *I think this Indian was here in this country before you, Indian*, Manny thought. He flip-flopped his way to the far side of the pool where he dropped into a lounge chair, the stares of the man still on him.

"Don't pay Gandira no nevermind." A woman in her thirties, perhaps early forties, popped her head up from the water and ran her fingers through her wet hair as she used the ladder to step out of the pool. Manny turned his eyes away from her fit body, not wanting images of Clara to dance in his head if he stared at the lady. She dropped into a lounge chair next to Manny and began drying herself with a beach towel with images of the Beatles on it. "Emily Mockingbird," she said as she thrust out her hand. "Like I said, pay him no mind—that blowhard is pushing his weight around like he already owns the place."

"You know him, then?" Manny asked after he'd introduced himself.

She stared back at the man as she lit a cigarette and blew smoke his direction. "That, Manny, is the next owner of the Best Western if negotiations pan out for him. He's been pressuring the owner to sell, and that horses' patoot over there swore he'd fire me the day he takes possession of the property. I just wish he'd go back to New Jersey where he came from."

"Fire you… I don't understand—"

"I'm the night clerk here and believe me that *Indian* looks down on *us* Indians. But for now, he has no say in me using the pool as he don't own it yet. It's one of the perks of working here." Emily shook her head and water dripped onto Manny.

"You live here at the motel?"

"The apartment next to the office. Been working here for ten years. What you do?"

"I'm an FBI Special Agent working out of the Rapid City field office."

Emily laughed and swept her hand around the pool building. "So, you are the agent?"

"Last I looked."

"I don't know what to feel—an Indian sitting next to an FBI agent. You feds and us from the rez aren't exactly friendly."

"You're from Crow Creek then?"

"Lower Brule Reservation across the river," Emily answered. "But in this case, I'll make an exception and be real friendly-like to you. But I would bet TripAdvisor didn't suggest you drive all the way from Rapid just to stay at our little home-away-from-home?"

Manny explained he had been assigned to assist local law enforcement with a drowning victim who might or might not have originated on the Crow Creek Reservation waterway.

Emily guffawed. "Drowning victim, my butt."

"You know something about it?"

"Just what I hear," Emily said. "Word on the street is the guy's been swimming with the fishes for decades and was snagged around the Amin area of the old American Island in the middle of the river. Got a hole in his chest, too, which I am almost sure the fishes didn't cause."

"Where did you hear that?"

Emily shrugged. "Like I say I just hear things from the moccasin telegraph." She leaned over and rested her hand on Manny's forearm. "You married?"

"In a manner of speaking."

Emily laughed. "Shacking up?"

Manny felt his face warm, and he was certain he blushed. He quickly changed the subject and said, "I intend to talk with Antionette Bear Paw tomorrow."

"You going to her house or to Bear Paw Trucking?"

"Trucking company. Why?"

"Watch your backside," Emily answered. "That Miles—Annie's son—is one gnarly bastard."

"He run the place?"

"With his mom. I dated him for a while in high school and I'm here to tell you he's got a dark side. He's likely to take a swing at you when he learns you're a cop."

"I'll make sure I don't get sucker punched."

"Not to worry," Emily said. "Miles is one to look you right in the eye before he stomps the air outta you. Walk carefully when you go see Annie. I'd hate to lose a paying customer."

Chapter 7

Shouting woke Manny earlier than he wanted to. He stood rubbing the sleepers out of his eyes as he opened the door. Down in the parking lot, Gandira stood looking up at a man wearing the utility belt of a service worker, finger jabbing the big man in the chest, ordering him to inspect a room on the far side of the complex.

"Damn fool's not going to let me sleep in," Manny said and turned to the dresser where he had stowed the contents of his suitcase yesterday.

He passed over three T-shirts and picked his only other shirt with any semblance of normalcy: a bright red and orange Hawaiian shirt, palm trees appearing to sway in the wind over a cove reminding him of Gilligan's Island.

He debated whether to wear shorts to match, then decided against it and picked the only pair of wrinkled jeans that he'd packed. At least the Senior Agent wouldn't see him dressed like a beach bum.

* * * * *

By the time he had shaved and dressed and made his way downstairs, Gandira and the handyman were nowhere to be seen, and Manny was satisfied with that. By the way the *Indian* was berating the man at the top of his voice, it would have been

Manny's nature to step between them and give the prospective motel buyer what-for for the way he yelled at his help.

Emily had given him directions to the trucking company yesterday, and he drove through town, passing stores on either side of the street opening for the day, many appearing to cater to people with a western interest. Manny could envision folks visiting this tourist-rich town entering stores and coming out looking like Roy Rogers or twirling their faux guns like Clint Eastwood, sending photos to their family in New York or Virginia showing how they'd assimilated to the western culture during their vacation. All to be tossed in the dumpster once they returned home.

He headed east, paralleling railroad tracks that had once serviced the town but that now appeared little used. Traffic was light this morning, but then Manny reasoned traffic was always light in the town of little more than 3,000 people. Situated right on the picturesque east bank of the Missouri River, the town drew people from all over who just wanted a relaxing stay in a western town. Or the countless fishermen who set their boats in the water for some of the best fishing in the state.

He had driven only a mile east of the main street when he spotted a tall sign in the shape of a black bear paw looming over the trees. Four semi-trucks stood parked in a line next to three gravel trucks off to one side of a mobile home marked as "Office." As he drove into the Bear Paw Trucking yard, shouts and screams reached Manny a moment before he saw eight or nine men standing in a circle watching two men fight. The taller of the two appeared to have a split lip and his bleeding misshapen nose told Manny he should have dodged a blow from the smaller, stockier man who circled, waiting for an opening. None paid Manny any mind as he parked in front of the office. He thought for a moment about calling the city police, then decided against it—the cops in this town responded to enough bar fights.

Especially when reservation Indians received their land checks each month, then it was the old cowboys and Indians battle until the drinking money ran out on both sides.

A cow bell tinkled over the door as Manny stepped into the office and closed it, the sounds of the fight left out in the gravel lot.

"We're not hiring," a woman's voice said from under a desk. "Unless you know something about computers."

"For one, I'm not applying. For another, I have people who know computers for me."

She used the edge of the desk to stand. Taller than Clara and nearly as tall as Manny, with her swept-back hair and expertly applied makeup, she looked a decade younger than Manny suspected she was. But then, he knew, Indians' genes sometimes made it difficult to guess their age.

He motioned to the door and said, "There's a heck of a fight going out there."

The woman stepped casually around Manny and looked through the window blinds before she shrugged. "That just Miles and the mechanic," she said as if that were the only explanation needed.

When Manny didn't respond, she added, "Miles is my son—I let him deal with the men we employ. Last week it was a teamster using old, rotten rope that caused a tarp to fly off a gravel truck and breaking a car's window behind him. That little scuffle you see outside now is a weekly occurrence—Miles needs to keep the mechanic straight. And Miles knows when the mechanic is slacking off—Miles used to work on all our trucks before I tapped him to manage the men. This time, the mechanic didn't do his due diligence and one of our Kenworth tractors trashed a transmission. Expensive."

"I'll make sure I never drive a Kenworth, then," Manny said, "but why not just hire a new mechanic?"

"You know how hard it is to find a decent diesel wrench

nowadays?" The lady turned and spoke to Manny as if seeing him for the first time. She stopped and eyed him up and down. "If you're not a mechanic turning in an application, who are you and why are you nosing around looking like you just woke up on some island?"

"They're the only clothes I had." Manny fished his ID wallet from his jean pocket and showed her. "I am looking for Antionette Bear Paw."

She put on glasses dangling from her neck by a gold chain and bent to look closer at Manny's identification. "Now what did we do? Some cock-a-mamie federal regulation we didn't quite follow to the letter and you're investigating it just before you guys fine us again?"

"I'm here to talk about your father."

She paused as she dropped her glasses back onto her chest. "Sit in Miles' chair." She motioned to a captain's chair beside a gun-metal gray desk. Behind the desk the walls were adorned with rusty artifacts—a ship's lantern with the globe still intact. A silver serving tray, the tarnish barely reflecting the light from the fluorescents overhead. Antionette said, "Don't knock the... crap off the walls or Miles will have a fit. Those are some of his *treasures* that he's found diving."

Manny nodded to a ship's wheel and asked, "looks like he's done some serious collecting from the river."

Antionette guffawed. "Miles doesn't dive the river here—too muddy. Can't see in front of your face. No, he and a couple old college friends take diving trips around the country, a lot in the lakes around the state. But you didn't come here to tour his private collection. You said something about my father?"

"His dog tags were found around the neck of a corpse in the river two days ago."

She pivoted on her heels and walked to a coffee pot. "Want a cup?" she said over her shoulder.

"Please," Manny answered.

When she turned around with two cups in her hands, her eyes had watered and she sat slowly in her chair behind her desk. "Let me get this straight—you think the drowning victim might be my dad?"

"Miss Bear Paw—"

"Jamieson," she interrupted. "I kept my husband's name even after the damn fool left me. But you can call me Annie. Now what do you wish to know about my father?"

Manny grabbed a notebook and pen from his briefcase as if he were prepared to jot notes during the interview. Which he had no intention of doing, instead concentrating on *how* the subject of his interview responded. Taking notes distracted him from gauging the person's reaction. "Deputy Christian says your father came to his school many times giving talks about his war experiences, so I am certain it is not him."

Annie forced a laugh and swiped her hand across her eyes. "Just as I am certain. I attended Dad's funeral fifteen years ago. Besides, I don't know anything about Dad's dog tags except the last I saw them that good-for-nothing husband took them just to anger Dad."

Manny remained quiet, knowing people inherently wanted others to know about themselves, and he was certain Annie would tell him more if he did not interrupt her. She did.

"Dad turned the trucking business over to me twenty-seven years ago. He stayed around Chamberlain and Crow Creek for a few years, but he just wasn't happy. So when he decided to pull up stakes and go into the assisted living in Pine Ridge, he was as happy as pigs in slop."

Manny thought about the only retirement home on Pine Ridge, the Cohen Home. The times that he'd been there Manny had been impressed with its cleanliness and the attention of the staff. "He must have liked the facility to want to move that far away."

Annie sipped her coffee delicately and said at last, "it wasn't a matter of Dad liking the facility so much. All his other friends around here had since died and his oldest friend, Amos Willow Bent, lives in the Cohen Home there. He was Dad's last friend." She dabbed at the corner of one eye. "Fifteen years ago, Dad died in his sleep at the home, so I can assure you the body found in the river is not my father's."

"I didn't figure so. Did you visit him often at Pine Ridge?"

Annie's mouth downturned in sadness. "Do we ever visit our loved ones enough? I thought I did until the day he was gone, then I realized I should have drove out to see him more times than I did."

She stood and walked to the window. "I kept telling myself it was because Pine Ridge is a two-hundred-or-more-mile drive and I had a business to run. A young boy to raise…" She faced Manny. "Miles. He was the one affected the most by Dad moving away—they used to do everything together when Miles was growing up." She laughed. "Dad boxed in the Army, and he passed on what he knew to Miles. He worshipped his grandpa." She tapped the window where the fight still raged on. "And that's where he got the urge to mix it up all the time."

"How do you suppose your father's dog tags wound up around the neck of another man?"

Annie shrugged. "Can't say. His dog tags were sacred to him. That good-for-nothing husband of mine, Buck—who Dad loathed for his philandering—used to screw with Dad. Grab the dog tags and hold them just out of his reach. Dad was a little guy, but Buck was a tall, strapping fellow and he'd tease Dad to no end. Of all the things he kept close from his Army days, his dog tags meant the most to him. So I can't tell you how they got into the river."

The door burst open and the stockier man Manny saw fighting earlier stepped through, tire billy jutting from his back pocket.

Blood mixed with dirt had caked on a slice above his eye, and it appeared as if a piece of his ear had been bitten off. Still, he wore a wide smile as if he enjoyed the fighting. Until he focused on Manny. "That your beater Mercury out front?"

"It is," Manny answered.

"Then in case my mother didn't already mention it, we're not hiring. Especially anyone coming around looking like they're auditioning for *Hawaii Five-O*."

"Funny you put it that way," Manny said and once more dug his identification and badge out of his pocket. Miles stepped back like Manny was contagious. "What the hell reg did we not follow to the ridiculous letter this time? You know, you sons a' bitches are always hassling us."

"He's not here for that," Annie said.

"Then…" Miles's brows furrowed and he glared at Manny. "Don't tell me he's here to look into that bunch of money what came up missing. Mom, I told you I'd get to the bottom of that."

"That's not it either," she said. "Now will you calm down? Sit and I'll tell you, but don't kick Agent Tanno out of your chair—you're dirtier than a hog."

Miles snatched a bandana from his back pocket and dabbed at the cut above his eye oozing blood.

Annie made no effort to help as if Miles getting cut from a fight was a natural occurrence. "Agent Tanno is here," Annie said, "because a drowning victim some kids found when the water went down had your grandpa's Army dog tags around his neck." She looked at Manny. "The victim was *he*, right?"

Manny nodded.

Miles stuffed his bandana back into his pocket and leaned close enough to Manny that he picked up on early-morning whisky breath. "What's your theory, Agent Man, as to how those dog tags ended up around a dead man's neck?"

"I was hoping you'd help me out with that."

Miles shook his head. "I can't remember the last time I helped a lawman, and I'm not so sure I would this time even if I had an idea."

"That's enough," Annie said. She turned her back on Miles and said, "I think what Miles is saying is we're mighty busy, but we'll be happy to answer questions when you have more information."

That wasn't what he'd heard Miles Jamieson say at all, but for now Manny had no choice. Annie was right: he really had no tangible questions to ask either of them at the moment. Not until he learned more from Quantico about Robbie Bear Paw's Army career and from Doctor Darden.

Chapter 8

Sam was still tied up with the funeral escort when Manny stopped by the sheriff's office, and he headed over to the motel. Emily emerged from her room, heading towards the pool room with a towel over her shoulder, when she spotted Manny and walked over to him. "By that sour look on your face I'm guessing you have had the displeasure of meeting Miles Jamieson."

Manny leaned against the fender of his car and popped a piece of Juicy Fruit. "That Miles has some attitude towards law enforcement."

Emily laughed and held out her hand for a piece of the gum. "Don't take it personally. That dude's got an attitude toward most everyone, like that great big chip on his shoulder is always going to be there. Blame his old man."

"Annie briefly mentioned her ex-husband's name in passing."

"And that's about all you'll get out of her about that SOB. When I was dating Miles, he told me all about how Buck had at least two women on the side while he was married to Annie, and how he'd come home drunk and wail on her. Miles was just a little boy when Annie kicked Buck out of the house, but the memories remained vivid."

"Buck still around?"

"Naw," Emily answered. "The last woman Buck shacked up with was some Argentinian here on a temporary work visa.

Annie figured when the woman's visa expired, she moved back and took Buck with her. But then, he was messing around with some banker's wife, too. Far as I know, no one's seen hide nor hair and that's a good thing for that town."

Emily stiffened when Gandira emerged from the office. He glared at her and ran a finger across his throat before climbing into his Mercedes and speeding off. "Word is that horse's ass is close to closing on a deal for the motel, and he wants to make certain I know my days here are numbered."

"Then where will you go?" Manny asked.

"Who knows?" Emily said. "Can't hardly go back to the rez—there's no work there. I was thinking of heading to Sioux Falls. Heard the meat packing plant is always hiring. What about you? You headed to the pool house?"

"I wish," Manny said. "I have some follow up calls to make. Have a good swim."

Manny walked into his motel room and punched in Reuben's number before shutting the door. Manny wasn't sure his brother would even answer—he had just joined the modern world and bought a cell phone just this last month. Reuben picked up on the second ring and yelled into the phone, "what the hell you want this time?"

"Just to visit with my only brother for a minute," Manny answered. "No reason to get mad."

"Oh," Reuben said. "I thought you were another telemarketer selling me anti-aging crème again."

"I'm afraid at your age, anti-aging crème would be a lost cause. Didn't my number show up on your phone contacts?"

"Somehow I wiped them out a couple days ago," Reuben said. "Philbilly's going to recover them for me."

"Philbilly?" Manny said. "As in Philbilly-the-dumbest-man-I-ever met Philbilly?"

"The same," Reuben said. "Seems like he's some kind of genius with phones. But you didn't call to give me hell about my phone."

Manny explained that he'd been assigned to either take over a possible federal case or assist local law enforcement with the decades-old victim found roped to what was left of a cabin on American Island. Either way, he was stuck in Chamberlain for a while.

"I loved that American Island."

"You were there?"

"Once," Reuben said. "Long before you were born when I was about five. The folks took me there right before the Corps of Engineers flooded the river to make the reservoir there in Chamberlain. They had these neat concrete animal statutes kids could crawl over and play on. Even had an ice cream parlor there as I recall, though that's been so long ago I don't know what I remember and what my mind's making up right now. Who was the floater?"

"I don't have an ID yet, but he had dog tags around his neck belonging to Robbie Bear Paw."

"The Code Talker."

"You knew him?" Manny asked as the line went dead. He stared at his cell phone for a moment when Reuben called. "My fat thumb disconnected me. But to answer your question, I met Robbie when I got paroled from prison. I just started my new journey to become a *Wicasa Wakan*. You know very little of that time as you were long since hired by the feds and living in Virginia."

Manny closed his eyes, recalling the hell that his brother Reuben had put him through. He had looked up to Reuben growing up, despite his involvement with the militant American Indian Movement. But when Reuben was convicted of a homicide just outside the reservation and sentenced to twenty-five years in state prison, Manny cut ties—and respect—for his older brother. Until Manny got reassigned to a case in Pine Ridge that brought him home and forced him to once again connect with Reuben. And to forgive him. Reuben had found religion in prison and studied to be a *Wicasa Wakan*—a sacred man. "I think you were telling me how you met Robbie."

"That first couple years after I was released, I stayed on the Red Road. Never got into trouble. Never touched a drop of booze. But about ten years into sobriety, I nearly backslid. I struggled to stay out of trouble and stay away from the liquor. My counselor suggested I volunteer at the retirement home... you do not know how I hate those little ping pong balls. If I never called another game of Bingo—"

"Robbie," Manny pressed.

"Sure. Robbie. He came right up to me one night after the games. I was stowing all the gear and he said, 'You got yourself a heavy heart, brother'. Just out of the blue. 'What you mean?' I asked him and he said, 'I'll pour us a cup of joe and we will talk about it, you and me.'

"We went to his room where he had a hot plate set up. 'Always keep coffee warming' he told me right before he poured me a nasty cup of coffee that had been simmering all day. He said he recognized in me that I was struggling with something bad, just like he struggled with things that happened during the war. And just like that, we bonded—him the World War Two Code Talker and me the Vietnam vet. I got to know him pretty well for those few years before he died."

"I just can't see how his dog tags were found around the floater's neck. But of course I can't talk with Robbie and ask him things."

"Next best thing," Reuben said. "Another Code Talker who served with Robbie in the Pacific lives here. Amos Willow Bent."

"Robbie's daughter mentioned him, but I wouldn't have ever imagined he'd still be alive. He'd have to be ancient."

Reuben laughed. "Not only is he alive, but sharp enough to

give the nursing home staff fits with his pranks. I go to the home now and again to visit with him. Not too often—I don't want the staff to get a room ready for me just yet."

Manny thought about talking with Reuben about his *other* problem when his brother said, "now it's my turn to tell someone that something is weighing heavy on them."

"You can tell?" Manny asked.

"Always can. What's the problem, *misun*?"

Manny explained that, when he and Willie stopped to look at the Corn Palace, a vision had swept over him. A terrifying vision that he needed a Sacred Man's help deciphering. He needed Reuben.

"When do you want to sweat?"

Manny didn't want to, but he knew he needed to enter the sweat lodge where his vision would come upon him once again and where a Sacred Man—Reuben—would be there to help him sort it through. "I'm fixing to check out now and drive back to Pine Ridge. I think I'll talk with Amos Willow Bent."

"Then I'd better prepare the sweat lodge for you," Reuben said right before he disconnected.

Chapter 9

Manny stopped at a high hill overlooking Wall Drug before driving south through the Badlands toward Pine Ridge. A soothing voice from the Records section at Quantico had left him a message, yet he knew the voice belonged to Abigail Winehart who was anything but soothing in the flesh. And there was a lot of flesh there, too. Abigail had courted Manny when he instructed at the FBI Academy in Quantico to the point where he felt she was stalking him. Now, half-way across the country, she sounded as if she still had a thing for him. "Call me about your inquiry, sugar," she'd recorded.

Forcing himself to sound pleased to talk with her, he recalled his academy instructor's suggestion with phone interviews: smile before you dial. "Abigail, it is so nice that you called me back. What did you find out about Robert Bear Paw?"

"I thought you Indians liked some small talk before getting down to business," she said.

Manny knocked his head against the steering wheel of the old Mercury "Of course. You are so right... tell me what you have been doing since I left the Academy."

"For one," she said, "I got a chin lift. You ought to see it—makes me look fifty pounds lighter."

Manny resisted the urge to ask *which chin* was lifted and instead said, "I am glad to hear that."

"You'll also be glad to hear I intend to take a vacation out west soon," she seemed to *coo* over the phone. "I've never seen the Black Hills. Mt. Rushmore. Crazy Horse memorial. I'm sure we'll be able to meet up somewhere. You owe me that romantic dinner, remember?"

Manny closed his eyes. *Does that woman ever forget anything?* Manny had promised Abigail a candlelit dinner last summer if she could dig deep and find out what she could about a murder suspect on the Wind River Reservation. "I recall the offer well," then added, "Robert Bear Paw…"

Computer keys clacked on the other end of the line. "Corporal Bear Paw was a Code Talker with the 320 Reconnaissance when McArthur returned to retake the Philippines in '44," she began, and Manny envisioned doughnut crumbs falling on to her computer keyboard. "The Department of the Army lists three unit citations and two personal citations for him." Keyboard keys *clacked* again. "Looks like he was mustered out after the war wound down." More *clacking*. "He had to return the following year to testify against Japanese soldiers in the War Crimes trials that the Philippine government held apart from the one our own government conducted."

"Anything else?"

"I am sure there's a bunch, sugar, but the Army takes its sweet time getting the information to us. Perhaps if you flew back here, used your influence to prod them along." She giggled. "Then we could have that dinner date you promised."

"Can't hear… losing reception." Manny scraped his fingernail against his phone. "Get back to me when you… have more on him," Manny said and quickly hung up.

He slumped in the seat; deflecting Abigail with her advances was as exhausting as going ten rounds with Mike Tyson. Manny had barely dodged the bullet, knowing Abigail had not changed one bit and he dreaded the thought that she'd actually vacation out this way to look him up.

He punched in Reuben's number. It rang until it went to voicemail, but Reuben called him right back. "Damned phone won't leave me alone even for a minute. I miss the times when a man could visit the outhouse without anyone interrupting him. Including people calling him. Whatcha need?"

"I'm at Wall and fixin' to head your way. I wanted to stop at the Cohen Home and talk with Amos Willow Bent."

"This would this be a good time to stop there," Reuben said. "If you hurry, we can catch supper. They always have meatloaf on Tuesdays."

"We?" Manny asked. "Did you want to meet me there?"

"I would," Reuben said, "but I don't have a car to get there. You know I don't have a driver's license."

"Wouldn't be the first time you drove without a DL," Manny said, "or took someone else's car."

"Is that what you want me to do, steal a car and meet you at the home?"

Reuben would, Manny knew, and not think twice about it. "Sit still and I'll pick you up once I get to Pine Ridge. Hate to see you in the hoosegow again."

* * * * *

They pulled off Highway 18 toward the Cohen Home when Reuben slipped his seat belt off. They were the only non-factory items installed that Manny had wanted when he bought the old car. "Hate seat belts," Reuben said, "but at least you bought a car old enough I can finally stretch my legs out in."

Manny drove into the parking lot of the retirement home and parked beside a new Chevy caked with dust from sitting close to the gravel road. "What's he like, Amos?"

"Affable," Reuben said immediately. "He'll talk your leg off about anything besides his time in the Code Talkers. He's a bit more guarded concerning his time during the war. Kinda like me with the 'Nam—don't much feel like talking about it. I'm not sure how much you'll get from him."

"As long as he can shed some insight on Robbie Bear Paw."

Manny followed Reuben into the assisted living home and to the receptionist's desk. A woman older than Reuben looked up from reading her *Cosmopolitan* and grinned at him. "Thought you forgot about us, been so long."

"Now how can I forget you, Henrietta?" Reuben said.

The woman blushed as she pulled a curl of white hair behind her ear. "Can you run Bingo tomorrow night?"

Reuben winked. "Will you be here?"

She shook her head. "Have to take my mom to Rapid to shop. She just loves to browse that Adam and Eve store."

Manny did the math in his head, hoping that Reuben wouldn't point out that Henrietta's mother had to be in her nineties. *Adam and Eve indeed.* Manny feared it would be a long time before he got that image out of his head.

Reuben exaggerated a frown. "Perhaps next week I'll work the game. For now, we're here to see Amos Willow Bent."

Henrietta motioned to a room past her desk. "He just went into the dining room."

Reuben smiled at her a last time and motioned for Manny to follow him into the dining room.

"What was that about?"

"Henrietta has been putting the moves on me ever since I started volunteering again."

Manny glanced over his shoulder at Henrietta. She chewed on the end of her pencil as she watched Reuben walk away. "Need I point out that she's damn near old enough to be our mother if she had lived?"

Reuben stopped before entering the dining room as he looked over the residents sitting waiting for their supper. "That's why I go out of my way not to get to close to her. I don't need some scandal—she was married to one of the firemen over on the Rosebud before he keeled over picking corn from his garden." He chuckled. "I think she flirts with me because of my reputation."

"You might have something there." Ever since Reuben was an enforcer for the American Indian Movement in the sixties and seventies—before he was sent to prison—people would whisper when he walked by for fear he would take notice of them with violence soon following. But since Reuben reconnected with the old ways and studied to become a sacred man while in prison, he had stayed out of the eye of law enforcement. Mostly. And now and again, he had saved Manny's bacon in tight jams. "Besides, you're a little long in the tooth to be interested in any woman."

Reuben looked down at him and beat his chest. "What, you don't think I still have *bloka*? I'm as virile as I always was?" he wheezed. "Besides," he motioned to the residents, "half the old folks here are messing around with the other half."

"No way?"

"Way. That's why you gotta watch yourself—there's other women here old enough to be our mother that'll drag you into their room and do the wild thing." He motioned across the room. "There's Amos. Let's grab a tray and join him."

Manny followed Reuben to the line of people holding trays. Besides meatloaf, the server plopped a scoop of potatoes on Reuben's tray, then looked around before giving another scoop. Reuben winked before digging into his pocket for money to put into the empty coffee can at the end of the line. "Best three bucks on the rez," he said. He threaded his way through the residents.

They stopped at the corner table and Reuben asked Amos, "Want company?"

The large man looked up from his meal and smiled. "Reuben." He offered his left hand to shake, the other armless side of his shirt pinned to the side of his breast pocket. "Been a while since you stopped to visit, son. Sit." Sit came out sounding like *sssit* through the old man's loose dentures. He pushed them up tighter into his mouth and looked at Manny. "That little feller with you can eat at my table as well."

Reuben sat across from Amos and Manny saw that sitting, the old man was nearly as tall as Reuben. With a full head of gray hair worn in a single ponytail and the stub of a goatee adorning his leathered face, Amos looked at Manny with a twinkle in his eye. "Is this your FBI-agent brother?"

"You've heard of him?" Reuben asked while he laid a checkered napkin across his lap.

"Who has not?" Amos dabbed at the corner of his mouth with his napkin before offering his hand. "Amos Willow Bent." His hand enclosed Manny's with a firm grip, and he saw Manny looking at the limp shirt sleeve. "Let us get this out of the way—my other arm is somewhere on Luzon in the Philippine jungle."

"I didn't mean anything—"

"Of course not, son." Amos waved the air. "Just human nature to wonder about such things when you first see 'em. But having only one arm did not stop me from living the rest of my life how I damn well pleased."

"Amos used to be hell on wheels in the rodeo circuit," Reuben said.

Amos' smile faded. "That I was. In my younger days. Before the war. Before I lost my arm." He looked away for a moment as if composing himself. When he looked back, his smile had returned. "I did all right after the war on that scrub land of my Pa's there by Potato Creek. I was not able to sit a bronc or a bull like I did before the war, but that didn't prevent me from being a successful rancher."

"Amos raised those buffalo you see around that area. If you ever get a chance to sample his buffalo meat, take it."

Amos patted his stomach. "I tell folks eating meat with no

more fat than buffalo is the reason I have lived so well for ninety-five years."

Amos looked twenty years younger. Still fit, but still needing a helping hand now and again if he were living in the Cohen Home. Manny hoped he looked so good if he made it as long as Amos has.

"You the one who got sentenced to investigate all sorts of crime here on the rez?"

"That be me," Manny said. "Living out my sentence until another Indian agent pops up."

Amos picked up his fork and speared some green beans when he asked Reuben, "Just in the neighborhood or here for a reason, 'cause Bingo is tomorrow night?"

"My little brother's got a murder case that you could help with."

Amos leaned closer to Manny and a wide grin engulfed his face "Any help I could be I will. I just love those CSI shows. I always thought I could do what they do if I were younger. What kind of murder?"

"A man's corpse was found floating in the Missouri River by Chamberlain."

Amos shrugged. "How can I help with that? I have not left the reservation for decades except to hop the casino bus to Deadwood whenever I can. Why do you think I could be of any help?"

"Because the victim had Robbie Bear Paw's dog tags around his neck."

Amos stopped with his fork mid-mouth. He dropped it on his plate and began trembling. "That cannot be," he sputtered. "I was a pallbearer at Robbie's funeral. He is buried right there at Holy Cross Cemetery. How—what does this even mean, Agent Tanno?"

"I was hoping you'd have some idea. Let's talk after supper."

After the other residents had left the dining room to flock to the large screen to watch reruns of *The Golden Girls*, Amos scooted his chair back. The old man took out a thin bladed pocketknife and began picking his teeth. "What can I tell you that might help you?"

Manny took out his notebook and pen, though he never actually wrote in it while he was interviewing anyone. He wanted to gauge their reactions to questions, like, "When was the last time you saw Robbie?"

"Fifteen years ago," Amos answered immediately. "Sitting just 'bout where you are now. He had just snookered me at dominoes and he laughed until I thought he would have a heart attack. Which apparently, he did that night, 'cause Robbie did not make it to breakfast."

"His daughter said you two were both Code Talkers during the war."

Amos closed his eyes, and Manny thought he'd fallen asleep when the old man finally opened them. "Robbie and me enlisted at the same time. Went through basic at the same time. Was shipped to Australia for advanced jungle training at the same time. He was my *kola*, and we were very close. So when he turned his business over to Annie, he really had no place to go. Nothing to do and he moved into the home here. He was from Crow Creek, but he fit in here just fine. His room was right down that hallway," he chin pointed to a row of doors.

"You two must have enjoyed talking about old times," Manny said, and out of the corner of his eye he saw Reuben shake his head slightly.

Amos slapped his empty shirt sleeve with his hand. "Robbie, he always felt guilty for this."

Reuben and Manny remained quiet, waiting for the old man to gather his thoughts.

"As a Code Talker, we went out on patrols that lasted up to a week looking for the Japanese. We would take turns, the code talker in the jungle with his security man watching for the enemy, relaying enemy troop movements to a code talker in the rear at company headquarters. The Japs never did decipher our Lakota language."

"You told me once," Reuben said, "that you and the other Code Talkers took turns going into the field on recon."

Amos studied the piece of green bean on his fork. "We were assigned to the Second Brigade, Robbie and me, and one day it was Robbie's turn to head into the brush to scout for Japs. But the kid had gotten into some confiscated sake and did his best to manage a raging hangover. Not me. I did not want that stuff, and I agreed to switch with Robbie—I was to go out into the jungle with a security man protecting me to relay what we saw back to Robbie in the rear, then the next time Robbie would pay me back and go out when it was supposed to be my turn."

Amos threw up his hand. "What could I do? Robbie was in no shape to head out as sick as he was. It was that time that I sprung a booby trap that blew off my arm. He always felt guilty about that, even when I tried convincing him it was the will of *Wakan Tanka* that it happened to me. For the rest of his life, Robbie never forgave himself. 'It should have been me' he said so many times. But I do not see how any of this helps you figure out who drowned with Robbie's dog tags around his neck."

"It appears," Manny said, "that the victim was shot in the chest before being tied to an abandoned cabin on American Island."

"Again, how can I help? Can't recall the last time I was east-river."

"I'm just clutching at straws at this point," Manny said. "This case is stalled until I find the identity of the victim."

"If I think of something, Agent Tanno, you will be the second to know."

"The second?"

"Sure, the second. The first one I tell is Robbie—we talk most every day. In a manner of speaking."

Chapter 10

"You sure you want to do this today?" Reuben swiped a bandana across his face. "It's hotter 'n hell outside let alone how hot it's going to be inside the *initipi*."

"I need to do it," Manny said, looking down the bank at Reuben's sweat lodge he always kept erected from canvas draped over willow sticks forming a dome. Some sweat lodges throughout the reservation were fabricated just for special occasions: for people to enter prior to their marriage. At the one-year anniversary of a loved one's death. For a young man's vision quest. Or for any other reason one had to get right with *Wakan Tanka*. This was one of those times Manny needed to get right with the Creator, to ask guidance and, with a sacred man's help, to decipher the vision Manny had had outside the Corn Palace. "I am ready, *kola*."

Reuben nodded and slipped out of the thick terry cloth robe. Even in his mid-seventies, Reuben's muscles rippled across his tattooed chest. Scars from wounds acquired in Vietnam caused ridges of scar tissue along his shoulder and down one side of his back. "Do you like what I did to the place, by the way?"

Manny did. Since the last time Manny had been here two months ago, Reuben had installed railing on either side of the steps leading down into the ravine where the sweat lodge stood. It made the decent almost pleasurable compared to sliding down the dirt bank on his butt like the other times, though Manny knew nothing pleasurable awaiting him down there. It was just something that had to be done.

Reuben handed Manny a towel to dry himself when he emerged from the lodge after the sweat. "The fire and the rocks are hot by now. Grab that bucket of water and head down there."

Reuben picked his way down the steps, planting each foot carefully so as not to fall. "Gotta take my time these days."

"Just be careful," Manny said. 'Old bones break easily' Manny's Uncle Marion had told him often when he'd gotten older. 'I needs to be a little careful—don't want to end up in one of those retirement homes nursing a broken hip.' But that's just what happened to Unc, and the old man never recovered from a fall off his porch steps. He spent his last days, like Robbie Bear Paw, in a home playing dominoes and whist with other old men. But Manny could not see Reuben confined to a retirement home. He'd be a nightmare resident for other residents.

As Manny followed Reuben down the embankment, he could feel the intense heat coming from the fire just outside the opening of the lodge. Reuben had arranged stones atop a metal grate over the fire to heat, the coals burning down. The rocks brittle-hot.

As he always did, Manny paused. Something in the back of his mind resisted entering the *initipi*, until Unc's teaching emerged in his memory. 'You got to sweat, Manny. If you want to walk the *Chunka Duta*, you need to get right with *Wakan Tanka*.' But after Unc died and Manny had moved to Quantico, far away from thoughts of walking the Red Road, he had abandoned his Lakota teachings. Until he reconnected with his sacred-man brother. Reuben had slowly and patiently led Manny back to his Lakota roots even as he had resisted the journey. Today though, he knew he needed *Wakan Tanka*. Today, he needed the Creator—and Reuben—to lead him into his vision.

Manny hung his towel over a nail sticking out of the stair

railing and walked around to the lodge entrance facing east, the source of life and power.

"Ready, *misun*?" Reuben asked.

Manny nodded and bent to the fire where he dropped tobacco for an offering before ducking through the low entrance. He brushed past the seven red prayer bundles Reuben had tied to the lodge entrance and set the bucket of water beside him before sitting cross-legged. Quiet. Reverent around the small pit in the center of the lodge awaiting the stones.

Reuben ducked through the entrance and crawled to the pit. He carried hot rocks in a small shovel that he'd used to lay them in the dirt in the center of the lodge. He made two more trips, the rocks immediately raising the temperature inside and Manny closed his eyes, breathing deeply.

After Reuben made the third trip with the rocks, he remained outside the lodge. Soft wails emerged from him, the sound of prayers to *Tunkasila*, Grandfather, thanking him for life and for the opportunity to enter *Unci Makha*, Grandmother Earth—the lodge. Manny could not see his brother, but he knew that he faced the four directions in turn and before praying to the Earth and Sky while he offered tobacco.

Soon, Reuben grew quiet and ducked low inside. He closed the flap and blackness engulfed the lodge. "The darkness represents human ignorance," he said as he sat cross legged across from Manny. The red-hot rocks cast eerie shadows off Reuben's face. "And the stones you see represent the coming of life."

Reuben told him such things each time they entered the lodge together, each time reminding Manny that he was two beings—the Catholic Manny, raised by his devout uncle, and the Manny with his Lakota roots. Outside Grandmother Earth, the two beings fought for control of him, always tugging at one another to go their way. Yet inside the lodge, Manny knew the two sides of him would come together. Inside the lodge, he would find help with the terrible vision he had that day outside the Corn Palace.

"*Mni, misun.*"

Manny dipped the ladle into the bucket of water and trickled it over the rocks. The water hissed, and Manny said, "the steam represents the creative forces of our world being activated."

"Good. You do remember some things," Reuben said. "More."

Manny dipped the ladle into the water again and trickled water over the rocks once more before hanging the ladle over the side of the water bucket.

He squinted through the steamy haze rising up from the pit.

Reuben hummed softly to the Creator while he sat cross-legged rocking back and forth.

As Manny often did entering the lodge, he doubted his ability to connect with the Creator, doubted guidance. He closed his eyes. Praying softly. Feeling the intense heat from the steam clutching at his lungs as he took in great gulps of air. Would he remain inside, even though the heat was becoming oppressive? Doubts once more filled him as they often did, and he fought them back down. Fought to surrender to the stifling heat that threatened to explode his lungs as cries reached him, then, and he opened his eyes. Had Reuben entered the lodge with him, for Manny could not see him?

Manny rubbed his temples, trying to remember how he had come to be inside Grandmother Earth when wails filled the tight space in the *initipi*. Cries of terror from unseen forces.

The mist rose from the rocks and seemed to swirl about him.

A wall of water. An angry wall of water rushing toward him. The roar of the deluge pierced his ears.

The deluge, neither malevolent nor righteous, neared but failed to drown out the screams of the man thrashing about.

Manny looked frantically around. Water rushed over a man struggling against ropes binding him to a cabin while other buildings crashed around him. A child's play set tumbled past in the torrent barely missing him. A soda fountain sign crashed close to the drowning man.

His cries became muted as the water swamped over him.

Manny tried standing. Fell back down, a hemp rope encircling his feet keeping him from reaching the victim. The victim.

Soon, the victim grew quiet.

His screams no more.

Manny reached out, the intense heat searing his lungs. He felt himself losing consciousness even as he tried crawling to the deluge. To the man he...

"...could not save him," he heard himself sputtering as light slaps woke him from his stupor.

"*Misun!*" Reuben squatted beside Manny, holding his head off the ground, trickling water over his head. Cooling him down.

With Reuben's help, Manny sat up and looked around. Reuben poured water over Manny's head and patted it dry with a towel. "You're okay, *misun*. Your vision has left you."

"It was horrible," Manny said.

"You want to talk about it?"

"I have to."

"Then let's go to the porch and we'll have some cold lemonade and talk, you and me."

Manny led the way up the steps, his legs shaky, his hands trembling as he thought back to his vision. A vision nearly identical to the one he'd had just outside the Corn Palace.

When he got to the top, he waited for Reuben to climb the steps and together they made their way to the back porch, Reuben's arm around Manny, helping him walk on wobbly legs. Reuben pulled the bug screen back and eased Manny into a lawn chair. "Be back in a minute," he said and disappeared inside his trailer.

Reuben soon emerged with two glasses and a pitcher of lemonade that he set on a small table made from a slab of cedar.

Manny's trembling had subsided enough that he could pick up the glass and sip without spilling.

"You okay now, little brother?"

Manny nodded. In what detail that he remembered from his experience inside the lodge, he told Reuben what he had seen in his vision. This wouldn't be the first time that Reuben helped him interpret his vision. Even though visions were highly personal and meant for the one *Wakan Tanka* had gifted the vision to, often a recipient needed a *Wicasa Wakan*—a sacred man—to help him realize what he had experienced.

When Manny finished, he sat back, the trembling in his hands returning with the telling of the vision.

Reuben set his glass of lemonade on the table and closed his eyes for so long Manny thought he'd fallen asleep when he opened his eyes and said, "I think that the drowning man represents more than just the case you are working on."

"But it was so vivid," Manny said. "I am sure it deals with the corpse those kids found."

"What did the man look like?"

"Well, he was... now that you brought it up, I couldn't see his face."

"Then what was he dressed like?"

Manny shrugged. "I don't remember what he was dressed like, either."

"Could the man drowning, pleading for someone to save him, also represent your life?"

"What are you getting at?" Manny asked.

Reuben wiped sweat off his forehead with a bandana before taking up his glass of lemonade again. "How's the job going?"

"It's going... all right I suppose."

"You don't sound so happy with it."

"It's just that I am nearing retirement and haven't been involved in one case that makes any difference to anybody. Ever since being reassigned to the Rapid City office all I've done is work reservation cases. I'd like to finish my career with something I can hang my hat on."

Reuben stood and slipped his T-shirt back on. He walked a cramp out of his leg and said, "You have caught several nasty bastards since you were transferred here."

"I know I have, but I still feel… something is missing. Something else is wrong with me."

"How's your relationship with Clara coming?"

"We put off the wedding again." Manny sipped his lemonade, feeling a cooling breeze coming through the screened porch. "I just couldn't go through with it just yet. Seems like every time I go into the office or every time I talk with Clara and agree to walk down the aisle I feel like—"

"You're drowning?" Reuben said. "Like there is no hope for you and like the man drowning in the water, you're reaching out in desperation for help?"

"That's just what it feels like," Manny said. "It feels like I'm sliding into the water, and no one can help me."

"No one in *this* world," Reuben said as he faced Manny. "When was the last time you attended Mass?"

Manny looked down at his feet, avoiding looking at Reuben, feeling like he was Unc giving him what-for for skipping Mass again. "It's been a while."

"As long as it's been since you entered the sweat lodge to get right with *Wakan Tanka*?"

"Longer."

"Then, *misun*, perhaps you need to start attending Mass once again. And enter the lodge more than a couple times a year."

"So, you think the drowning man—"

"Represents you *and* that victim found in the Missouri. When you find the killer, perhaps you will find yourself along the way. Worth a shot, no?"

Manny rubbed his temple and his headache subsided. "I'll speak with *Wakan Tanka* in the lodge more often. And talk to God when I attend Mass this Sunday."

"Mass with Clara?"

Manny nodded. "Mass with Clara."

Chapter 11

"I still think the key to finding out who that floater is lies with Amos Willow Bent," Manny said over breakfast. He had stayed at Reuben's last night after calling Clara and telling her he would not drive home to Rapid City in the dark. She had sighed deeply over the phone and Manny knew she was aggravated with his absence, both at home and in their lives. "I promise," he told her, "after I get back home, we'll have an evening out. Have a nice supper. Maybe go to Spearfish to the Passion Play." When the line had gone silent, he added, "I just had a sweat at Reuben's and don't feel safe driving. Besides, I need to talk with a man here in Pine Ridge in the morning."

"Promise to come home after that?" Clara asked.

"Promise," Manny answered, knowing Reuben was right when he said he was drowning in his relationship with her. He would make a genuine effort to make things right with Clara. And later, he'd have a come-to-Jesus moment with the Special Agent in charge of the Rapid City Field Office and lobby to be assigned non-reservation cases.

Reuben stiffened at a noise Manny couldn't hear, and his brother grabbed an ax handle beside the door when Manny said, "what're you jumpy about?"

"Someone just pulled up outside."

A loud knock on the door startled Manny as Reuben hid the ax handle beside his leg before opening the door. A kid with his hat turned around backwards and a nose ring looking like some dusty pirate, stepped back as he looked up at Reuben. "This the place needing a water pump for a '55 Merc?"

Reuben relaxed but not much as he said over his shoulder, "your part's here from Skeeters. Pay the kid."

The water pump blew the seal when Manny started the car this morning, spewing antifreeze under the hood, and he cursed himself for not driving directly home after returning from Chamberlain and taking his government car. As the closest auto parts store was in Chadron, Nebraska an hour across the state line, he had no other option than to wait for the part. He was just lucky that Reuben was a mechanic and agreed to install the new pump.

After Manny paid the parts runner and tipped him for the trip, he called Willie for a ride.

"You're welcome to stay right here until I swap out the water pump," Reuben said.

"I'd love to," Manny answered, "but I need to talk with Amos. The sooner I wrap this investigation up, the sooner I can go home and talk with Clara. And go to the Senior Agent with some overdue demands, like giving me a case that's important, not routine."

"Maybe this is *the* important case, and you just don't know it. After all, it doesn't get much more *unroutine* than investigating a seventy-year-old murder."

Manny shrugged. "Anyway, I'll come back after I talk with Amos and pick up the car."

"You owe me," Reuben said as he gathered the paper plates and tossed them in the recycle can. "I never thought I'd be working on a cop's car. Especially an FBI ride."

"Old memories die hard," Manny said.

"That they do."

When Reuben had belonged to the militant American Indian

Movement that was festering on reservations in the late sixties and into the seventies, people thought that, as an enforcer, he had been responsible for many of the bodies that popped up in roadside ditches along Pine Ridge. But Manny always doubted it, even up to the time that Reuben was sentenced to the state penitentiary for an off-reservation homicide.

Manny drew the curtain back and watched for Willie. "Ever want to go back to that time of the murder outside Hill City, the one that sent you the state penitentiary and… and want to do things differently?"

"You mean, do I think Jason Red Cloud deserved to get murdered? I did then and I do now, though I wouldn't change a thing about that night or the trial afterward."

Manny closed the curtains of Reuben's trailer when he spotted Willie turning off the BIA road and onto the long drive leading to Reuben's place. "I'm outta here. Be back after I talk with Amos."

"Later, *misun*."

Willie's Expedition kicked up dust as it skidded to a stop in front of Reuben's trailer house. When Manny climbed in, Willie asked, "That crazy-ass brother of yours ain't going to stick a gun out the window at me?"

Manny laughed and buckled himself in. "You know it's illegal for a felon to own a gun."

"Since when did a law ever stop Reuben Tanno?"

"You got a point there," Manny said.

They drove past Oglala Lake on their way into town, the east side of the bank lined with kids out of school for the summer. Some had cast their bamboo poles with nightcrawlers out into the water, while others sat on the ground holding theirs and laughing amongst themselves. "That'll be you with Precious in a few years," Manny said as he pointed to the kids fishing.

"But we won't make a single catch if she smells as bad as she does now. She'll scare all the fish away."

"Smell?"

"Diapers," Willie said. "Thank God that I don't have to change her more often than I do. I leave that up to Doreen when I can."

"That's kind of wimping out," Manny said. "What's the matter, the great Hunter and Gather of the North can't stand a little odor?"

"It's more than a little odor. I can bring down a deer or an elk. Get elbow-deep gutting it out and not flinch. But Precious… she's a world class stinker the way she fills her diapers. Speaking of, how long will you be in the home talking with Amos?"

Manny shrugged. "For as long as he'll visit. He tired out yesterday and couldn't talk much."

"I just wish I could talk and get around like he does at his age. I see him walking on Cohen Road in the mornings sometimes. He's got a cane, but he seems pretty spry for his age."

"I got the impression," Manny said, "that his mind is just as spry, and I'm hoping he has some insight into the body found in the Missouri, if I ask the right questions to jog his memory."

Willie slowed to allow a doe antelope and her fawn to cross the road. "I never actually talked with Amos, but I'd have loved to. I took an elective course in college about the war in the Pacific and Code Talkers but interviewing any wasn't part of it. Mind if I sit in?"

They pulled into the parking lot of the Cohen Home. A resident sat off to one side eying a big cottonwood with a murder of crows perched wing-to-wing. She held a stick of charcoal while she looked at the birds before sketching them to her tablet, paying Manny and Willie no mind as they walked past her and went inside.

The receptionist looked up over half glasses and said to Willie, "You here to take another stolen car report?"

Willie turned to Manny. "Henrietta here had her car stolen from the parking lot a few days ago. But they were nice thieves and brought it back. Parked it out in the visitor's parking lot. I'm leaning towards some resident taking it and going to Deadwood for some gambling. Half the residents here are slot-machine addicts."

Henrietta put her cigarillo in the ashtray and leaned over the desk. She eyed Manny with a cloudy eye, the other one looking somewhere just past him. "I didn't much mind them taking my old beater Pinto wagon. But they ran it out of gas. Left it in the parking lot on empty. Have you priced gas recently? That was the real crime there."

Manny knew. He had just spent seventy-five dollars filling up the old Mercury at Big Bat's before driving to Reuben's. It had been sitting on empty when he last gassed up in Chamberlain and he was surprised he didn't run it dry going these two-hundred-plus miles. "I know just how pricey it is," Manny said before asking, "Is Amos awake?"

Henrietta laughed. "That old coot's always awake. You'll find him playing pinochle with some other duffers in the commons area."

Manny and Willie walked down the hallway and into a large room with tables occupied by residents filling out crossword puzzles and reading the latest copy of *Lakota Country Times*. Two residents hunched over another table as they picked up pieces of a jigsaw puzzle, while the table next to that one hosted two women playing cribbage.

And in one corner, Amos Willow Bent played pinochle with two other men. He dealt cards to the other old man to his left, flicking them out effortlessly with his one good hand, before giving himself four cards. He laughed and laid his cards on the table. "Three-hundred points for me boys," he said.

The two other players looked at the score sheet and stood. "That is game again," one said and handed Amos a can of Right Guard deodorant. The taller and thinner of the two dug a tube of

Polident from his vest pocket and dropped it on the table. They stood and left shaking their heads.

Amos looked up and spotted Manny and Willie. He motioned to the table and said, "Care for a friendly game?"

"You mean a not so friendly game, don't you?" Manny said.

Amos leaned back and looked warily at Manny as he sat opposite Amos. "I do not understand."

Manny picked up the four cards Amos had just set on the table. "Double pinochle," he said. "High score. What's the odds of a player getting that?"

Amos shrugged, his thin grey braid bouncing on his chest. "People get Double Pinochle now and again."

"Probably more likely if the dealer double deals. Like you just did."

Amos slumped in his seat. "You saw that?"

Manny nodded.

"How—"

"I worked carnival fraud when I was on the police force here many years ago. You're good for a one-armed dealer, which I suspect is why they let you deal the cards. And what's with the deodorant and Polident?"

"They don't let us play for money here," Amos answered. He looked from Willie to Manny and said, "you going to turn me in?"

"I'm not," Manny answered. "You'll have to deal with your conscience after you cheated those two."

Amos waved the air. "They will win it back at checkers this afternoon. I am terrible at checkers. But you did not come here to give me hell for my… indiscretions."

"We came here to talk some more about your friend Robbie Bear Paw. How his dog tags got around the neck of that corpse 'cause it's not Robbie those kids spotted in the river."

Amos used the edge of the table to stand and grabbed his cane made from a bull's penis. He grabbed a small bag of popcorn sitting on the table and stuffed it inside his bib overalls. "Follow me."

He led them past the commons area to a sliding glass door and to Adirondack chairs on a concrete pad outside. "Have a seat, boys." He eased himself down and leaned his cane on an arm of the chair before reaching inside his bag. He came out with a piece of popcorn, and pigeons that had been roosting in a nearby maple fluttered down to compete for the treat Amos threw them. He looked at Manny and said, "I wish I could be of help identifying the body in the water, but like I said about the time that man was murdered I was just getting my ranch started."

"Let's start with who Robbie hung out with who might have access to his personal dog tags."

Amos tossed another piece of popcorn at the pigeons, and they scurried over to fight for it. "Me and Robbie… well, after the war, we never saw each other much. He always felt guilty for this," Amos flopped his empty shirt sleeve.

"Can you tell me about you losing your arm, or is too painful?" Willie asked.

"Not really." Amos snatched a handful of popcorn and flung the kernels into the flock of pigeons. "That Japanese General Yamashita made life hell for us in the Philippines. They didn't call him the Tiger of Malaya for nothing. Me and Robbie were two of six Lakota Code Talkers assigned to McArthur when he made that dramatic entry back into the Philippines at Red Beach. More a photo op than anything else, but we were proud to be part of it."

"In college, we studied about the Sioux Code Talkers," Willie said. "The professor said you guys were invaluable in relaying information about enemy positions and movements."

"We liked to think so. We took turns going out on recon

patrol. When me and my security man went out that last time—the one that cost me my arm—Robbie was manning the radio back in the rear. I would radio what I saw, and he would interpret. Then hand it over to the officer transcribing it and from there the intel would work its way up the chain. But that time was different."

Amos popped a couple pieces of popcorn into his mouth before tossing the rest of the bag into the pigeon fray. "That time we saw a Japanese staff car drive the road. Chrysanthemum flags on the fenders. Two trucks of soldiers following for protection. Another loaded with… I am not sure what. We had heard rumors of the Japanese hiding pillaged gold and jewels and precious items looted from China and across Asia on the island. We always poo-poohed it off. But I got a vibe that day they were doing just that: stashing precious loot the way those soldiers grunted and worked their keisters off toting it down into that cave."

"That was when you tripped the booby trap?" Willie asked.

Amos leaned back in his chair. "No. I told Robbie what I saw and his man transcribing it told us to forget it. Ordered us to press on further into the Coraballo Mountains where we suspected the main Japanese soldiers were holed up. Later that day when we located a Japanese unit right above Nueva Viscaya, *that* is when I ran into the booby trap. All I can say is I was damn sure lucky my security man knew enough battlefield doctorin' to tourniquet me and get me back to an aid station or I would have bled to death."

"Ever talk with him after the war?" Manny asked. "My brother Reuben still keeps contact with some of his old Vietnam buddies."

Amos shook his head. "Sergeant Kimbre was wounded on Luzon two weeks later when our unit entered Manilla to relieve the city. He was shipped to a field hospital, and I heard he died in surgery. Shame, too—he was about the only one of the few in the unit bigger'n me and we got along. But Robbie was the only one I talked with after the war." Amos looked away. "I miss him, too, though I always figured he cheated at dominoes."

"You guys stayed buddies all those years?" Manny said. "Just like Reuben has with his pards?"

Amos stood and grabbed his cane while he hobbled a few feet off, then back. "Get these damned nocturnal cramps now and again that knot my legs in the daytime, too. But as for buddies with Robbie, we were not that close after the war until he moved here after he turned the business over to his daughter."

"You never saw him until he moved into the home here?" Manny asked.

"Once," Amos said. "A year after the war he stopped by and visited me at that ranch I was working up by Interior. I could still sit a horse and mend fence with one arm, though roping was out of the question so I made a passable living."

Willie stood and walked his own cramp out of his leg. "Sounds like he wanted to stay in touch."

"Not like that," Amos answered. "Robbie felt a powerful guilt that it was me who got his arm blown off taking a patrol that he was scheduled for."

"Is that why he came to visit you that day?" Willie asked.

"In a manner. After the war," Amos said, "Robbie's father died and left him some bottom land on Crow Creek with the stipulation that Robbie give me half when he sold it. He gave me half to start a ranch and used his portion to start that trucking company in Chamberlain."

"Was that the only time you saw him until he moved in here?" Manny asked.

Amos nodded. "It was. He lived with that terrible guilt, and it took all those years to convince him I did not blame him for losing my arm. If anything, I was eternally grateful to his father for the gift—it allowed me to start my buffalo ranch."

"That you deeded to Oglala Lakota College when you moved in here," Willie said.

Amos shrugged. "I never married. Never had kids. Had to do something with the ranch. How did you know?"

"There's a plaque on the wall of the college thanking you," Willie said.

Manny popped a stick of Juicy Fruit and offered Amos a piece of gum. "It sticks to my dentures," he said.

Manny pocketed the gum and asked, "in all those years after he came back here, did he ever mention anyone who might have gotten close enough to steal his dog tags? Mention any friends?"

Amos dug down into his bibs and brought out his own set of dog tags. "We always wore them as a badge of honor. I was upset when I was not wearing them."

"What did he say happened to them?" Manny asked.

"All he said is 'some horse's ass is wearing them now' and how pissed he was that his former son-in-law often took them just to tease Robbie. You have no idea, Agent Tanno?"

"Can't say," Manny said. "All I know is the dog tags were stuck in that floater by Chamberlain. But there must be something or someone Robbie talked about when he moved in here."

"He kept quiet on most things related to his business or Chamberlain, and he was always happy when his daughter and grandson visited him. On one trip his daughter said Robbie had a ton of friends in Chamberlain that missed him, friends he developed through his trucking business," Amos answered. "Everywhere he went, people sidled up to him. There was something about that little guy people were just drawn to. Guess half the town of Chamberlain are your suspects."

"Sounds like what Sam, the deputy sheriff there in Brule

County, said about when Robbie would come to school giving talks about the Code Talkers. Sam said kids couldn't get enough of him."

"That was Robbie," Amos said. "I sure miss him."

Chapter 12

The color drained from Willie's face and he pocketed his phone.

"You look like you just saw a ghost," Manny said.

"Worse," Willie answered. "Doreen needs to go to the church for an emergency council meeting. She'll meet me at the Justice Building and hand the baby off."

"That's it?" Manny said. "You're scared 'cause you get to spend time with your little girl?"

Willie looked at his phone as if blaming it for the dire news. "Doreen says Precious is *fussy* today."

"Of course, she's fussy. She's a baby."

"Fussy," Willie explained, "is Doreen's euphemism for Precious having unusually frequent and runny BMs."

"Welcome to parenthood," Manny said. "But why meet you at the Justice Building instead of at home?" Manny asked.

"She was there looking into an application for a dispatcher opening when church called."

Manny smiled. "Wait until the guys see big ol' Willie cradling a baby."

Manny wasn't sure if Willie slowed to keep kicking up dust on his cruiser or to prolong the inevitable as they drove the road south toward the Nebraska state line. Toward White Clay. Toward where so many Oglala Lakota had bought their alcohol that continued to destroy their lives. Until the state of Nebraska, under pressure from the Pine Ridge Tribal Council finally closed the four liquor stores some years ago.

When they pulled into the Justice Building parking lot, Doreen stood leaning against her car waiting for Willie. She held Precious wrapped in a multicolored fleece blanket close to her. Doreen's smile faded when she spotted Manny. He was—in her eyes—her main competition for Willie's time. She said to Willie while she continued glaring at Manny, "I shouldn't be more than an hour unless Velma Two Kettles starts flapping her gums about Sunday school, then I'll be longer."

"Doreen," Willie seemed to plead, "I'm working. I can't be tied up with Precious that long."

Doreen jerked her head in Manny's direction as she passed the baby to Willie. "But you have time enough to ride around with *him*."

"Manny's with me on business—" But Doreen had already ran to her car and hopped in.

"An hour," Willie groaned as he rocked the bundle back and forth. "An hour."

"What can happen in an hour?" Manny asked. "Besides, maybe Doreen just needs a break. I wouldn't worry about her being gone for too long—she didn't even leave a diaper bag."

"I carry my own diaper emergency kit wherever I go," Willie said. "Here."

He handed Precious to Manny before popping the hatch of his Expedition. When he came away from his government SUV, a black tactical bag was slung over one shoulder. Manny eyed it while he handed the baby back. "A tack bag for diapers? Not exactly like you're going to war."

"No? I hope not. But believe me, this bag contains everything I need in case Precious declares war and unloads. Let's get in out of the heat."

Manny followed Willie into the Justice Building. As he walked past Dispatch, the two young girls manning the phones and radios snickered when they saw Willie holding Precious. He led Manny past the police dispatch and into a large conference room.

Willie rocked the baby back and forth, singing softly to her just as Police Chief Lumpy Looks Twice waddled in. "What the hell's this?"

"Doreen had to run to the church for a meeting."

"So now the taxpayers are footing the bill for you to babysit?"

"Lighten up," Manny said. "You're just worried one of the councilmen will barge in and see Willie doing something terrible—holding his child."

"Not so much that," the Chief said. "The baby's a distraction."

"Distraction how?" Manny asked.

"Listen?" Lumpy said.

Footsteps rapidly approached the conference room. A moment later the door flung open. Two dispatchers and an animal control officer entered the room, each woman crowding the other to get a closer look at Precious.

"That distraction," Lumpy said.

"Can I hold her?" a dispatcher asked.

Willie breathed a deep sigh of relief and passed the baby to her. "I'll be talking with Agent Tanno and the Chief if you need anything."

Willie set the tactical diaper bag on the floor and walked to the end of the long conference table. Manny and Lumpy plopped into chairs across from him and Willie leaned back, beads of sweat forming on his forehead.

"Relax," Manny said. "They'll be gentle with Precious."

Willie wiped his forehead with his hand and said, "that's not what I'm worried about. What I'm concerned with is, the longer Doreen is away, the more likely Precious will… do her thing. And that's not pretty."

Lumpy looked at the three ladies fussing over the baby before

DEATH UNDER THE DELUGE

turning back to Willie. "Why are you here anyways? Thought you were following up on that car theft from the Cohen Home."

Willie stuffed his lip with Copenhagen and wiped the excess tobacco off on the cuff of his trousers. "I'm still not convinced it was theft. Whoever took the car brought it back. I'm thinking more of a prank. Joy riding at the most. My guess it would be kids—Henrietta said she leaves the keys in the ignition. Says the Pinto's anti-theft device is the way it looks."

"Guess it failed that one time," Lumpy said.

"Apparently," Willie said. "Besides, Manny needed to interview Amos Willow Bent concerning a case he's been assigned to in Brule County."

Lumpy threw up his hands. "Not again? I got the Fifth Member of the council on my butt for that car theft and two other car jackings and you're wasting time with a federal case? Didn't I tell you not to get involved with cases not in our jurisdiction? And especially with this goofball," he nodded to Manny.

Manny felt his face flush. *Goofball.* Ever since Manny and Lumpy worked as tribal policemen together decades ago, the short, round mound of sound Lumpy Looks Twice had been at odds with Manny. But once in a blue moon Lumpy came through to help with a case so, for that reason alone, Manny didn't jump in his shit. "My car crapped out at Reuben's, and I had to leave it there for him to fix."

"If you want a violent felon working on your car," Lumpy said, "that's a chance you'll have to take."

"Can we talk about something else until Doreen comes back," Willie said while he watched Precious being passed amongst the women. "I'd hate to be the one who had to break up a fight between you two."

Lumpy walked to the coffee pot on a cart in one corner of the room and picked it up. After sniffing it, he set it back down. He turned to Manny and asked, "Just what is this monumental case you roped Willie into helping with?"

Manny explained about the corpse being discovered in the Missouri River by Chamberlain when the water receded due to the drought. "The dog tags said Robbie Bear Paw, who so happened to live a long life until he passed away at the Cohen Home."

"That," Lumpy said, "sounds like a mystery."

"You are so astute," Manny said. "But then, I'd hate for you to contribute anything to solving that *mystery*."

"Like I said before, it is way out of our jurisdiction. But if you must know, I talked with Amos many times when I volunteered at the home."

"You volunteered?" Manny said. "As in helping someone out?"

"Don't tell anyone," Lumpy said.

Willie looked over at the three women lording over his baby. "The Chief runs the whist tournament they have at the Cohen Home every week. He's the official judge." He nudged Manny. "They put on a feed every night after the games."

"Where'd they find a referee shirt that'd go over your big belly?" Manny said.

Lumpy glared at Manny before shaking out a cigarette and lighting it.

"A Virginia Slim," Manny said. "How appropriate."

Lumpy flicked his ash in a tray made from a car piston. "Enough of me. What the hell you need to talk with Amos Willow Bent about?"

"That victim—Robbie Bear Paw—was a Code Talker stationed with Amos during the war."

"With the 1st Cavalry. 302 Reconnaissance," Lumpy said.

"Does everyone know about these Code Talkers but me?" Manny said.

"Guess we're just a lot smarter than some hot shot FBI agent," Lumpy said.

"All right," Manny said. "I'll bite. Just what do you know about the Lakota Code Talkers."

Lumpy looked away. "Just what Amos said when I was playing the tournament. Had to prod him, though. He's not one of those heroes that brag about it, so you might have a hard time getting anything out of him."

"So, you really don't know much?"

"I know there were nineteen tribes during World War Two who were employed as Code Talkers to confound the enemy. That's about all Amos told me. Like I said, he's not exactly forthright about his war days."

The animal control officer holding the baby at arm's length walked to Willie and handed Precious to him. She scrunched her nose up and said, "I think she needs changing."

Willie took the baby for just a moment before handing her to Manny. It took him even less time to realize that she, indeed, needed her diapers changed. "I need to go to the restroom," Manny said, even as Willie was digging into his tactical diaper bag. "Here." He handed the baby to Lumpy.

Lumpy held the baby away from him and yelled at Manny leaving the conference room, "Don't leave me with the baby—" but Manny had already escaped.

He waited in the men's room long enough that he figured Willie was finished changing the diaper before Manny ventured back into the conference room. The dispatchers and animal control officer had fled, and Lumpy was nowhere to be seen. "Guess everybody left you."

"Including you, you coward." Willie took off a clothes pin pinching his nose and stripped off his elbow-length pregnancy-tester gloves used to check cows. He held a plastic garbage sack out and said, "Precious is done doing her thing. Watch her while I take this dirty diaper out to the dumpster."

"Is she done?"

"It's safe," Willie answered.

A small star quilt covered the baby and Manny chanced a look. He pulled the blanket back and the baby looked at him while she sucked on a pacifier. When Willie came back into the room, Doreen stormed right behind him. She scowled at Manny as she took the baby back.

Willie motioned for Manny to follow him, and they left the conference room. "She's not happy that I gave the baby to you even for a minute. She says you wouldn't know what to do with Precious other than interrogate her."

"As long as the baby doesn't fill her diaper again," Manny said, "I'm your guy."

They walked to the parking lot and headed to the Cohen Home. "We're going to talk with him again, but Lumpy's right—it'll be like pulling teeth getting any more information from Amos."

Willie rolled the window down in his patrol unit. "Air conditioner went on the blink. If what I learned in that college class is right, Code Talkers—regardless of what tribe—were forbidden to talk about their service until just recently."

"Lumpy mentioned there were other Code Talkers besides the Navajo and Lakota."

"There were, though the ones you hear about the most were the Navajos," Willie said. "The Army used some members of the Choctaw tribe in World War One to confound the Germans. Later in the Pacific during World War Two, the Marines took note of that. There were over four hundred Navajo Marines in that theater of war, which most people are familiar with. At Normandy, Army Comanche Code Talkers confused the Germans. But from what I've studied, every Code Talker was humble about their service even after they were allowed to talk about it."

"Every Code Talker except Robbie Bear Paw, if Deputy

Christian was right about him."

* * * * *

They pulled into the Cohen Home and Willie parked beside a wheelchair-accessible van with the ramp down. As they entered the side door, an orderly wheeled a lady out of the home and toward the van. She looked up at Manny with clouded eyes as she puffed on a cigarette, and Manny wasn't sure she actually saw him or not.

They entered the home and stopped at the receptionist's desk. Henrietta looked up from her *Woman's World* magazine and pulled a thin tendril of white hair behind her ear as she flashed a semi-toothless grin. "You never said before if you are married?"

"I am not," Manny said, "but I'm spoken for."

The receptionist's smile faded, and she picked up her magazine again. She looked at Willie. "You're not here to take another stolen car report, 'cause I ain't had it taken since last time."

Willie shook his head. "We want to see Amos again."

"He's out back feeding the damn birds," Henrietta said. "Just follow all the pigeon shit."

Manny stopped at the soda machine long enough to grab a bottle of water for him and Amos and Willie before walking through the sliding glass doors. Amos sat in an Adirondack chair while pigeons milled around him waiting for him to toss the next popcorn kernel. He spotted Manny and Willie and set the sack of popcorn aside while he swished the birds away with his cane. "Figured you would be back."

Manny handed Amos a bottle of water and scooted a lawn chair close.

"I cursed you last night," Amos said as he opened the water bottle with his teeth.

"How so?" Manny asked.

"When you and Reuben stopped by yesterday asking about Robbie, that got to bothering me. I haven't thought about the war much these days. Never wanted too. Never talked much about those times with anyone except Robbie when he was alive. Unlike him, I just wanted to forget."

"Did you remember anything in those talks with him that might indicate who might have stolen his dog tags or who he would have had issues with?"

"That a-hole son-in-law of his, Buck," Amos said immediately, "but he was long gone from his daughter's life by the time Robbie moved in here. Annie says Buck hung around Chamberlain whoring some women for a while before he ran off with some banker's wife. Tell me, Agent Tanno, did your medical examiner determine much, like how big the victim was?"

"Not yet. The long bones were missing, and he has to contact a bone specialist and run the measurements by him. Why do you ask?"

"Just that some soldiers we served with were big men. Like me. Unlike Robbie who was a little guy. Perhaps one of his old wartime pards came back for a visit."

"Perhaps out of friendship, Robbie gave him his dog tags?" Manny asked.

"Doubt it. Those tags, like mine, were the one souvenir that Robbie treasured."

Manny sipped his bottle of water and leaned close to Amos. "You do remember some of the men back in the war?"

Amos nodded. "I can see their faces, but not their names." He rubbed his forehead before setting the bottle of water down and picking up his sack of popcorn again. "Believe me, I would tell you if I could. Whoever that man floating in the river is, he is sure to have people wondering about him. Even after all these years he would have relatives wanting closure. Perhaps the Department of the Army has records."

"I'm going to put a request into the Army archives after we leave. Do you recall anything about the men you and Robbie served with?" Manny pressed.

"Some big ol' boy—from somewhere in the south I think—who was with him that day in the rear transcribing what I radioed to him that time I lost my arm. One of those assigned to transcribe what one Code Talkers in the field relayed to the Lakota Code Talker in the rear."

"But you don't remember his name?"

Amos flicked a dozen popcorn kernels at the pigeons and grinned at the fight that ensued before setting the sack back beside his chair. "I wish that I did. Hate to think his family does not know the man's fate, if he was your floater."

Willie turned his seat to face Amos. "*Tunkasila*," Willie said, using the term of Grandfather out of respect for the old man, "maybe it might jar your memory if you talked more about that day the booby trap took your arm."

Amos closed his eyes as he took another sip of his water. "Sergeant Kimbre—that was my security man they sent to make sure I wasn't captured alive—and I were nearly spotted that day. We didn't expect a Japanese staff car to be traveling the muddy jungle road, especially with a couple trucks filled with soldiers following." He used the arm of the chair to stand and grabbed his cane while he paced in front of Willie and Manny, his armless sleeve batting his side. "Like I said before, the Japanese soldiers struggled most of the day to unload whatever it was. We watched them and relayed back to Robbie what was going on. Even hours later—when we saw all the soldiers had finished and disappeared into the cave—Robbie's man transcribing all this ordered us to forget it and to continue looking for the main Japanese defenders."

"I've never been a soldier," Willie said, "but that makes sense to me to call you guys off to look for the main Japanese Army units."

"But did it make sense that the Japanese commander set explosives in the cave," Amos said, "when their own troops were trapped inside?"

Manny did not think it made sense, unless… "Perhaps they didn't want anyone to know just what was stashed in that cave."

Amos nodded. "I thought of that many times since, but still have no logical reason besides just that."

"I have read," Willie said, "about Yamashita's Gold. About all the loot stolen from around Asia being hidden in the Philippines, but nothing ever proven."

"I thought so as well," Amos said, "and said as much to Robbie. But war was war and we both could care less about stolen loot back then. We were too concerned with coming back alive. So, me and Sergeant Kimbre moved on like Robbie's man ordered."

"Was it later that day you tripped the booby trap?" Manny asked.

Amos rubbed his stump with his one remaining hand. "One of those hanging traps the Japs were wont to set up on trails. They would set a trip wire chest height and hope some damn fool like me didn't spot it until it was too late."

Amos motioned for his bottle of water. When Willie handed it to him, Amos said, "this heat and talking with your fellers has plumb tuckered me out. I believe I will go in and take a nap. Come back another time when I am feeling better," and headed into the home.

* * * * *

Willie pulled into the Crazy Horse Housing complex. Phil "Philbilly" Ostert sat on his steps whittling on a piece of wood. He stood when Manny and Willie neared. "Whatcha think of this?" he said as he handed Manny his whittling project. "I'm making progress."

Manny turned the piece of wood over in his hand, struggling

to figure out just what it was supposed to be.

"Well?" Philbilly asked.

"Looks like the makings of a fine flute," Manny said and handed it to Willie.

"Flute!" Philbilly sputtered. "It's a rattlesnake stretched out."

Willie handed the project back to Philbilly and said, "looks like just a piece of wood you were whittling on. Like you were just making kindling for a fire."

Philbilly snatched the wood and stuffed it into his pocket. "You want your phone fixed or not?"

Philbilly didn't wait for an answer but stumbled into his house as Manny shook his head. When Phil was barely out of middle school, the Ostert family had been passing through Pine Ridge returning from the lettuce fields in Oregon. As they headed back to Arkansas, they stopped at Big Bat's for gas. It was a reservation-wide discussion for years whether his parents left him to fend for himself on purpose or merely forgot to check if he was in the station wagon when they pulled out of the gas station. Either way, they must have figured to cut their losses and leave him to make his own way as they never came back for him. And he had tried making his own way here, selling meat from the back of his ratty pickup with *You Can't Beat Phil's Meat* plastered on the side, which had failed. He had tried his hand at a food truck selling *Sizzling Hot Indian Tacos*, but it had failed like his other ventures. Still, Manny admired the man's persistence in searching for *something* he could succeed at. Perhaps as a phone guru if Willie was right.

Lights flicked on Philbilly's Christmas tree which he kept up all year as he was too lazy to take it down. Tiny rabbits still hung on the faux branches that Philbilly called it his Easter Tree. *Guess he was too lazy to take it down after Easter, too*, Manny thought.

Philbilly sat at a table with one short leg propped up by a phone book and held out his hand.

Willie laid a five-dollar-bill in his palm, and said, "hope you can fix it."

"Shush," Philbilly said as he began punching numbers. "Geniuses need quiet."

Willie shrugged and made a motion to zip his mouth when Philbilly said, "By the way, Officer With Horn, when does the police department auction the impounded vehicles?"

"Usually late summer," Willie answered. "But you wouldn't want any of those. Most people leave their cars in impound 'cause they're not worth paying the tow bill. Besides, you already have a pickup."

"Had," Philbilly said. "I wrecked it rushing back up to Rapid City. That cousin of mine with that triple mastectomy had complications and I rolled the truck right outside the hospital."

Manny wanted to ask for clarification on the triple mastectomy but thought better of it.

"Any car would be better than nothing," Philbilly laughed. "Even that rusty old Pinto wagon that picked me up would be better than nothing right now."

"A Pinto station wagon you say?" Willie asked.

"Yeah. Thought the fenders would fall off, all rusted and flapping every time we hit a rut in the road."

"When was this?"

Philbilly stared into the corner of the room as if he had forgot to load film for his photographic memory. "A week ago. I was walking back from Rapid City when a Good Samaritan picked me up in that old beater."

"That'd be about the time that Henrietta's car was taken the last time," Willie said to Manny.

"No doubt," Manny said. "Not too many Pintos still on the road anymore."

"There," Philbilly said and handed Willie his phone. "Just keep me posted on that impound auction and we'll be even."

"Thanks," Willie said as he slipped his phone on his belt

holder. "Who was the driver who picked you up?"

"Didn't recognize him," Philbilly answered.

"What'd he look like?"

Philbilly shrugged. "Can't say that either, 'cept he was bigger 'n me. But then most everyone's bigger 'n me."

"Let me get this straight," Manny said, "you rode all the way back from Rapid and don't know what the driver looked like?"

"Hey, it was dark, and the damn dome light didn't work. Besides, my focus wasn't hardly on the driver. It was on his phone."

"This I gotta hear," Willie said. "Exactly what were you focused on?"

"His phone," Philbilly repeated. "He had a flip phone laying on the dash. When was the last time you saw a flip phone?"

Chapter 13

Manny's phone rang just as Reuben came into the back porch with a pitcher of iced tea. He set it and the glasses onto the coffee table while Manny answered the call. He put his hand over his phone speaker and said, "Department of the Army Records Office." After Willie and Manny left the Cohen Home earlier, he had called Abigail and sweet-talked her into a records check of soldiers serving with Robbie who were tall men.

Reuben nodded knowingly and quietly sat on the other lawn chair in the screened porch.

After the caller identified himself as Colonel Curtis, he asked for Manny's federal identification number before he continued. "I have the information your records department requested."

Manny grabbed his notebook from his back pocket. This was too important to trust to memory. "Please continue."

"With regards to who fit the height criteria of men serving with Private First Class Robert Bear Paw," the colonel began, "there were five. One Code Talker and four regular infantry."

"I'm ready for the names now."

"You want the ones still alive?"

Manny thought about Amos, finally realizing most soldiers who served with Robbie were probably dead by now. "No, just the living."

"You mean *presumed* living."

"How's that?"

"Three," the colonel began, "are dead for certain. We know that because they are all laid to rest in veterans' cemeteries. The other two we have not had any information on for decades."

"Tell me what information you have on the other two," Manny asked.

"Not much, except they fit the parameters you wanted us to search for. Charles McKnight from Wheeling, West Virginia, and Corporal Amos Willow Bent from Pine Ridge are the only ones."

Manny explained that Amos was alive and still quite active for his age living in a nursing home, but this was the first Manny had heard about McKnight. "Can you tell me anything at all about his activities after the war?"

A computer keyboard clacked on the other end of the line before Curtis said, "McKnight was mustered out in Little Rock. He joined the American Legion post there and there's no indication he ever left that area. But, there hasn't been any activity in his file since the '50s." More keyboard noise. "McKnight was ordered to the Philippines after the war, along with PFC Bear Paw, to testify in the war crimes trial. I haven't researched where Bear Paw was discharged as your office hasn't put in an archives request for him."

"Can you fax me what you have on McKnight and PFC Bear Paw?"

"You will have to submit another official request," Colonel Curtis said, "but I can have that as soon as the request lands on my desk."

Manny thanked him and disconnected with a groan.

"Not what you wanted to hear?" Reuben asked.

"No," Manny answered, "it's not that. Colonel Curtis sounds as professional as they come with military archives. It is just that I have to call the Bureau records office and channel a search of Robbie's post military activities that way."

"Is there a problem with that?"

Manny put the sweating-cold glass of iced tea to his temple to ease a rising headache. "The problem is that I have to talk with Abigail Winehart in Bureau records."

"That hunk of burnin' love you told me about?"

Manny nodded. "And it's just a matter of time before I will have to pay up and take her to dinner."

Reuben grinned and said to Manny, "The solution is really very simple."

"How?"

Reuben winked. "Marry Clara. Then you will be officially spoken for."

* * * * *

That evening, Manny and Reuben entered the *initipi* once again. Although it felt good to sweat out toxins in his body, Manny did not experience any vision this time. "That's how visions are," Reuben explained as he toweled himself off afterward. "*Wakan Tanka* gifts visions only rarely. You, *misun*, have an inordinate ability to please the Creator and receive them. Just not this time."

"Funny," Manny said, tossing Reuben his pair of jeans, "my visions do not feel like gifts. Be different if my visions were pleasant, but they're not. They're frightening."

Reuben motioned for Manny to take a lawn chair by the coffee table before disappearing inside his trailer. He came out within moments with a plate of fry bread and a saucer of warm honey that he set on the table. He didn't wait for Manny but broke off a piece of bread and dipped it into the honey. "It's not Clara's home cooking, but it'll have to do."

When Manny said nothing as he dipped his own fry bread into the honey, Reuben said, "You're going to have to confront her eventually. You cannot live in the same house with the elephant-in-the-room of marriage not being addressed."

"I know. But damn it, I've made it this long without tying the knot—"

"If she walked out the door and left you tonight, how would you feel?"

"Devastated," Manny answered immediately. He wiped his mouth with a napkin and slid the saucer of honey toward Reuben. "I've heard that a man is incomplete until he's married, then he's finished. I mean, look at you: you've never been married either."

"I'm saving myself for the right woman," Reuben said.

"You wait much longer for the right woman," Manny said, "and you'll have to chase her down with your walker."

"I am not that old yet," Reuben said as he rubbed his trick knee. "What I'm saying is that you can hang out here at my place every day if you like. I welcome the company. But it's just putting off the inevitable. You can only use the excuse that that old beater Mercury broke down on the rez so many times."

"Speaking of beaters—"

"You're changing the subject—"

"Obviously," Manny said. "Philbilly caught a ride from some guy driving the road from Rapid to Pine Ridge a couple weeks ago. Phil couldn't tell me a thing about the guy except that he drove a Pinto wagon and had a cell phone on the dash."

"I know the car. It's Henrietta's from the nursing home."

"You've seen it around the rez, then?" Manny asked, excited. "Who was driving it?"

"I said I know the car. I've never even seen anyone driving it besides her."

"Then how do you know it was hers?"

"Last week—just when she said someone stole it—she called me. Bawling, poor old gal. She got off work at the home and was going to drive to Sioux Grocery for a few things, but it wouldn't start. She called practically begging me to come fix it."

"What was wrong with it?"

Reuben chuckled. "Nothing. Whoever stole it brought it back on empty. Soon's I put some gas in, the old wagon fired right up. You would have thought I was some national hero, glad as she was."

"Did you see a flip phone on the dash?"

Reuben shook his head. "Only thing on the dash was that sand-weighted ash tray near overflowing with cigarillo butts. Couldn't hardly see how Henrietta could even reach the ashtray, as far back as that seat was."

Chapter 14

Manny headed east past Oacoma situated on the west side of the Missouri. He drove across the river towards Chamberlain and dropped down into a shallow valley. As he started across the I-90 bridge, he marveled at the beauty of the Missouri River, at the trees lining the banks, at the boats making small wakes in the blue-green water, at small kids standing on the banks with their fishing poles anticipating a big catch.

He turned into the Chamberlain city limits and motored towards the sheriff's office. As he passed St. James Catholic Church, he thought back to his Uncle Marion. Wherever he went, he always made it a point to attend Mass. Unlike Manny. Reuben was right: Manny needed to get right with God even as he was getting right with *Wakan Tanka*. Even as he needed to get right with Clara. He needed to heal his relationship with the Creator as much as needed to heal his relationship with Clara. Soon, he told himself.

He parked in front of the sheriff's office and started towards the door when a voice called out, "Sheriff Bain and Deputy Christian are out on calls."

He turned and faced a woman twice his size pushing a walker in front of her as she exited the courthouse across the street. An eighty-ounce Big Gulp rested in a cup holder she had rigged up on the side of her contraption, while a garbage bag slapped the other side. The bag clanged with empty aluminum cans as she neared. "They might be back later," she said pointing to the county jail.

"You sure they're not in there?" Manny asked.

"Sure, I'm sure. That Sheriff Bain… you couldn't corner him in a round room. Slick. In and out. Leaves most of the real work to Deputy Christian." She jerked her head toward the courthouse and the waddle under her chin continued to shimmy. "I work in vehicle licensing, and we tried getting hold of both of them an hour ago to check a vehicle's VIN number. No luck. Had to call a city cop to verify the number."

Manny thanked her and climbed into his car before checking his address book. Annie Jamieson lived on River Street a few blocks away and Manny punched her address into the Garmin. Marge blared over the speaker, "turn left." Manny wanted to defy the Garmin voice and turn right, but knew she would only spew more hatred and tell him to make a U-turn.

A dozen blocks down River Street he pulled into her circular driveway just as one door of the double garage was shutting. Annie quickly ducked under it before it closed and approached Manny's car. "Thought that was you, Agent Tanno. I bet you want to talk more about my father?"

"I do."

"Then come on inside. The place is a bit messy, but I got called to the county courthouse to make bail for Miles before I could straighten things up."

"Your boy in trouble?"

"Got himself arrested by the city police last night for fighting again. He was drunked-up at Charly's Lounge when he felt like hitting on a woman. Problem was, her husband took offense, and the fight was on. That makes twice this month I had to bail Miles out." She looked around the street and lowered her voice as if there were people close enough to hear. Which there wasn't. "What I wouldn't give to have some tough guy come into town and just clean Miles' clock. That's the only way he'll ever grow up and get this fighting out of his system."

Annie led Manny through the front door of the bricked home, and he looked about. He didn't know what the inside of the house looked like before she went to bail Miles out, but Manny didn't see a speck of dust or a chair out of place. "Have a seat at the breakfast counter and I will make us some tea. You do drink tea?"

Manny wanted to tell her that he choked it down when coffee wasn't available, but said, "Tea will be fine, and I think I'll stand. Give me a chance to stretch my legs. Drove straight in from Pine Ridge."

She snatched a canister from the cupboard and said over her shoulder, "I get my love of tea from my dad. He got hooked on it during the war in the Pacific."

Manny walked to a bay window looking out onto the Missouri and he could see why she had picked this spot to build a home. He admired the view of the Missouri with the boats and fishermen, the undulating river gentle. The whole scene serene. Calming.

Annie saw Manny looking at an inside shadow box overflowing with luscious pink orchids, and she said, "That's my one vice. Or rather hobby—gardening. Especially flowers."

"They're beautiful." Manny bent and took in the essence of the orchids before looking out the window. "Is that the old bridge across the river?" he asked, pointing to concrete pylons sticking out of the water.

The tea pot whistled just as Annie said, "It is. Usually, you can't see that much of it. But with the drought, the water's down." She turned around and set a cup of tea on the breakfast counter. "Sugar?"

"Please."

She put two cubes into Manny's cup and joined him at the window. She handed him the tea while she cradled her own cup in her hand. "Guess that's how those kids found that man right over there," she pointed. "You can just see the tip of that old cabin poking up from the water. There was one cabin Dad had to leave as it was rotted down and no one wanted it."

"Had to leave? Explain."

Annie sipped her tea, and the steam fogged her glasses. "That was one of Dad's first big projects he bid on and won when he first started his trucking company right after the war. He moved houses since back then, but that project earned him people's respect. There were eleven other cabins that folks won in the auction and he was contracted to move them before the Corps of Engineers flooded American Island." She faced Manny. "You ever been in business?"

Manny forced a laugh. "That'd be more like work."

"It is. Especially for an Indian living just off the reservation. After the war, Dad made a decision to live off Crow Creek. He felt living on the rez would prevent him from building his trucking business, what with people's prejudice towards us Indians. He thought he'd be passed over for bids just because he was Lakota."

"Wouldn't be the first time we were treated differently," Manny said.

"It was even worse back then. Think about it—it was right after the war. People were bigoted to the nth degree. Dad had to overcome that if he expected to successfully bid on projects, and he did. He built his business into the biggest trucking outfit in five counties."

Manny sipped the tea lightly before turning to the breakfast counter and adding another sugar cube to it. "Amos Willow Bent said Robbie's father bankrolled him and your father to start their businesses."

Annie smiled. "Dad said that grandfather—who I never knew—died leaving money to Dad to start a business and to Amos for taking that booby trap he felt was meant for Dad." She walked to the tea pot. "A refill?"

Manny waved the air. "I'm good."

Annie put another tea bag into her water and sat at the breakfast counter. "Have you made any headway identifying that body those kids found?"

"The medical examiner feels the victim would have been six-one to six-four. The records colonel I talked with narrowed it down to five soldiers who served with your dad who would have fit that criteria. Three have since died. The other two—Amos, and a Charles McKnight, were the only ones the colonel had no status on. He could be alive or dead. Does McKnight ring a bell?"

Annie shook her hear. "Dad never mentioned him. For that matter, he never mentioned anyone he served with except Amos."

"Then I'm back to square one identifying the body. Just how your father's dog tags got onto the man in the river is beyond me."

"Me, too." Annie walked to a China cabinet where she displayed mementos: A blue-green vase with cracks running through flying cranes. A trophy announcing Miles as the star running back in his senior year of high school. And a large, framed photograph that Annie took out of the cabinet. She handed Manny the picture. A much younger Annie Jamieson smiled at the camera as a man's arm draped over her shoulder, palm trees and the ocean as a backdrop. "That is my ex-husband, Buck."

Manny held the photo to the light. Buck smiled wide for the photographer, revealing two sparkling gold teeth. A pencil-thin mustache ended just at the corners of his mouth, and his angular face set off a small nose like a tall Clark Gable.

"Looks like a model, don't he?"

Manny handed the photograph back. "He is a handsome guy."

"You mean *was*." Annie put the picture frame back into the cabinet and turned to face Manny. "I had to go to court and declare him dead after he never came home. Damn fool was a womanizer. Even when I caught him sleeping around right after Miles was born, he still continued doing it."

"Any particular woman he take up with?"

Annie shrugged. "Banker's wife, Jaz Halverson, or so the town rumor went at the time. I had kicked him out, but he hung around town. Worked at the Standard Gas Station pumping gas. One day he left work and just never came back. I've never heard from him since. I keep that picture of our honeymoon in case he comes back one day." A dreamy look crossed her face. "Even after all this time and after the way he cheated on me I still love him."

Chapter 15

Sirens blaring, nearing, and Manny pulled to the side of the road. A Brule County Sheriff's truck sped by, lights bouncing off the walls of the businesses on Main Street and disappeared north through town. Manny sped up, dodging cars, curious why a sheriff's truck would need to run code at eleven o'clock in the morning.

The sheriff's patrol truck turned into the American Creek Campground just across the small bridge in Chamberlain and headed north with Manny close behind. He spotted the sheriff's unit parked at the campground's small beach and pulled into the parking lot. A dozen people stood in swim clothes crowding a man in uniform as he squatted beside a body, water sloshing over the victim. Manny climbed out, elbowing his way through the lookie-loos eyeing the victim lying on the sand. A man older than Manny with "Sheriff Bain" embroidered on his tan uniform shirt knelt beside the body and he looked up through red-rimmed eyes.

Manny slipped his ID wallet out of his pocket and showed the sheriff. Tears filled his eyes. "Why... he was as good a deputy as I could ever find."

Manny moved to one side and saw the face for the first time: Sam Christian. Manny sucked in a breath. "My, God, what was he doing in the river, 'cause he sure wasn't swimming with his uniform on."

Sheriff Bain started to speak, then stopped and looked at the crowd.

Manny turned and faced them. "Go on home now. The sheriff has his hands full without people crowding him."

When no one moved, Manny showed his badge around and snapped, "Damn it, get the hell outta here, all of you, or you'll be spending the night in the hoosegow."

One man clenched his fists and started toward Manny when a woman beside him took his arm and pulled him away.

The others reluctantly left, some glancing over their shoulders to get a last look at the dead man.

When they had cleared the beach, Manny turned back to the Sheriff still kneeling beside Sam's corpse. "What do you know about this?"

"Just that the city dispatch called saying there was a drowning victim popped up on the beach at American Creek." He drew his arm across his eyes and Manny fished a bandana from his pocket and handed it to the sheriff. "I never imagined it would be Sam. How the hell he got into the river is beyond me."

Manny helped the sheriff stand on wobbly legs.

"May I... look at Sam?"

"Of course."

Manny squatted beside the body and turned him over. A large bruise had formed along one side of his cheek and it appeared as if his cheekbones were fractured, while his flayed nose rested to one side of his face. "I'm not sure what caused his death," Manny said, "But it sure wasn't by drowning. I would say Sam here was beat to death. We'll know for sure at autopsy."

"Autopsy?" Sheriff Bain said. "We'll have an autopsy conducted on Sam?"

"Your call, but if you don't order one, the DCI will step in and order one."

Sheriff Bain handed Manny his bandana back and said to him,

DEATH UNDER THE DELUGE

"I don't think I could witness Sam being autopsied."

"As unpleasant as it will be," Manny said and put his hand on the sheriff's shoulder, "I'll attend the procedure in your place. If you like."

"Would you?" the sheriff seemed to be pleading.

"I will call Doctor Darden and tell him he has another one," Manny said.

"Doctor Darden," Sheriff Bain said. "At least I know he'll be in good hands."

* * * * *

The courthouse was dark by the time Manny drove from Hickey Funeral Chapel to the sheriff's office where only a dim light burned. The door stood slightly ajar to get air into the office and Manny entered, a cup of coffee from nearby McDonald's in each hand. Sheriff Bain sat on a chair slumped over a cardboard box. The old man looked up, his eyes still red with pain. "Just gathering Sam's things to give to his sister living in Letcher. Police Academy certificate. That time he won that Tough Man contest down in Winner. A spare box of ammunition he always kept for emergencies." He forced a laugh. "Guess the boy won't have to go to any more emergencies now."

Manny set the cups on the desk and gently eased the sheriff up and away from the box. "Why don't you take a little break. It's been a hard day for you."

"Been harder for Sam."

"Can't argue there."

Manny handed the sheriff a cup of coffee. He took the top off, sipping lightly, steam clouding his glasses. "The autopsy is complete I take it?"

Manny nodded and took out his notebook. "Doctor Darden was as upset as you are—he genuinely liked Sam."

"Everybody liked Sam," Sheriff Bain said.

"Everybody except the one who murdered him."

"So, it was a homicide?"

Manny nodded.

The sheriff set his cup down and opened a desk drawer. He came away with a pouch of tobacco and a meerschaum pipe, the milky-white stone stained brown from the many years of use. Sheriff Bain packed the bowl and tamped it down with the end of a pencil before lighting it. When he spoke, his voice was measured, calm as if the pipe gave him strength to ask, "why does Doctor Darden believe Sam was murdered?"

Manny laid his notebook on the desk and flipped to a page. "Sam's face and temporal region of his skull had been fractured. The indent and bruising looking like a pipe. A piece of hard wood. From something round like a pool cue but bigger around. But it was his internal injuries which probably caused the most damage. Someone beat Sam until he couldn't defend himself."

"Who would ever want to hurt him? Everyone liked the kid."

Manny finished his coffee and dropped the cup into the round file beside the desk. "Perhaps it had something to do with the cases he was working on. Sam told me a couple days ago that Annie Jamieson reported she suspected someone embezzled money from the trucking company."

"I gave Sam that case," Sheriff Bain said. "Kid had an accounting degree and if anyone could figure out who stole the money it would have been Sam. But he said he didn't have anything to report as of yesterday, though he had some suspicions that he never shared. He was like that—never accused anyone until he had proof positive."

"What other cases was he working on? When I stopped earlier today a lady from the courthouse said you were both out of the office on calls."

"I was at a family fight in Kimball. Sam was following up on a tip down in the Bijou Hills where we've had a dozen cattle thefts this last month. The dispatcher tried getting hold of him down there but had no luck. But that doesn't mean anything—the service is pretty sketchy down thataway."

The old man swirled his coffee around as he looked into the cup. "And a hit and run by the truck stop that killed a girl on a mountain bike two weeks ago. I don't believe he'd developed any substantial leads on that either, but he may have." He crushed the Styrofoam cup and tossed it into the trash can. "But none of those cases warranted Sam getting beat to death."

"My opinion is no one warrants a gruesome death like that," Manny said. "Can you think of anything else, anyone who might have a grudge against Sam? Anyone he had a fight with recently perhaps."

Sheriff Bain looked at his pipe that had gone cold and tapped it against the side of the metal trash can. "Not recently, but he killed a man in an attempted robbery six years ago and his brother vowed he'd return and get even with Sam."

"Know where we could find this brother?"

"Sure I do," the sheriff answered. "The state penitentiary. The guy's name is Jake Duddy. He was in on the robbery with his brother when Sam shot and killed him."

Chapter 16

Manny walked down the steps of the Best Western and headed to his car when a voice called out, "That's a pretty dull looking car you're driving this time. Where's the cool old one?" Emily Mockingbird emerged from a room wearing a beach towel slung over her shoulders and a minimalist bikini.

Manny averted his eyes and said, "This is what the government issues me. Can't be choosy."

Emily approached Manny and smiled wide. A breeze coming off the river blew across her and Manny took in her cologne. "No one in the pool today. You could keep me company."

Manny felt his neck and face warm and he was sure he blushed at the younger woman flirting with him. "I need to do some research today."

"About Sam Christian getting hammered to death?"

"Figured as many people who saw him washed up on the beach that word would get around," Manny said. "Have you heard anything?"

Emily shrugged. "People tell me things. All sorts of things. A night clerk at a motel is like a barber or hairdresser—people just flap their gums when they come in. But about this… not a word. A shame—I liked Sam. A lot. When Miles and me dated, we had an awful row one night. Sam showed up at the bar and Miles calmed down right off. Sam might have been the only guy that crazy bastard Miles Bear Paw was afraid of. Guess it goes back to when they were in school together and Sam would kick Miles' keister on a regular basis." She chuckled. "Now the city police will have to hire more officers."

"And why is that?" Manny asked.

"Because," Emily said, "Sam could talk Miles into coming into jail when he got into a bar fight. It'll be Katy Bar the Door whenever the cops are called now."

"If you hear anything—"

"You'll be the first one I whisper it to," Emily said and sashayed toward the pool.

Manny climbed into his *dull* government car and drove the few blocks to the public library—more exact, the Cozard Memorial Library after one of the town's beloved mayors. Two boys no more than ten years old bounded along the sidewalk toward the front doors and disappeared inside a moment before a girl about the same age followed. As Manny started through the doors, he noticed a flyer that proclaimed that every day during this summer vacation the library conducted reading time for young children.

When he walked to the reception desk, a librarian looked over the top of her glasses and said with a grin, "You look a mite old to sit listening to someone reading adventure stories."

"If it gets me out of this heat I'll sit and listen to most anything." Manny dug his ID wallet out of his pocket and showed the lady.

"This have something to do with Sam Christian being found drowned?" she asked.

Does everyone know? he thought to himself. "It ties in. I'm here for some research on American Island."

"Then you've come at about the right time. Alice—that's the senior librarian—will be in shortly. She knows just about everything about the island. In the meantime, you can sit and listen with the children."

"Or I can read your local newspaper until Alice comes in?"

"Of course."

Manny picked up a copy of the *Chamberlain Oacoma Sun* and scanned the front page. The Chamber of Commerce called for entries for the upcoming July 4th parade. Bear Paw Trucking and Jackson Trucking out of Ft. Pierre to the north had submitted identical bids to move eight houses to make way for a new road on the north end of town adjacent to St. Joseph's Indian School compound. The Chamberlain-Oacoma Gun Club advertised a sporting clay shoot at their range next Saturday, while the police blotter mentioned Miles' arrest for fighting. He wasn't alone: three others had been arrested for disorderly conduct over the weekend but, unlike Miles, they apparently had no one to bail them out. Sam's homicide would probably be covered the following day, Manny was certain.

A short, compact lady with long, graying hair approached Manny and offered her hand. "I'm Alice. Batty said you were interested in American Island."

Manny opened his notebook on the table and grabbed his pen. "I am sure by now that you have read about the body found in the river at the old American Island?"

"The newspaper said Sheriff Bain released very little information, and folks just figured it was another drowning victim. We get several a year," Alice said as she pulled a chair out and sat across from Manny. "When the Corps of Engineers opens the gates of the dam up north, small boats have been known to have been sucked under." She leaned closer and said under her breath, "but it wasn't a drowning victim, now was it?"

"If you have information—"

"I don't know squat," Alice said, "but I do know the FBI doesn't investigate drownings."

It wasn't Manny's place to release information to the public: it was Sheriff Bain's. But if Manny ever wanted to identify the victim in the river—and perhaps find Sam's killer—he had to trust someone local. Manny explained to Alice how the body in the river had a rope tied to its wrists at the time of the murder and it apparently had gotten snagged to an old cabin on what used to be called American Island. He concluded that the victim had been shot prior to being tied up.

"Hot damn!" Alice said, slapping her leg. "I knew it was a murder." She looked around the library, but the only other people here were a dozen children sitting on the floor listening to Batty reading an adventure story. "Your secret is safe with me."

"Until Sheriff Bain releases it officially?"

Alice made a gesture as if she were zipping her lips. "But what has this got to do with American Island?"

"I don't know if it has anything to do with it except the body was found there. And he was probably alive when the Corps of Engineers flooded the reservoir," Manny said.

"You said the victim was a he?"

Manny nodded, watching the children out of the corner of his eye wildly waving their hands to get Batty's attention.

"The victim was a man," Manny explained. "The medical examiner feels he may have been in the water for approaching seventy years. Or, he may have been in there as little as thirty years. Water deaths with people who have been under for some time are difficult to age."

Alice stood and paced in front of the table before stopping and facing Manny. "You think American Island may have some connection to the victim?"

"I might be clutching at straws, but at this point I'll take any straw I can grasp."

Alice looked at Manny's notebook and asked, "Can I have a piece of paper and your pen?"

Manny tore a sheet off and handed Alice his pen.

She began drawing and a few moments later she explained as if Manny were the group of children at story time. She continued sketching while she said, "Lewis and Clark came onto the island in 1804. They noted there were cottonwood and aromatic cedar trees. Wild berries that they compressed into pemican." She turned the map she drew so Manny could see it better. "Here's about where we are now and here's where American Island was. My father said he and mother used to take a ferry out there a couple times a month in the summer. They would rent a cabin and walk around the island, though no bigger than it was it didn't take long to walk it."

Manny tapped his finger on the map. "Then the whole Island was no longer than what, a couple miles?"

"Not quite that, but close. And a half-mile wide. Dad said they had a ball field where baseball teams used to compete. Swimming pools. The auditorium even had an ice cream parlor. Later, it became a CCC camp in the thirties. He said it was quite the place to visit in its heyday. Now the only thing left of the island are those concrete statutes you see around town."

"What statutes?"

Alice put several marks on the map. "They used to sit at the entrance to the island and were rescued prior to the big flooding: a squirrel here," she pointed with the pen to the map of town she'd drawn. "A rabbit on this corner. A fawn here."

Manny turned the map around to orient himself with the statues. He had seen them when driving around town, but never knew they came from American Island. "Tell me about the cabins there."

Alice shrugged. "Not much to tell, at least, my father never mentioned them much. They rented for a night or a week, but they were auctioned off before the reservoir was flooded in the early fifties."

"Where'd they go?"

"Can't say," she said. "All I know is Robbie Bear Paw got the bid to move them and from then on his trucking company took off, according to my father." Alice stood. "Unfortunately, there is scant little information in the library about the island. You might check with the newspaper just a couple blocks down on Main Street."

The children still sat enthralled by Batty's reading and paid Manny no mind as he left the library and started walking towards Main Street. He passed antique shops along the street where tourists stopped and examined items displayed on the sidewalk. He could tell they were tourists—they wore Hawaiian shirts. Just like him when he did the tourist thing. One man walked the sidewalk proudly carrying a jackalope mount he had bought in one of the shops.

Manny entered the office of the *Chamberlain Oacoma Sun* to the tinkling of a cow bell over the door. A lady in her twenties stood from her desk and approached the counter. Large beaded hoop earrings dangled from her ears partially hidden by her thick, black hair. "*Hau.* What's the FBI want with the Sun today?"

"How do you know I'm an FBI agent?"

The woman laughed and tapped her head. "Us Indians are sort of mind readers. Actually, I can't lie. This is a small town and word travels with the speed of gossip, 'specially when an FBI agent is in town. I would wager you want to find out about Robbie Bear Paw. Trying to figure out who that floater is those kids found by the old American Island."

"Why do you think I want to research him?"

"His dog tags were around the victim's neck, weren't they?"

Manny thought about who might have leaked information that he didn't want public. The only others who knew about Robbie's dog tags being found on a corpse were Doctor Darden, Sam and Reuben. Sam was dead. That left Doctor Death, and Manny recalled how the doctor belted down beer after beer. Manny could imagine him at one of the local watering holes getting schnockered and shooting off his mouth. Manny would have a talk with the good doctor when he had the chance.

The woman, Shandy Comes Flying by her name tag, grabbed a notebook and asked, "What can you tell us about that body? And about Sam Christian's murder?"

"No comment."

"Come on, Agent Tanno—you need to give us something to print. Now what's the skinny on the victims?"

"No comment," Manny said, then asked, "You sound as if you have heard things. What things?"

"No comment," Shandy said and put her notebook down. "Soon's you come clean with something we can print, I might just remember things I might have heard. Now is there anything I can help you with. Officially and on the record?"

"Robbie Bear Paw," Manny said. "I understand he was something of a local celebrity."

Shandy grabbed a can of Copenhagen from a desk drawer and stuffed her lower cheek. She wiped the excess off on her jeans and said to Manny, "He was before my time. But folks hereabouts brag that they had a living, breathing Code Talker walking amongst them. I would wager you are curious as to who Robbie hung with who might have worn his dog tags."

"That mind reading trick again?" Manny said.

Shandy chuckled. "Just simple deduction this time, gleaned from things I've heard recently. Just figured you'd be nosing around about him." She swung the gate away and motioned to Manny. "Our old articles are archived on a microfiche machine. And before you say it, we know that microfiche is a little outdated, but this is a small newspaper."

"But," Manny said as he followed her, "the articles your newspaper has been putting out aren't outdated from what I've read. Pretty professional reporting I'd say."

Despite her dark complexion, Manny saw Shandy blush.

She led Manny into a small room off to one side of the office.

She pulled a plastic cover off an old microfiche machine, the tall hood with sloping sides meant to allow someone to look for hours, if necessary. Shandy bent and grabbed a box from under the machine and took the lid off. "There's articles dating back to the first world war." Her fingers glided over the squares of plastic with words too tiny to be read unless the sheets were placed into the machine. "Here's dates you might be interested in, starting just before World War II and ending in the 90s when we went digital."

She showed Manny the procedure to connect to their printer if he wanted to print an article. "Would you like some coffee, maybe soda? I suspect you'll be here for a while."

"Coffee's fine," Manny said and pulled a chair close to the microfiche reader. It had been years since he'd had to read anything on such a machine. The last time was when he was a tribal policeman in Pine Ridge before he'd been hired by the Bureau.

When Shandy brought Manny a cup and carafe of coffee she said, "I figured you'd be needing more than just a cup, long as it might take you."

* * * * *

Sometime on his third cup of coffee, Manny found an article that praised Robbie for having been one who testified at a war crimes trial in the Philippines, along with a former Army Lieutenant Charles McKnight. Robbie was welcomed home with a parade on Crow Creek Reservation after the trial but there was no mention of McKnight being a decorated vet.

Manny went through three other sheets of microfiche plastic before finding another article about Robbie. A year after being discharged from the Army, Robbie had moved to Chamberlain and annually rode a Code Talker float in the 4th of July Parade.

The article went on to recap and reprise Robbie's time as a Code Talker in the Pacific. A photo attached to the newspaper article was the same photo that Sam pointed out hanging on the wall of the sheriff's office.

However, the caption underneath was not cut off like the picture in the one hanging in the SO. This caption identified Robbie, looking dour, and a visiting soldier he had served with during the war—Charles McKnight. He rode the float along with Robbie, towering over the shorter man, smiling and waving at the crowd as if *he* were the local hero the parade was dedicated to.

A sidebar noted that, during the community luncheon following the parade, Charles McKnight started drinking heavily and the police were called to remove him. And even before the parage began, the police responded to the D&D Bar where McKnight had picked a fight with two Indians from Crow Creek, and was escorted out before they got a chance to hurt him.

"Maybe that's why he was grinning like a Cheshire cat on the parade float," Manny said to himself. "Maybe he was already tuned up. That would account for Robbie looking so grim—he might have been truly angry at his old Army buddy's drinking. Embarrassed by McKnight's actions."

Chapter 17

Shandy poked her head into the viewing room and said, "I'm about ready to lock up for the night." She stepped into the room just as Manny gathered up his notes. "Find anything that might help you?"

"I'm not sure," Manny answered. "Now, if I could just talk to someone in the parade the day this photo was taken—"

"Not too many people left alive. That was the early fifties. Closest you'll get is Freddy Geddes down at the D&D. His grandfather sponsored that float Robbie and that friend of his rode on that day."

"The D&D?"

"Sure." Shandy laughed. "We used to call it the Death and Destruction before it got civilized. Bar at the north end of main street. When you stop there, tell Freddy I am not going to go to the movies with him Saturday night."

Manny gathered his notes and put them into his car before walking the few blocks north. The sign above the D&D sported chipped blue paint, cracked like an egg, as if it hadn't been painted in decades. Which it may not have been by the looks of it. Manny entered the dimly lit saloon and stood to one side of the door to let his eyes adjust to the low light. Two cowboys hunched over the table playing pool. The bigger of the two looked up before laying his pool cue on the table and approaching Manny. Even as the man neared, Manny could smell the thick odor of beer, recognized the saunter of a man looking for trouble. "Is it payday already?" the man asked and tilted his head back and laughed. His partner did the same and the big cowboy stared at Manny. "Well, is it payday? That why you're off the reservation?"

Manny ignored him. Even if Manny were an Indian living on Crow Creek, his land payments were no business of this drunk.

Manny started around the cowboy when his hand shot out and grabbed Manny by the arm. Manny jerked back and swept his foot under the cowboy's boot. He tumbled to the floor, knocking over a chair, his hat rolling across the floor a moment before his head hit the floor.

The man's partner grabbed his pool cue. He cocked it like he intended hitting a baseball and advanced on Manny. The first cowboy used the edge of the pool table to stand when a blur whizzed by. From Manny's right, the man with the pool cue went sprawling. Peanuts littering the floor *poofed* up when he landed face down.

Manny looked over at a man small in stature but obviously big in courage. He held a tire billy in his hand and said to the cowboy, "You know damn well I don't allow fighting in here. Now pick Earl up and get the hell out."

The big cowboy nearly fell over again as he stooped to retrieve his Stetson. With his finger he poked the air in Manny's direction and said, "You ain't seen the last of me, Indian. And you either, Freddie."

"Go on, Wayne" Freddie said. "Get Earl out of here before he bleeds all over my floor. And get him up to the ER for some stitches."

The cowboy picked up his companion, a round indent on his forehead leaking blood, and they stumbled out of the bar. Freddie looked after them before walking back behind the bar and stashing his tire billy. "That was the Heinous Horris brothers—Earl and Wayne. They're just pissed 'cause they lost a lease on some reservation land they were bidding on up by Ft. Thompson. Now all they got is a quarter section down by the Bijou Hills. Needless to say, they're crappy ranchers. They'd rather be here in town getting beered-up than doing hard work. You watch your backside around them—they're bullies who don't cotton to being embarrassed." The man leaned over the bar and offered his hand. "Freddie Geddes."

Manny introduced himself and said, "Shandy's not going to the movie with you."

"How you know that?"

"She just told me."

Freddie laughed. "Since when does FBI agents relay information from lonely girls? Hell, she'll go to the movies Saturday. She does every week. She's just teasing me. Want a drink?"

"Diet cola," Manny said as he patted his stomach. "Gotta be careful with my diabetes."

"Coming up." Freddie filled a glass with ice and soda before grabbing a *Grain Belt* and popping the top. He saw Manny eying the bottle of beer, reminding him of Doctor Death drowning his *Blatz*, and said, "So I like cheap beer." He swallowed half the bottle before setting it on the bar. "If you didn't come in for a drink, why did you come in here?"

Manny took off his Stetson and ran his fingers through what was left of his hair. "I guess I'm always clutching at straws." He explained to Freddie what would be in tomorrow's newspaper: Deputy Sam Christian was murdered with a blunt instrument.

"I already knew that."

"How?"

Freddie winked. "Shandy. She can't keep a secret. She also told me that corpse those boys found by the old American Island was murdered as well."

"Guess word does get around quick here." Manny sat on a stool and leaned his elbows on the bar. "Shandy said your granddad sponsored this float." He unfolded the copy he had made from the microfiche article on the 4th of July Parade in 1952.

Freddie nodded and stared at the photo before handing it back. "Granddad—and Dad as well when he was running the bar—talked constantly about Robbie Bear Paw. About what a good guy he was, always giving to this charity or that cause. Granddad was more than happy to sponsor a float for a war hero like Robbie."

"Did they ever mention this other guy riding on the float with him?"

"Did they!" Freddie turned around and grabbed a dusty frame hanging above the back bar. "They said that a friend of Robbie's, that Charlie McKnight, was some character. Got into a scuffle that first time with some locals but he mellowed out. The man came in the bar here most every night after that and the first thing he'd do is buy a round for everyone. By the end of the night, he'd have put down more beer than just about anyone Granddad saw who ever came in here. Generous." Freddie handed Manny the frame and smiled. "Yeah, quite the character. He gave this to Granddad one night. 'Here's a nice gold coin for your hospitality.' Granddad said Charlie lit out of town the next day and never came back."

Manny plucked a bar napkin from the holder and brushed the dust away from the frame. He held it to the light, though he couldn't make out many details through the old glass. "That was pretty generous of Charlie to give your granddad a gold piece."

Freddie laughed. "That's why it's still hanging above the bar—it ain't a real gold coin. Granddad and later Dad kept it displayed as a conversation piece."

"Have you ever had it appraised?"

"For some goofy medal that's merely painted gold?"

"Mind if I take it out of the frame and look at it?" Manny asked.

"Suit yourself," Freddie said. "Just make sure you put the dust back when you're done."

Manny turned the frame over and worked out the toothpicks holding the back. He carefully picked up the coin by the edge and turned so the light hit the coin. He fished his reading glasses from his pocket and asked, "Do you have a little flashlight?"

"I have a big flashlight," Freddie said before reaching under the bar. He handed Manny an aluminum-bodied flashlight that was dented much like his tire billy and Manny thought there was still old, dried blood by the head of the light.

Manny shined the light from an angle and saw struck on the face of the coin a man on horseback. He wore no armor as he fought and speared a dying dragon on the ground. Manny handed Freddie his reading glasses and said, "Take a look."

Freddie bent to the coin and brushed the glasses aside. "Guess I'm still young enough I don't need them. Now what is it you want me to look at?"

"That man battling a dragon is a depiction of Saint George—after King George the III. Notice how his hair flowed in back of him under his helmet?"

Freddie shrugged. "Sure. What of it?"

"The designer, Benedetto Pistrucci, was ordered to remove St. George's helmet in 1821—"

"You're acting like this thing is a genuine gold coin."

"It is," Manny said. "Probably struck in England in or around 1819 but few survive today. This was at the time when England flirted with the notion to get rid of all coins and issue paper currency instead."

"It can't be real," Freddie said. "People just don't hand out gold coins."

Manny carefully set the coin on a napkin and sipped his cola. "They do if the price of gold isn't as high as it is today. Think about it... McKnight was here throwing around gold in 1952.

The price of gold then was about forty-dollars an ounce. He could afford to be generous. Did your granddad or dad mention other gold coins Charlie McKnight had? Maybe he paid his bar tab with gold."

"He did not," Freddie said, picking up the coin again and turning it over. "At least they never mentioned it and that's something that would have stood out."

"Especially since FDR made it illegal for private citizens to own gold. Lasted until Tricky Dick Nixon and Gerald Ford got rid of that outdated law."

Freddie whistled. "So with the price of gold nowadays, this is worth upwards of two grand?"

Manny gently took the coin from Freddie and wrapped it in a bar napkin. "I worked a case up in Crow Agency a couple years ago where artifacts were stolen. Historical artifacts. One being a British Sovereign. Not quite this old, but still valuable. It was appraised at $90,000 at the time. This one... I'd say more in the ballpark of a $125,000."

"Damn," Freddie breathed. "I'm rich. Where would I ever sell it?"

"Freddie," Manny said slowly, "I'm afraid I'm going to have to seize this."

"What the hell for?"

"Charlie McKnight gave this to your Granddad. When you say he disappeared after that, he must have had more gold coins to spread around. To live off of. I need to know where he got this coin. It might lead me to the killer of that man in the river. For all I know at this point, Charlie shot that feller and lit out of Chamberlain right afterwards."

"Now why would he do that? Granddad said Charlie was friendly. Never got into any fights after that day of the parade."

"Maybe someone recognized it as a true gold coin. Maybe McKnight had more. Maybe someone jumped him to steal it.

Maybe—just maybe—he's that man found murdered in the river."

Freddie's hand grasped the flashlight tightly, his knuckles white. "I don't know as if I'll let it go."

"You have no choice," Manny said, his hand going inside his jeans, feeling the butt of the small revolver that wasn't Bureau issue. "I'll give you a receipt and speculate that I can return it to you if I can't trace its origin."

Freddie's hand relaxed and he finished off his bottle of beer. "I'll hold you to it, Agent Tanno. And I'll be expecting it back soon."

Chapter 18

The drive from Chamberlain to his office in Rapid City had been a long one, and all Manny could think about was the gold coin he had seized from Freddie Geddes. At the time that Charlie McKnight gave the gold coin to Freddy's granddad, spot price of gold was nowhere near the price as it is now. Still, Manny wondered as he drove, just where McKnight had come into possession of a British sovereign. And if he had had more.

Manny turned his desk light to avoid the glare as he sat back in his chair and examined the notes he'd just taken. On the way back to his home in Rapid City, his office had called—St. Louis PD had information on Charles McKnight. As soon as Manny arrived at his office, he'd called the St. Louis liaison officer.

"Our records show that Charles McKnight owned a small taxi company here in the city," Officer Waits said. "He bought the business right after he came back from World War II—long before my time. Seems that his aunt gave him the money to buy the taxis, though I don't know what her name is. Or was."

Manny knew the chances of McKnight being alive was slim: he would be as old as Amos. "I can't say if he's still living or not," Waits said. "He pulled up stakes and left town."

"When?"

Paper shuffled on the other end of the line. "Last contact our officers had with McKnight was 1952. There's several police reports of him and his girlfriend fighting, and it looks like he was a suspect in dealing drugs in the city."

"Could you fax over those reports?"

"Sure," Officer Waits said, "though there's nothing here that would help you."

It was those reports that Manny now studied as he sat back in his chair. He would be late for his dinner date with Clara, but he prayed that the police reports from St. Louis might contain some pearl of information. They didn't. Knight's live-in girlfriend called twice when he came home "drugged up" as she put it. The follow-up report developed information that McKnight was dealing downers and uppers via his cab drivers, and he was an associate of the city's most ruthless dealer at the time. "How the hell did you get involved in drugs?" Manny said to himself, then answered his own question. Combat veterans returning from the war suffered what they called shell shock back then, what is now recognized as PTSD. And like modern warriors, returning World War II vets drowned their agonizing memories in drugs and alcohol. McKnight might have seen an opportunity to deal himself to support his habit.

Manny picked up another report from an undercover officer assigned to follow McKnight whom the officer referred to as "Charlie." McKnight had entered a pawn shop specializing in antiquities and pawned two pieces of pottery dated from the Chinese Kangxi period of the 1700s. On yet another occasion, he sold the shop a rolled-up oil painting depicting a Taiwanese country scene. Another time selling six gold sovereigns that sounded much like the one McKnight had given to Freddie's grandfather.

"It would appear," Officer Waits had said, "that Charlie McKnight was running out of money to feed his drug habit. The officer assigned the case had suggested the detective division of the St. Louis PD apply for search warrants and arrest warrants for McKnight.

The St. Louis PD report outlined that they never got the chance to execute the search or the arrest warrant—McKnight suddenly went missing. His girlfriend reported that he had locked his office up one night and called her to say he was stopping by a nearby tap room for a brewski. He never made it home. The department had alerted all officers to find the flight risk, but McKnight could not be found. The Detective Division commander concluded after a year of fruitless searching that McKnight had crossed his dealer and was wearing concrete galoshes somewhere in the St. Louis river.

"But you popped up in Chamberlain, Charlie," Manny said to himself. "Visiting your old war buddy. Were you on the lam from the law or that nasty dealer you double crossed? Did that dealer follow you to Chamberlain and kill you and toss you in the river?"

As Manny closed up the office and turned off the lights, he figured this would be something to kick around with Clara. After all, he had been with her so long that she was almost an extension of him. He knew he had put off long enough a serious talk with her. Would he agree on a wedding date tonight? Would she give him the ultimatum tonight? Either way, he knew that he could not risk losing her.

Chapter 19

"Amos told me before that Robbie never had a proper sending-away ceremony," Reuben said. "I should have done this long before now. Cow."

Manny laid on the brakes and the government Crown Vic skidded to a stop inches from a black white-faced heifer crossing the road.

"Want me to drive?"

"You don't have a driver's license," Manny answered.

Reuben chuckled. "Even without a license and blindfolded I would get in fewer wrecks than you have."

Manny ignored him and continued along Highway 18 toward the Red Cloud School complex. "Why would Robbie Bear Paw never have a ceremony?" Manny asked. "Seems like someone in his family would want one performed."

Reuben grabbed a leg and repositioned it away from the dashboard. Cars never seemed to fit him. "Maybe Robbie was like you were before you found your way back to walking the Red Road. Did you see any sacred artifacts when you stopped by his daughter's house? Any dream catchers or photos of our fallen warriors?"

"Nothing to indicate she even identifies as Lakota."

"Some Indians are like that," Reuben said. "When I was serving my time in the state penitentiary, there were a lot of Indians who wanted nothing to do with the old ways. I always figured they would rather continue their life of crime when they got paroled rather than return to our traditions."

"But you turned your life around," Manny said.

Reuben nodded. "I was lucky. If I hadn't met that sacred man while in stir and studied with him, I would have surely been rearrested many times over after I was released."

Manny turned on to the Red Cloud Indian School compound road. As they passed two children picking up litter along the side of the road, they looked up and waved as the government car passed. Coming upon the Holy Rosary Catholic Church, Reuben said, "That is a great church, done in traditional ways but I miss seeing the original one the Jesuits built. Not that I much went there before I started walking the *Chunka Duta*."

"I was teaching at the academy in Quantico when the old church burnt down," Manny said. "A shame too: Unc used to take me there for Sunday Mass every single week."

"It burned down the same day my sentence was complete and I was released from the penitentiary—Good Friday in '96. I always wondered if *Wakan Tanka* had sent me some kind of message that my old ways were burned up, saving me the fires of perdition, and I would be rebuilding my life in an honorable way. As many times as I've entered the sweat lodge, I have never been lucky to have the Creator speak to me like He does you."

"Believe me," Manny said, "when I get a vision He sends me, I don't feel very lucky."

They took the road leading to the cemetery. Manny had been here several times with his Uncle Marion. This had been Unc's yearly pilgrimage, paying respect to the great Oglala Lakota leader Red Cloud who was buried on the hill overlooking the school he fought the Jesuits so hard to establish.

At the entrance to the cemetery, Manny parked and waited outside the car as Reuben unfolded himself from inside. He groaned and said, "Not a spring chicken anymore. Damned arthritis."

As they walked past gravestones, looking for Robbie's marker, Manny saw tiny red prayer bundles hung over headstones. One marker showed *U.S. Army Scout*, another declaring an Oglala had died at the Wounded Knee Massacre in 1890, while others were so old and weather-eroded the dates were unreadable. Manny counted at least three with dates that were barely readable, each with the inscription that the child had died while attending the Holy Rosary School. They passed the headstone of one priest alongside two belonging to Catholic sisters who'd died while working and living at the school.

"There," Reuben said and chin-pointed to a headstone newer than most others.

Manny joined his brother as they stood reverent looking down at Robbie Bear Paw's marker. An orchid like the one he had seen in Annie's house hung wilted over the side of a small vase at the base of the headstone. "Annie grows those flowers. She must have been out here in the past month."

Reuben placed his canvas shoulder bag on the ground. From his pipe bundle, he unwrapped a clay pipe in two parts. He reverently fit the bowl and the pipe together before filling it with tobacco from a small pouch in his bag. He tamped the tobacco down with what Manny recognized as a Sun Dance skewer—a bone that had pierced Reuben's chest as he participated in a Sun Dance the year he was released from prison. He dug into his pocket and grabbed a crusted and dented Zippo lighter embossed with the eagle, globe, and anchor of the Marine Corps. He paused when he saw Manny eying him. "Zippos ain't traditional but I figured with this wind I couldn't keep a match lit."

Manny remained quiet, praying to Wakan Tanka, praying that Robbie's *sicun*, his guardian spirit, had escorted him along the *Wanagi Tacanku*, the Spirit Road, upon his death.

Reuben turned to each of the four directions in turn, offering the pipe before addressing the sky, Mother Earth, every time chanting *hanbloglaka,* the sacred words only *Wicasa Wakan* holy men knew.

He lit the tobacco and blew on the embers before taking a long draw and handing the pipe to Manny. He had struggled to quit smoking some years ago and avoided any contact with tobacco, but this was different. The Creator would help him get past this point, for it was the taking of tobacco for a sacred reason and he drew in a long pull of the smoke before slowly releasing it. He handed the pipe back to Reuben who, after once more offering prayers to the four directions, the zenith and nadir, tamped the tobacco out of the bowl and allowed the wind to carry it across Robbie's grave site.

After they'd stood quiet in front of the headstone, Reuben dismantled the pipe and carefully rewrapped it in the leather cloth that he stowed in his bag.

Manny and Reuben stood for a moment longer, praying softly when Reuben interrupted the silence. "Code Talkers were heroes, you know. Amos told me a lot about how they would go into the field with only one other soldier to watch their backs. And to ensure they were never captured alive and reveal the Lakota language. They put their life on the line every day."

"Kind of like you did in Vietnam," Manny said.

"Same but different," Reuben said. "At least we knew that—unless we got our asses shot off—we'd be back in the world in thirteen months."

"Maybe Robbie and Amos and the other Code Talkers liked pulling the strings against the Japanese."

"Doubt they enjoyed it. My guess is they couldn't wait to be back in the rear."

"Or maybe they were like you," Manny said. "Enjoyed the action."

"Who said I enjoyed the 'Nam?"

"You served three tours," Manny said. "Voluntarily. Means you actually liked the fighting." Manny tried many times to get his older brother to open up about his time in Vietnam, but he rarely did. Manny finally concluded some time ago that Reuben wanted to bury his horrific years over there much like Manny had wanted to bury his Lakota roots for so long.

Reuben slung his bag over his shoulder and started out of the cemetery when Manny's vision suddenly blurred. He looked about and a hollowness inside his mind came over him. He staggered and nearly tripped over a marker when strong hands held him up.

"*Misun.*" Reuben wrapped his arm around Manny's waist and held him erect. "Maybe we should leave."

"I'll be okay in just a minute… let me sit."

Reuben eased him onto the ground and squatted next to him. "What is it?"

Manny forced a smile. "*Wakan Tanka* just… gifted me with more images of souls wandering the Spirit Road than I can handle. Just give me a minute."

Manny rubbed his temples and took deep, calming breaths, looking about when his mind cleared enough that he could read the names and dates on the headstones. *Wakan Tanka*, he was certain, guided his gaze to a marker close to Robbie's: Emanual Bear Paw. Manny did a quick calculation on the dates chiseled into the concrete marker and saw that Emanual had been thirty-seven when he died. "That name ring a bell?" Manny asked Reuben.

Reuben turned to the headstone and brushed dust away with his hand. "Never heard of him. Must have been Robbie's uncle if my calculations are right. Sure couldn't be his father—Robbie would have been three or four at the time of his death."

Manny agreed. Annie said Robbie's father had lived a long life, establishing a farm near Kimball, Nebraska. He'd been successful enough that he gave Robbie enough money to start his trucking business and for Amos to buy buffalo to start his herd.

Manny felt the fog leave him and he held up his hand. Reuben helped him stand and he started for the car. "Let's get out of here before the Creator has any more *gifts* for me."

Chapter 20

Clara sat across from Manny, oblivious to other Chop House patrons seated and waited upon. "I thought we'd never get a night out."

"It's this odd case they dumped in my lap," Manny said. "It's been taking up a lot of my time—"

"All your cases take up a lot of your time." Clara squeezed the slice of lemon in her water and sipped lightly. "But this one has been keeping you out of town and down on Pine Ridge more than most."

Clara knew that Manny was the de facto Reservation FBI agent, the one the Special Agent in Charge assigned all reservation cases to. Even when Manny explained how he had been at the wrong place when the body was found in the river and how it could still be federal jurisdiction, she was upset. "I'm thinking maybe you have been avoiding me so as not to talk about marriage."

Manny looked away and she rested her hand on his forearm. "That's it, isn't it?"

Manny turned back, wondering if Clara was a mind reader. He finally concluded his avoidance of the subject was quite obvious and even a little child could see he was uncomfortable with it. "You know I was a confirmed bachelor until I met you."

"A bachelor who backed out of a marriage date twice." She picked up the menu and said as she looked over the top, "I don't know if you've noticed, but we're both not getting any younger."

Manny took her hand and said, "You'll always be beautiful to me. You never get old."

"Then what's the hold up?" she asked.

Manny hesitated before telling her, "Maybe I'm a little gun shy of having kids."

"Kids! You think at my age we'd be having any children? My time has peaked long ago, and I doubt you have many swimmers left who could get the job done. Do you really think we could get pregnant?"

"Possibly. Look at Felix Unger—"

"Who?"

"That guy in the *Odd Couple*...Tony Randall. He was seventy-eight when he had his last baby."

"Oh, for Pete's sake."

"But what if... let's say I do have that one little swimmer strong enough and we do have a baby. Just think of all the diapers we'd have to change. Not to mention it's expensive raising a child nowadays. Especially with my retirement from the Bureau approaching."

Clara leaned back in her seat as the waitress came to their table. After they had ordered and the waitress left, Clara said, "This all about changing diapers? You've been hanging around Willie too much."

Manny's face scrunched up recalling the last time he'd held Precious at arm's length. "Believe me, the last thing we want to talk about is Willie's baby and her... incidents."

Their food arrived and they agreed to postpone the discussion of marriage and—dirty diapers—until they'd gotten back home. As Manny sliced into his prime rib steak, Clara said, "How can you even eat that stuff?"

"I'm a carnivore." Manny cut the fattiest piece off and savored the aroma for a moment before letting it slide down his throat.

He pointed to Clara's plate with his fork and said, "I'd ask you the same question: How can you even eat that stuff?"

"Collard greens and bean sprouts are good for you. Kale, too, especially if they are in a nice salad like this."

"That's just my point—it's a salad. It's rabbit food."

"So the mighty Lakota hunter-gatherer only eats meat?"

Manny winked. "Mostly."

He felt heartburn coming on and he set his fork down while he sipped water. "You were going to tell me what you found out about the Philippines in World War II." Clara had gotten her history diploma from the Oglala Lakota College in Kyle, and she forever loved digging into the past. Manny had asked her to research the Philippines during the time when Robbie and Amos fought there.

Clara withdrew a small spiral notebook from her purse and opened it on the table. "It appears as if Amos Willow Bent was the lucky one when that booby trap nailed him. Being injured and evacuated to a medical station in the rear prevented him from joining the fight for Manilla. The Manilla Massacre, as it was called, cost 100,000 civilian deaths at a minimum. Most killed and mutilated in horrendous ways. Rear Admiral Iwabuchi Sanji was ordered to vacate Manilla, but he refused. He had 16,000 sailors and marines under his command, and they wreaked havoc on the civilians. The commander of the Japanese forces at the time, Tomoyuki Yamashita, was held responsible for the massacre and later hanged after the war crimes trial, even though he'd left Manilla before the slaughter."

"The Tiger of Malaya," Manny said. "The one Robbie and Charlie McKnight testified against?"

Clara nodded and motioned for the waitress. After she ordered fried ice cream to split between them, she turned a page in her notebook. "After McArthur's troops finally drove out Japanese forces, he started hearing rumors of treasures that the Japanese pillaged from their conquests across Asia. Treasure the press dubbed *Yamashita's Gold*."

Manny thought back to the gold sovereign that he had seized from Freddie Geddes, the one that Charlie McKnight had given to Freddie's grandfather. "Did General Yamashita ever reveal where he had hidden all the stolen loot?"

Clara tapped the notebook page with her fingernail. "He denied it ever existed, but others think that was all a bunch of bullshit. 'Scuse the language. Although some gold pieces and pottery and paintings and other antiquities were stolen when the Japanese conquered territory, there's no proof positive that such a large-scale theft and cover-up was going on within the Japanese War Department."

Manny told Clara what Amos had witnessed that last time he went into the field, about a heavily armed convoy carrying large boxes into a cave only to be interred with soldiers within when the cave was purposely blown.

Clara picked up her spoon when the waitress brought their fried ice cream and she daintily picked at the luscious dish in the center of the table. She dabbed at the corner of her mouth with her napkin and said, "I'll have to do some additional research it would seem. What Amos saw—or thought he saw—has never been proven. If the Japanese looted on a large scale and somehow managed to stash it in the Philippines, it hasn't been found. And believe me, from what I found out there have been treasure hunters that have gone over every inch of the Philippine countryside until there's hardly a spot of ground that hasn't been searched."

"None of the alleged stolen loot has been found?"

"Oh, there's been some items recovered," Clara said. "But certainly not enough to warrant such a heavily armed convoy driving into the Philippine jungle."

"You mentioned a moment ago," Manny said, "that rare pottery was rumored to have been looted by the Japanese."

"Just rumor. Pottery from China and Taiwan and Korea. Pottery, it's said, that was the most exquisite ever made. But once again, there's no proof. Why do you ask?"

"A vase I saw on Annie Jamieson's mantle was very… unusual." He described the almost translucent vase, but Clara knew nothing about pottery. "You're going to have to hook up with a pottery expert. Do you think it's important, or is it just that Tanno curiosity?"

Manny shrugged. "Maybe both. Guess it's like pornography— I'll know it when I know more about it."

Chapter 21

Manny turned off St. Patrick Street and pulled to the curb. He took the note out of his shirt pocket and checked the addresses of the houses around him. He had left his Garmin in his old car and actually missed Marge telling him where to go. When he stopped at the library earlier asking for information about Asian pottery, the research lady smiled. "We have nothing on Asian pottery, but we are lucky to have a lady who just lives for pottery. She gave just the best presentation last year…" Her hand shot to her mouth. "I just hope she's still around."

"Did she move?" Manny asked.

The librarian shrugged. "Can't say. What I was concerned with was if she was still… *around*. She was eighty-five when she presented here." She lowered her voice. "You can never tell with those elderly folks if they're going to be on this side of the grass or not."

As Manny double-checked the address for Sylvia Dovonski he, too, hoped she were still *on this side of the grass.*

He drove another block and parked at the curb in front of a two-story brick house. He craned his neck up at the tall cupola looking out onto historic West Boulevard, one of Rapid City's earliest housing developments catering to miners when the town was founded.

The front had no doorbell, and Manny raised a heavy, black door knocker in the shape of a dragon and let it fall several times. When no one answered, he raised the knocker again just as the door opened. A petite woman in her fifties wearing a starched white skirt with white stockings and shoes looked up at Manny. She said nothing until Manny broke the silence. "Sylvia Dovonski?"

"I am Helen. Sylvia's home care professional. What is it you want with her?"

Manny showed Helen his ID wallet and she handed it back with no sign of emotion. "Unless this is important, I would prefer Sylvia not talk with you. She's had a bad morning."

Manny pocketed his ID. "If it wasn't important, I wouldn't be here."

"What is it, Helen?" a woman asked from another room, her voice loud. Clear.

A lady hunched over a walker approached the front door and stood looking at Manny. "What is it?"

"This is FBI Agent Tanno. He wishes to speak with you, but you've had a bad day—"

"Nonsense! All I did was fall against the couch. Not like I hurt myself. Just my bursitis flaring up. Now let him in. And bring us some tea and those little cookies you make." She motioned to Manny. "Come this way."

She led Manny down a hallway that opened into a large living room. A sectional couch as white as Helen's uniform hugged one side of the room, while two curio cabinets full of pottery took up two other corners of the room. Silvia backed into a recliner across from the couch and used her walker to ease herself down. "Helen's just a little protective of me. I think she figures as long as I'm breathing, she'll have a steady job."

"I just don't want you falling and hurting yourself." Helen entered the room carrying a tray with silver cups and a tea pot beside a tray of small cookies. She set them on the oaken coffee table and turned to Manny. "My main job—besides cooking and cleaning and baking cookies—is to make sure Silvia doesn't wind up in a nursing home. You don't want to wind up in a nursing home, now do you?"

"Oh, God, no," Sylvia said. Her face softened and she added, "You think I want to set around with other drooling old people as they try holding their cards or try figuring out their cribbage score? Or comparing the fit of our dentures? Not on your life. And I won't, either, as long as you take good care of me. Now run along to the grocery store before they close."

She watched Helen grab her sweater and leave the house.

Sylvia bent and plucked a cookie from the tray. "I don't want her to get a big head, but she really is the reason I'm not rotting in an old folk's home." She cocked her head and looked at Manny out of her peripheral vision. "You're staring trying to figure out my lineage?"

Manny felt himself caught like he had been when he and Lumpy raided the Sioux Grocery for apples when they were kids and the clerk spotted them. Manny felt only slightly guilty then as he outran Lumpy who took the fall for the apples. "I was… wondering just that. Call it professional curiosity."

"Not to worry. Lot of folks question my heritage." Silvia waved her hand as if to dismiss it. "For your edification, I am Russian and Korean. My father was a Russian archaeologist during the Second World War. The Japanese recruited him to authenticate items looted from the Koreans and Chinese and the Siamese. I get some of my looks from my mother, Iki, that father met while in Korea during the Japanese occupation." She stopped nibbling and looked at her cookie. "Unfortunately for her, she caught the eye of a Japanese Colonel and soon disappeared."

Manny sipped his tea, jasmine and ginger. Soothing as he remained silent. He'd learned long ago that if he kept quiet, people often opened up. And like the Lakota and Cheyenne and Arapahoe, one often made small talk before getting to the reason for the visit. He felt Sylvia would like to do so as well. "Father tried finding her... I was but a year old at the time when they took mother. My father did not give up but kept up inquiries. He later learned the colonel who had taken her had tired of my mother and sent her away to be an *ianfu*—a comfort woman to Japanese troops. Nothing more than an unpaid prostitute and she died during the war. He somehow managed to sneak us out of the country where we made our way to Hawaii." Silvia used her walker to stand and she arched her back, stretching. "I can only assume the FBI wishes me to authenticate some piece of evidence seized, for why else would you visit an old woman?"

Manny explained about how a Code Talker's dog tags wound up around the neck of a homicide victim. He explained that Robbie had lived many years after the deluge swallowed the cabin where the victim had been tied. "When I visited Robbie's daughter, I saw an unusual vase in her curio cabinet. My fiancée did some research and learned one of the things that the Japanese looted during the war was rare pottery."

"And you think this vase will lead you to the killer?"

"At this point, I'm thinking the killer is long dead. If not, he'd have to be—"

"As old as me?" Silvia said before she broke into a wide grin. "Not to worry." She bent and picked up another cookie before asking, "What was it about this vase that piqued your curiosity?"

Manny shrugged. "It was just something I'd never seen before. It looked... exotic." Manny explained the pale blue-green color of the base, the lines throughout the vase that indicated some imperfection in the firing of the clay.

"There was no imperfection when the vase was put into the kiln," Silvia said. "Those lines are subtle depictions of bamboo."

"How do you know that?"

Silvia motioned to one of the curio cabinets. "That top shelf... I can't quite reach it."

Manny stood on tip toes and took a vase off the shelf. And swore to himself that he was looking at the same vase that Annie possessed.

"Korea was the first Japanese conquest and it was declared a colony of Japan in 1905," Silvia said. "They employed the vicious *kempeitai*—the military and secret police, and the gangsters from the various *Yakuza*—to steal everything they considered valuable. Including pottery like you hold in your hand."

Manny turned the vase over. "What makes this valuable?"

Silvia ran her finger lightly over the vase, tracing the delicate constricted base, the bulging center, the tiny opening at the top. "Royalty used this to contain tea. Or plum blossoms. This vase dates from the Joseon Dynasty. More precisely the middle period from 1500 to about 1700." She lovingly, almost reverently, pointed to the other side. "See the Ming influence?"

Manny shook his head. "I have to plead ignorance. I know little about pottery."

"Then it is sufficient to tell you that this Korean pottery surpassed even China's Tang porcelain and is quite valuable. If Robbie gave this to his daughter," Silvia said, "then she has a rare and valuable vase that was most likely looted."

Chapter 22

Lumpy lumbered into the conference room at the Pine Ridge PD and plopped into his chair that groaned under his weight. "If you have a meeting in my police department, I need to be notified."

"You might clean your uniform shirt off," Manny said and handed Lumpy a bandana. "Filled long john again?"

"Never mind what pastry the dispatchers brought to me this morning," Lumpy said as he rubbed some vanilla-colored filling that had dropped onto his shirt front.

Manny grinned. Since the Tribal Council ordered Lumpy to lose weight, claiming he was a liability working law enforcement and at risk of a heart attack, he had struggled with losing. But then, he was fighting an uphill battle. The police dispatchers, who constantly complained about Lumpy's heavy-handed running of the agency, had been less than helpful. Every morning they brought a dozen pastries and left it where they knew Lumpy would have to walk by them. And sample one or two. Or three. At last weigh-in, he had gained four pounds.

"Well, Hot Shot, why the hell are you here?"

"I need to drive back to Chamberlain and needed someone to follow-up with Amos at the Cohen Home. Since Willie's already talked with Amos and has some rapport with him—"

Lumpy turned to Willie and said, "I told you that you don't get paid to investigate crimes that ain't ours."

"Chief Looks Twice," Manny said, drawing out Lumpy's name like he was addressing royalty, "how many times have tribal cases been cleared because Willie helped me with one of mine?"

Lumpy turned away and mumbled under his breath.

"I didn't hear that," Manny pressed.

"All right," Lumpy said. "All right, so more than a few cases have been cleared. But there's still nothing that Amos could tell Willie that would crack any cases we have open right now."

"Henrietta's stolen Pinto wagon," Willie said. He stood and walked to the Wheel of Death in the corner, the vending machine that contained all sorts of *tasty* sandwiches and hoagies. All put there sometime this last week when the salesman came in to restock it. Willie scrunched up his nose and dug into his trouser pocket for some dollar bills. He fed money into the machine, taunting his mortality. "Henrietta had her car stolen and she might tell me something she'd forgotten. Henrietta keeps a hawk's eye on the gas—figures she had about 300 miles left in the tank before it ran out of gas. Thought someone had to have seen it—driving 300 miles around here someone's bound to notice a beater like that, but no luck so far."

"And you plan to just happen to run into Amos while you're there?" Lumpy said.

Willie peeled the plastic wrap back from his ham and cheese. He sniffed it and bit off a corner to see if he died of food poisoning before taking a bigger bite. "Might as well. Help clear up Manny's case so he can get back to doing rez FBI stuff."

Lumpy wheeled his chair to a metal coffee tray. And what was left of last week's doughnuts. He tapped one hard Bismarck with his finger and turned around. There were things even Lumpy wouldn't eat. "What is it you need Willie to ask Amos? Maybe I could interview him."

"He wouldn't talk with you," Willie said.

"Why the hell not?"

"Because he doesn't trust many folks," Willie said. "For some reason he trusts me. Maybe it's 'cause I went there with Reuben once to talk with him."

Lumpy threw up his hands. "The felon? You're trusting your solidarity with the ex-con to get information from old Amos?"

"For starters," Manny intervened, "my brother did his time and didn't ask for a day off his sentence for parole. Since then, he's been—"

"Less than stellar," Lumpy argued. "What with him driving around the rez with no license. Beating someone up now and again."

Willie chuckled. "No one that didn't deserve it. So what you say—am I good to help Manny out?"

Lumpy started for the door and said, "you'll do what you damn well please anyways. Officially, you'll be talking with Henrietta to find out about her stolen car. If you happen to run into Amos while you're there," and left the subject hanging as he slammed the door on his way out of the conference room.

Willie slid a chair out from under the conference table and grinned. On a plate on the seat were three fresh pastries and he set them between him and Manny. Willie tossed his stale sandwich in the trash and grabbed a donut. "Gotta hide them from the Chief. Now what do you want me to ask Amos?"

Manny explained about the vase that he had seen at Annie's and how—according to the expert Silvia Dovonski—it was quite valuable. If it were authentic. "You know I don't believe in coincidences. Robbie giving his daughter a vase that might be looted and Charlie McKnight passing gold sovereigns to a bar like it was a tip has to have some connection. I need you to find out if Robbie ever told Amos about that trip he and Charlie took when the government sent them back there for the war crimes trial."

"You'll be driving back to Chamberlain then?"

"I have to," Manny said. "For one, I need to examine that vase more closely. If it is authentic and Annie's only explanation is her father gave it to her, I'll have to seize it."

"Because it was stolen during the war?"

Manny nodded. "And believe me, I don't look forward to her reaction to me taking it. Or that wild-ass son of hers."

* * * * *

Manny pulled into the circular drive and sat in his car for a moment gathering his courage. He had called Annie when he passed Murdo headed east and set a time to meet her at her house. How would she take it? Manny had sized her up the few times he'd spoken with her and concluded she was one tough lady. She had to be, taking over the trucking business with a bunch of rowdy men under her. He would assume nothing less when he talked with her in a moment.

Annie stood at the door waiting even before Manny climbed out of his car. She held the door for him and said, "You sounded like this was urgent over the phone. Would you like tea?"

Manny shook his head. "This is an official visit."

"Now I am worried."

"No reason to," Manny said. "*You* did nothing wrong."

"Someone must have," Annie said. She stood with arms crossed as she looked Manny in the eye. "Miles get in trouble again?"

"Not Miles." Manny pointed to the curio cabinet. "I need to look at something in there."

Annie waved her hand. "Feel free."

Manny walked across the hardwood floor and opened the curved glass door of the curio cabinet. He took out the blue-green vase, depiction of bamboo and blossoms looking just like the one Silvia had showed him. He was certain it was an authentic antiquity, one that may have been stolen by the Japanese during the war. "Did your father say where he acquired this?"

"He bought it from a local Filipino one day when he and his security man were entering a village in the mountains. Why do you ask?"

"Because I think it is one of the many artifacts looted from Korea by the Japanese during the Second World War."

"That may be, but what has that to do with the FBI?" Annie said as she reached for the vase.

Manny turned so it was just out of her reach. "There is a federal law that prohibits people from owning antiquities such as this unless they came about it legally. Tell me your father had some paperwork showing where he bought it. Some provenance—"

"Now who the hell would stop in the middle of a war with Japanese all around him to ask for a receipt? Either way, my dad gave me that and you can't have it."

"I have no choice, Annie. I'll do my best to see if it can be returned—after all, it's nearly impossible to tell who even fired this vase. But I can't guarantee anything."

She crossed her arms and glared at him. "You think my dad had something to do with stolen loot? The man was honest. Hard working. From the moment he was discharged, he worked his tail off to build up his trucking company. And he wouldn't steal from anybody."

"I'm not besmirching your father's legacy, I just question how he came about this," Manny said as he headed for the door. "Like I said, if it can be returned, I will do it."

* * * * *

Manny laid on his hotel room bed and punched in Willie's number. "Your voicemail didn't tell me much."

"I talked to Amos a little more as we fed the pigeons," Willie began. "He didn't know much about Robbie's trip back to the Philippines for that war crimes trial except he and McKnight did a little sightseeing while they were there. Robbie told Amos he was just glad to be able to look the country over without being shot at."

"Do you think it's a matter of Amos' memory fading after all these years or because he's holding something back?"

"Can't say," Willie answered. "But then I can't say I get bad vibes from him, either. He is an old man, after all."

Manny agreed and hoped that he would be as active and sharp as Amos when he got to be in his nineties. If Manny made it that far.

"The important thing is I found out more about Robbie's father. The one who you said started Amos and Robbie both in business," Willie said. "And it didn't come from Amos."

"Sure, right after the war. I understand why Robbie's father gave Amos seed money to start his buffalo herd. Like he said, Robbie told him how grateful his father had been for taking Robbie's turn in the field and losing his arm to that booby trap. But you said you found out more besides what Amos told you."

"I had to dig into Tribal records. The consensus is that Robbie's father must have been successful in his ranching to have given them both money to start their business," Willie said. "Except he wasn't."

"How's that?"

"Robbie's father didn't own a successful ranch. He was a farm hand at a small spread just outside Kimball, Nebraska. His name was Emanual Bear Paw."

Manny sucked in a breath, recalling the headstone close to Robbie's, the one Manny and Reuben thought must have been an uncle or other close relative. But not this close. Manny did the mental math and said, "then Robbie would have been just three or four when his father died."

"Bingo," Willie said. "There's no way he could have given either Amos or Robbie money to start their business."

"Then where did Amos say the money actually came from?"

"I don't think Amos knows," Willie answered. "When he told me Robbie's father's name, I started searching archives and found the truth. When I returned to the Cohen Home to talk to Amos about what I'd learned, he looked as dumbfounded as I was when I remembered you and Reuben spotting Emanual's headstone at the Holy Rosary Cemetery. When I told him the date on Emanual's headstone would have put Robbie an infant, he was genuinely surprised if I read him right."

"Then where did the money come from?"

"As Chief Looks Twice would say, that's for the feds to find out."

Chapter 23

Manny pulled into the driveway at the Brule County Sheriff's Office. Sheriff Bain stood outside waiting for him. He hitched up his belt that had sagged over his belly. Yet, for his age, the sheriff was in decent shape, and he would have been a handful when he was a younger lawman, Manny figured.

"Now what's this about needing backup?" The sheriff asked.

Manny explained that he needed to notify Annie Bear Paw at her trucking company that FBI agents would be coming by this week to conduct a forensic audit of their books. "If that crazy kid of hers don't jump them."

"But that's Annie," Sheriff Bain said. "Why does the FBI need to audit her? She ain't done nothin' wrong," he said as he climbed into the old car.

"Never said she did." Manny backed into the street to horns blaring and a driver with his middle finger jabbed high in the air. Manny nearly had one more of his accidents that he swore he'd never have again. "It all comes down to where Robbie got the money to start his trucking company."

"His pappy gave him the money."

Manny explained that Robbie's father would have to have given his son the money when he was a toddler. "Besides, Emanual Bear Paw never owned a place of his own. Never had enough money to spare when he was alive. The guy worked himself to death on someone else's farm and died when he was thirty-seven."

"Still doesn't explain a federal audit."

"It does if Robbie returned from the Philippines after that war crimes trial with antiquities looted by the Japanese. Enough to start a trucking business and give his friend Amos Willow Bent seed money for a buffalo ranch. If the audit reveals that's where he got his start-up money, reparations are in order."

"Reparations to who?"

Manny shrugged. "That'd be for the federal courts to decide."

"Slip by McDonalds drive-through," Bain said as he rolled down the window to allow his pipe smoke to escape. "I'll spring for coffee."

Manny drove the couple blocks and pulled behind a pickup piled high with hay bales. "Tell me how Sam's homicide investigation is coming along."

Sheriff Bain took off his Stetson and ran his fingers through thick hair. Manny was envious. "South Dakota DCI has been close-lipped about it. They don't even tell me much, probably 'cause they don't know much yet. The one thing the Senior Agent did say was that those Horris boys were real a-holes when they interviewed them."

Manny remembered them from the D&D and how one threatened Manny. And how Freddie Geddes made it a point to tell Manny the Heinous Horris brothers were crappy ranchers barely hanging onto their ranch by a thread. And how they would hold a grudge against Manny for embarrassing them in the D&D. "Why interview them?"

"That rustling case Sam was working on. We found their names in his notebook under people on his suspect list he needed to interrogate. But he never got the chance. Cream, no sugar."

Manny stuck his head out the window and ordered the two cups of coffee before taking the five-dollar bill from Sheriff Bain to pay. "What do you know about those two peckerwoods?"

"They're bad news." The sheriff blew on his coffee. "Now I see why McDonalds was sued—this coffee is hot enough to scald chickens. Anyway, Sam had a run-in with the youngest Horris, Earl, two summers ago at the County Fair. He was pissed 'cause his steer didn't get the blue ribbon and he started a fight with whoever was handy. Just happened to be Sam was there off-duty and Earl sucker punched him. Wrong move. Sam stomped a mud hole in Earl's ass. A week later Sam was responding to a disturbance call at the Silver Dollar and got waylaid soon's he ran into the bar. Got the boots put to him bad, too. He never saw who attacked him and no one at the bar had the stones to say, but Sam was pretty sure it was the Horris boys."

"I'd put them at the top of my suspect list on Sam's murder, then."

"I wouldn't," Sheriff Bain said. "Jake Duddy would be just above them."

"That brother of the one Sam killed in that attempted strong arm robbery?"

"The same."

"But he's in the state pen. He's not even in this area."

"He is now. Pretty Obese—"

"Who?"

Sheriff Bain chuckled. "Sven Targa, but we call him Pretty Obese as you'll see if you ever meet him. He's Duddy's probation officer. Anyway, the PO called me yesterday and said Duddy had stopped by the parole office to talk with him as was required by the parole conditions. It was his initial check-in after he *just* got paroled."

"Tell me he was still in Sioux Falls at the time of Sam's murder."

Bain wiped coffee off his chin. "Duddy was released from the state prison a week before Sam was killed. He absolutely could have been the one."

"Did the DCI interview him?"

Bain nodded. "Duddy told them to pound sand and denied even holding a grudge against Sam. Duddy said he was a free man and didn't intend to go back in stir."

"But you don't believe him?"

"No more than I believe those damned televangelists wanting money on TV."

They pulled into the Bear Paw Trucking lot, nearly empty this morning with all the trucks out hauling. "Bear Paw got the contract to haul gravel to county roads," Sheriff Bain said. "We might luck out and that crazy-assed Miles won't be around the office."

They weren't. As they entered the office, Miles came from around the desk, his face instantly flushed. Veins in his forehead throbbed in time, it seemed, with the clenching and unclenching of his fists. He stopped inches from Manny's face. "You got nerve coming here after stealing Mom's vase Grandpa gave her."

"Back off, son," Sheriff Bain said, his hand on the Taser on his belt. "Agent Tanno is here officially to talk with your mother."

"Talk about what?" Annie emerged from the restroom, drying her hands on a paper towel.

"You might want to sit for this."

"I'll stand. What're you here for?" Annie asked.

"Tomorrow," Manny began, keeping an eye on Miles, "four FBI auditors from our Minneapolis field office will come here. They will serve you with a search warrant and conduct a forensic audit of your books."

"An audit for what?"

Manny explained that Annie's father may have started the business using money he had acquired from antiquities looted by the Japanese during the war. "I'd like you to give them your full cooperation."

"The hell we will!" Miles stepped closer, his fists clenching and unclenching. "I'll be damned if I'll let them see our records.

Opening our books to Sam to find our embezzler was bad enough but having a bunch of strangers pawing around here—they better come armed."

Manny stepped back out of spittle range. "I was afraid that'd be your attitude. Now I have to request a security team, and you don't even want to brandish a gun around those guys."

Annie stepped between Manny and Miles and said to him, "why don't you step outside for some air before you're tossed in the pokey again."

Miles grabbed a scuba tank from behind his desk and glared at Manny as he headed out the door. "I need to do some adjustments anyway."

"Now I see why he gets into fights," Manny said as Miles slammed the door. "He bulled-up right off."

"He has my Lakota blood," Annie said. "Just looking out for the family, that you have to know is top priority for the *Oyate*. But you can't blame him—he wasn't happy that Sam spent a couple days nose-deep in our books even though it was at my request. And now FBI agents have to get in the way?"

"This has nothing to do with someone recently skimming the books," Manny said. "My guess is it won't take the auditors long, not with two of them. But you could ask Miles to take a little hiatus until they're gone, 'cause I'm not kidding—the security men the Bureau sends to protect the auditors will be hard men."

As Manny drove Sheriff Bain back to his office, he got a call. After a brief conversation, he said, "That was dispatch. Seems like Minnehaha County deputies found our hit-and-run car in a trailer court north of the state penitentiary in Sioux Falls. Soon's I get back to the office I'll call the SO over there and ask them to contact the owner and request that he come in for an interview when I get there. So, with my only other deputy living twenty miles away in Kimball, you'll have to do."

"Have to do what?"

Sheriff Bain shrugged. "Be the local law until I come back."

"Maybe you didn't hear," Manny said. "I am a federal agent. You know I can't be involved in local law enforcement."

"You might as well do something while you're here."

"That's my point—I won't be here. I'll be back home gearing up for my life sentence."

"Life sentence?"

"Yeah," Manny said. "I have to get fitted for a tux. My wedding date has been set."

Chapter 24

Reuben's tuxedo had rose over his slight paunch and he pulled it back down as he looked into the mirror. "Still don't know why I have to give the bride away."

Manny stood beside Reuben in front of a full-length mirror. "Because you're the only duffer I know old enough to be Clara's father."

"Rather be a best man. They usually get to sidle up next to a bridesmaid. Maybe I'll get lucky."

"Luck for you," Manny said, "is crossing the room without tripping over something that'd break one of your old bones. Besides, this is my wedding, not a date night."

"Well, it took you long enough to get used to the idea of being *Mrs. Clara*."

"So now that I'm used to it I want it to go off without a hitch," Manny said. "For Clara's sake."

"Alright. Alright. I'll only respond if the bridesmaid pinches my butt or something. When you go home tell Clara I'll be on my best behavior."

"She's gone."

"Already? What did you do to piss her off?"

"Not that," Manny said. "She took a few days off to be with Georgiana Little Wound on the Rosebud. She figured this might be the last time she'd have to spend quality girl moments together."

"Where's that leave us?" Reuben asked.

"Spending quality guy-time at your place," Manny answered. "If you're up for having a bum sleep over again."

* * * * *

Manny toweled dry and handed another one to Willie before yelling down to Reuben, "You get any slower and we'll have to cart you out to the home where you can bunk with Amos."

"Damn arthritis or I'd have beat you both topside," Reuben yelled.

They had all three entered the sweat lodge, the *initipi* cleansing them. "To clear our heads," Reuben said, explaining why he'd invited Willie. "Maybe all three of us can get a handle on that river homicide and at the same time brainstorm who might have killed that young Brule County deputy."

Willie and Manny waited just inside the screened porch until Reuben trudged up and entered. "Don't wait on me," he told Manny. "You know where the iced tea and cookies are kept."

He went inside Reuben's trailer and grabbed a pitcher of iced tea from the fridge and a pack of Oreos from the kitchen table. He returned to the porch and set them on the coffee table.

"No visions this time?" Willie asked Manny.

Chewing his third cookie—since Clara wasn't here to give him what-for about his diabetes—he said, "not this time. This time it just felt good to sweat."

"Did it clear your thinking?" Reuben asked.

"It did."

"Me too." Reuben filled his glass before scooping sugar into his iced tea. "I think I might have an angle on Sam Christian's murder."

"We're all ears," Willie said, wiping frosting from his upper lip and mouth.

Reuben broke open an Oreo and started licking the filling. "You said that Jake Duddy character was chummy with Miles Jamieson that night at the steakhouse."

"He was," Manny answered. "Seems like they went to high school together." That last night in Chamberlain he had stopped by Charly's Steakhouse for their prime rib special. Duddy and Miles sat at corner table talking, not paying anyone any attention. Not seeing Manny sitting alone.

"Have you ever thought that Duddy killed Sam on Miles' request?"

"That's a far stretch," Willie said.

"Is it?" Reuben stood and walked off a leg cramp. "Back in my former life—you know, the one where I muscled opposition to our American Indian Movement—one of our… soldiers came up dead on the side of the highway by Batesland. Bud Robinson. The cops weren't interested in doing much investigating—"

"There were a lot of dead bodies along the roads on the rez," Manny said. "Cops couldn't do diligence with all of them. Especially since they were assumed to be victims of rival reservation factions."

Reuben looked down at Manny. "Don't cover for the law here on the rez in the seventies. They were crooked as a corkscrew. My point is that we—meaning others in the movement—learned Bud was killed by a perfect stranger. One of our soldiers asked his friend from Minnesota to off Bud and he did. As a favor. Just like Jake Duddy might do for his friend, Miles Jamieson."

"Whatever happened to the guy who killed Bud?" Willie asked.

Reuben swept his hand in the air and said, "He ran away, never to be found."

"In other words, he was killed and stuffed someplace?"

Reuben shrugged. "That was the rumor at the time, though I was not privy to exactly what happened."

Manny figured Reuben knew just where the killer had been secretly buried, but he already had one decades-old homicide to worry about in addition to Sam's murder. "You might have an angle there worth pursuing." Though deputy Sam's murder was state jurisdiction, Manny liked him. It was personal now. "When I get back to Chamberlain, I'll ask his Parole Officer to bring Duddy in for questioning. And the river homicide victim? Did the *initipi* give you any insight into that?"

"I'm working on it," Reuben said as he poured more tea and heaped more sugar into his glass.

"I already know who your victim is," Willie said. "Or I'm nearly certain."

Manny pushed the plate of cookies closer to Reuben as he sat back in the lawn chair. "Let's hear it."

"Buck Jamieson," Willie began slowly. "Allegedly, he came up missing when he ran away with that banker's wife. But what if he made it no farther than American Island?" Willie stood and paced in front of the table. "Buck was tall—like your Doctor Darden found out in his research with that bone specialist. Buck may have been in possession of Robbie's dog tags, probably stole them when he was still married to Annie."

"How do you square that Buck was alive and married to Annie long before American Island was flooded?" Manny asked.

"Like Doctor Darden pointed out, people being in water for any length of time makes them hard to age. There might be decades separating when we think a victim went under water than when they actually did."

Manny resisted the urge for one more Oreo, then gave in and took two. Buck Jamieson being the victim had crossed his mind more than once, but he couldn't connect Buck to anyone who wanted him dead bad enough and he said so.

"Annie would have loved her philandering husband to take a wet nap," Willie said. "And we still don't know if the banker would be capable of killing him for having an affair with his wife."

"Then how did he get into the river?" Manny asked. "How did someone kill Buck and tie him to that abandoned cabin in the river when the reservoir was full?" Manny asked, then answered his own question: Miles was an avid scuba diver. But he would have been in his teens is all when Annie kicked her husband out of the house. Was Miles even a killer? Manny knew the man had a violent streak, especially if Reuben was right that he asked his friend Jake Duddy to kill Sam. Manny thought back to his vision at the Corn Palace—he had clearly seen a man unable to get out of the way of a wall of rushing water. Buck being the victim didn't square with Manny's vision. Perhaps he would need another sweat to sort things out.

* * * * *

After Willie left for home, Reuben and Manny sat around the fire. He prodded the embers with a stick and said, "I have to go back to Chamberlain tomorrow."

Reuben laughed. "Is there such a thing as frequent driving miles like there are frequent flyer miles?"

Manny shrugged. "If there were I'd have won a new toaster by now. Maybe a blender."

"And you're going to pull Jake Duddy in for questioning on that deputy's murder?"

Manny nodded.

"Even though it's county jurisdiction and not federal?"

"I can justify it with my Senior Agent in Charge by telling him it might connect to the river homicide victim."

"But why even get involved?"

"Dammit, I liked the kid," Manny blurted out. "He was a good lawman by all accounts, and he didn't deserve to die like that.

And if you ever met Sheriff Bain, you'd see why he's not much of an interrogator. If he learns anything from that hit and run suspect by Sioux Falls, I'd be surprised. Sometimes a feller just has to bend the rules a bit to reach justice."

Reuben put his hands up as if in surrender. "Alright. I see that you're passionate about it. But this time when you're in Chamberlain I'll be with you."

"What for?"

"That Jake Duddy's already went up for one homicide connected with that botched convenience store robbery where Sam killed his brother. And from what you told me about Miles, he's got some kind of violent attitude. Duddy or Miles might decide you're getting too close. I'll tag along to make sure my *misun* doesn't get the boots put to him."

"You'll ride back there with me for what, protection? No! Absolutely not. The Senior Agent in Charge will have my shield, and my retirement, if he catches me driving halfway across the state with a felon."

"Ex-felon," Reuben corrected.

"Much as I'd love company for the long ride, you are not going back with me. Besides, I think I can take care of myself. I just can't have you riding along."

Chapter 25

Manny sat across from Pretty Obese. He had just finished his second Big Mac when the door of the probation office opened. Jake Duddy took one step inside before he stopped dead. He jerked his thumb at Manny. "What the hell's he doing here?"

"A visit," the probation officer said. "Just a little visit. Sit."

"I'll talk with you but not him."

"Would you rather I revoke your parole and you can talk with the intake officer back at the state penitentiary?" the probation officer said. "Now sit."

Despite his apparent bulk and soft-appearing manner, Pretty Obese projected no-nonsense and Duddy reluctantly sat across from Manny. "Now what the hell would I want to talk with an FBI agent about?"

The PO wiped his hands on a napkin and picked up his milk shake. "Whatever he wants to talk about, and you'd better be honest in your answers." He nodded to Manny. "Ask away, Agent Tanno."

Manny opened his notes as if he needed to get the date right. "Sam Christian killed your brother in that botched robbery."

"Old news."

"And you've hated him ever since."

"I hated him when we went to high school together. That was no big secret," Duddy said.

"Hated him enough to kill him?" Manny asked.

Duddy leaned over and said to Pretty Obese, "Can he even talk with me about this?"

"Is Duddy a suspect?" he asked Manny.

"Just a person of interest I wish to talk with."

Pretty Obese turned to Duddy. "Then he can talk with you about it."

"But ain't Sam's murder a state offense—"

"That might tie in with Agent Tanno's investigation into that river death?" The probation officer said. "Just answer him or my new set of license plates will be made by Jake Duddy."

Duddy took off his ball cap with the *DeKalb Feeds* barely readable for all the dirt and grime. "Is there a question in your accusation?"

"Bluntly," Manny began, "where were you when Sam Christian was murdered?"

"I was out of town delivering feed—"

"Your boss said there was a two-day period where you never answered your phone," Pretty Obese said.

"Like I said I was out of town—"

"Where?"

Duddy hesitated and Manny gauged his answer, concluding he was lying when he said, "I was selling feed around Parkston. I laid over in a motel."

"No, you weren't there," Manny said.

"Hell I wasn't."

"How's about we check your trucks mileage log that day."

"What log?"

Now it was Manny's turn to lie. He had no way of knowing if the feed store kept vehicle logs but he said, "The log your boss keeps on all his trucks."

Duddy looked away.

The probation officer leaned over his desk and said, "If the logs don't match, that proves you were somewhere else—maybe here in Chamberlain all the time with the intent to kill Sam Christian—"

"All right, damn it! Get off my ass. I was in Winner at the time of Sam's death."

"You got proof?" Manny asked.

"The best." Duddy nudged a piece of lint with the toe of his boot. "I was in jail. Under a different name."

"This I gotta hear," Pretty Obese said.

Duddy ran his fingers through his hair again, gathering his thoughts. "I drove the company truck down thataway. Needed a drink real bad, but I knew if I went to the tap room here I'd get busted. If I bought even a beer from the liquor store here, I'd get busted."

"You were in the steakhouse that night you were yuckin' it up with Miles Jamieson," Manny said.

"Just eating. I never ordered even so much as a beer. Don't that count for something?"

"If you actually did that," Manny said. "Why did you get tossed into the hoosegow in Winner?"

"Bar fight. Some cowboy came up to me and started making fun of my hat. My bib overalls." He shrugged. "We didn't make fun of a guy's threads in prison." He jotted a name on a pad on the desk. "Call the Winner PD—they'll confirm I was in for fighting. They'll confirm I was there at the time Sam was murdered." He slid the pad over. "You going to revoke me?"

"Let me think it over," Pretty Obese answered.

Duddy left the officer, leaving Manny and Pretty Obese to discuss revocation. "You going to send him back to the penitentiary?" Manny asked.

Pretty Obese leaned back and scratched his ample belly. "I ought to but… well, I got glowing reports from the state pen about Duddy. He was a model prisoner. He has a knack for figures and they even put him in charge of the prisoner's commissary. That's why he was paroled early. I'm just going to have to ponder that for a bit."

As Manny headed out of the courthouse, he passed the Clerk of Courts office. A lady stuck her head out the door and said, "Agent Tanno, you have a message."

She handed Manny a note that read, *Come to the airport. Come Quick!!!*

"What's this all about?" Manny asked.

"Can't say," she answered. "But Butch, the airport manager, sounded desperate."

* * * * *

Manny had no idea what to expect as he drove out of town towards the airport. He pulled up to the only building beside the only runway. The small facility was barely big enough to have a windsock. Manny watched a crop duster take off. The biplane's powerful engine nearly drowned out a man's screams as he ran from the building towards Manny's government car.

"You Agent Tanno?" the man said, the whites of his eyes showing like he was a frightened bronc about to get rode as he kept watch on the building.

Manny stepped out and glanced over at the airport's office. "Take it you're Butch. You sound… scared of something."

"You would be, too, if some big bastard lumbered into your office claiming he was starving. Wanting to be fed. Right before he demanded we find you."

"I don't get it—"

"Him!" The man pointed at a man emerging from the building walking toward them. "Some goofy bastard flew in on a gooney-bird landing—I thought that damn Cessna would wreck—and *he* somehow climbed out after it landed."

Reuben clung to an overnight bag with one hand, the other wiping mustard off his lip as he sauntered toward Manny and Butch. He moved away as Reuben neared, making a wide berth as he made his way back to the airport office. "Give me a lift?"

"How… how did you get here?"

Reuben looked after Butch scrambling to retreat into the airport building. "Willie. He flew me here from Pine Ridge."

Manny hung his head. "Not again. The FAA took his license."

"I can see why, too. I had chopper insertions into a hot LZs in 'Nam that weren't as frightening as flying with Willie."

"How'd you ever talk him into flying you here?"

"I told him you needed some additional protection while you're here." Reuben smiled. "So, can I have a lift?"

"What am I going to do with you while I'm working? I can't leave you to your devices or you'll get in trouble."

Reuben's hand went over his heart. "I'm crushed that you would leave your only brother and *kola* to make his way back home on foot."

Manny shook his head and nodded to the car. "Climb in. With any luck my Senior Agent in Charge won't find out a felon's riding around with me."

Chapter 26

"Who's your big friend?" Emily Mockingbird asked. She toweled dry from her swim session and walked across the parking lot towards Manny's car. She stopped in front of Reuben and smiled wide as she looked up at him. "You're kinda cute, in a senior kind of way?"

"Thanks, I think," Reuben answered before turning to Manny. "I'm going to the room and take a nap. That's we seniors do—take afternoon naps."

When she stared at Reuben walking away Manny said, "Emily! He's old enough to be your dad."

"But he just got... *bloka*. That," she pointed to Reuben disappearing into the motel room, "is a *man*."

"The last thing I need is a brother having a heart attack doing the wild thing."

Emily batted her eyelashes. "I could have some intimate moments with you first."

"I'm spoken for."

"So you claim."

Manny felt his face warm, and he quickly changed the subject. "Hear anything more on Sam's murder?"

"Figured you did, pulling Jake Duddy into Pretty Obese's office."

"Can nothing be kept secret in this town?"

"Some things are." Emily sat on the concrete curbing and

shook out a cigarette. She blew smoke rings upward and said, "like those Heinous Horris boys. They have been busy doing some midnight shopping, but most folks hereabouts don't know it."

"What kind of shopping you talking about?"

"The really expensive kind. They've been adding to their herd and some rumor is they *found* some cows on a spread north of Kimball. Going to go shopping and find some more soon, so I hear."

"Who told you that?"

"The resident deputy over in Kimball heard it from someone," Emily said.

"And he didn't stop it?"

"He claims he was busy in other parts of the county. But," she lowered her head as if there was someone close enough to hear, "he's a retired state trooper and just wants to ride out the next few years until he can draw social security. Don't count on him for anything."

Manny popped a piece of chewing gum and knelt beside Emily. "Have you heard where their next shopping spree will take place?"

"Don't know where, but I know when—tonight. An ambitious lawman might be able to follow them from their ranch and find out how many cows will be added to their herd."

* * * * *

Reuben brought the binoculars down and handed them to Manny. "That's how they do it so slick—they're using dogs."

Manny and Reuben had waited in the darkness watching the Horris' ranch house until they left pulling a small cattle trailer that would hold no more than twenty head. Small enough to make their theft quick. Clean. And get away before the farmer or rancher realized anyone had been rustling in the pasture. Manny squinted, finally picking up the brothers standing outside their trailer with two Border Collies sitting on the ground beside them.

"I'd ask again, why the interest in those rustlers?" Reuben asked.

"Because Sam was investigating them. Because Sam might have gotten close to making a case. Because if you'd have seen their eyes that day I knocked one down in the D&D Bar, you'd know they were capable of it."

"But it's still a case for local law enforcement. I did learn some things in prison."

Manny handed the binos back to Reuben. "Let's just say I liked Sam. He did the bulk of the work for Sheriff Blain and did so diligently. And the Horris brothers might have killed the kid."

"That hit-and-run driver might have killed him, too, if Sam got too close to exposing him."

"Can't argue there. Maybe this is just a... pleasant distraction from a true mystery."

"You giving in and admitting there might just be some cases you can't solve, like a homicide victim found in the river?"

"Not yet," Manny answered. "Let's say in the spirit of assisting law enforcement the Bureau will help out tonight."

"You can't do anything about this cattle rustling except call in local authorities, and it appears the only one to call is that old, retired trooper disguised as a deputy sheriff in Kimball."

"The resident deputy? Emily was right—the man's just biding his time until he hangs up his duty belt. We can't count on him for anything."

Manny reached in the back seat and grabbed a case. He opened it and took a night vision recorder from the case. Dialing in adjustments, he said, "At least I can document what they're about to do. Here, plug this into the power outlet."

Reuben plugged the cord into the power and the green screen lit up. "This isn't going to help you find the killer of that poor slob in the river. You thought any more about him?"

"That's all I've been thinking about."

"So, who you like as the prime suspect?"

Manny tested the recorder to make sure it worked before setting it on the seat between them. "I still don't know who the prime *victim* is. Doctor Darden did what he could, but until we know the identity of the victim we'll never know why someone shot him and tied him to that cabin. *If* he was tied to it and didn't just drift from upstream to get snagged. There! Looks like they're fixin' to send the dogs."

Reuben took the night vision recorder and looked through the reticle. "Relax. They're just giving the dogs a little treat—a preview of what they'll get once they round up the cows."

Reuben handed the recorder back to Manny and uncapped a Thermos bottle. He poured coffee for each. "From what you told me, Buck Jamieson is most likely the victim in the river."

"It's too easy," Manny said. "Buck Jamieson running off with that banker's wife. Still, someone would have run across him sometime if he were still alive."

"You punched her into NCIC?"

"Her?"

"Her," Reuben said. "That Jasmine Halverson. Whatever became of her?"

Manny thought of that, instantly realizing that he was glad Reuben was along, for who else besides a violent man would even factor in the banker's wife. As Manny started the recording, he made a mental note to give Jaz Halverson's name to Abigail and see if she could find out if Jaz were still alive. If she were, she might know just where Buck Jamieson was living. Unless he was the victim swimming with the sturgeons.

Chapter 27

Sheriff Bain sat hunched over his desk looking at fresh wanted posters when Manny and Reuben entered the sheriff's office. Bain looked up and leaned back in his chair. "Who's the big guy?"

"Reuben." He extended his hand.

"You a friend of Manny's?"

"Trainee," Reuben said immediately.

Manny nudged Reuben behind his back hoping his brother wouldn't play this trainee thing. Even Sheriff Bain would find it hard to believe the Bureau hired someone Reuben's age. The government wasn't that desperate yet.

The sheriff didn't buy it as he looked up at Reuben and squinted. "Mighty old to be in training."

Reuben shrugged and sat in a chair in front of Bain's desk. "The Bureau's gotta recruit where it can—short staffed and all."

Manny quickly changed the subject and blurted out, "Tell me—us—what that hit and run driver said."

"He didn't say anything. Want a Perrier?"

"I'm a carnivore," Reuben said.

"I could use one," Manny said and accepted the bottle of water.

Sheriff Bain took a short pull from his bottle and said, "The driver was dead in his trailer. Gunshot wound to the head."

"Does the Sioux Falls deputies know who killed him?"

"They ought to," Bain answered. "Looked like the guy killed

himself." He sat in his chair and sipped his water. "One of the Minnehaha County detectives had called the guy and arranged for him to meet us at the Sioux Falls sheriff's office for an interrogation when I got into town. When the guy didn't show after two hours, we drove to his place and broke in to see him leaking all over the carpeting. They're going to have a hell of a time getting that stain out. Rules out that guy as Sam's killer."

"Not necessarily," Manny said. "Guy might have felt remorse after murdering Sam. Especially if he hit a lady on a bicycle and killed her not two weeks ago. Did he leave a note?"

"He did not." Sheriff Bain tipped his bottle of Perrier up and finished it. "I have my doubts. The driver was a little guy—can't see him getting the best of Sam."

"He could if he used some kind of Shaleigh on Sam," Reuben said. "Wouldn't be hard. Manny said Sam was beat to death by some object—ball bat. Maybe a pipe or stout tree limb."

Bain's eyebrows raised ever so slightly. "Sounds like you know something about beating folks and what to look for."

Reuben smiled. "Manny is a good mentor."

"We have something else," Manny quickly interrupted. The last thing he needed was Reuben playing up this FBI agent-in-training thing. "We have the Horris boys dead to rights rustling cows north of Kimball."

Sheriff Bain leaned across his desk. "How dead to rights?"

"The deadest." Manny took a flash drive out of his pocket and handed it to the sheriff. "I put the surveillance video on this. It'll be enough for you to get an arrest warrant. I'll enter the master copy into your evidence files for court."

Bain spun his chair around and inserted the flash drive into his computer. Within seconds, the screen was filled with the Horris brothers standing beside their cattle trailer while their dogs rounded up eighteen head of black-white-face heifers before calmly driving off. "I can get a warrant this afternoon."

"Good," Manny said. "Then they'll be in your lockup and you can interview them about Sam's murder."

Bain shrugged. "I'm not much on interrogations. Could you interview them when I have them in custody?"

"Be a pleasure," Manny said, recalling the first run-in he had with the brothers at the D&D. "Is your Kimball resident deputy going with you when you serve the warrants?"

"Don Johnson would just come up with some excuse—his back is out or his grandkids are missing or some excuse not to come along."

"Don Johnson?" Manny said, "Like the *Miami Vice* Don Johnson?"

Bain laughed. "More like *Miami Nice*. When I hired him, he made it perfectly clear he was just riding out his time until he could draw social security."

"Then why even have him?" Reuben asked.

"He's a county commissioner's brother-in-law is why. As long as I have ol' Don on the payroll, I get about what I ask for at budget time." Bain sat back in his chair. "Would you back me up when I go to arrest the two?"

Reuben smiled. "Of course we would. Be our pleasure."

Manny scowled at him and turned to the sheriff. "We can come along when you make the arrest." He glanced at the clock above the computer. "Shouldn't take too long to cut a warrant once the judge sees this. And the drive down to Bijou Hills takes about thirty minutes—"

"I'm not going to arrest them at their ranch."

"How's that?" Manny asked.

"The Horris Ranch," Sheriff Bain began, "is like a fortress. Their doors are reinforced and they have markers along their drive marking the exact yardage for their rifles for anyone approaching. No, I'll get the warrant today, but I'll hang on to it. They won't know there's an active warrant out for them and will eventually saunter into town for supplies or just to raise hell. That's when I'll get hold of you and we'll put the *habeous grabus* on them. By the way, FedEx dropped a packet off for you. Sounds like the motel desk where you're rooming refused it."

"Damn *Indian*," Manny said under his breath.

Sheriff Bain took a manila envelope from his desk drawer and handed it to him, the St. Louis Police Department logo prominent on the return address.

* * * * *

"What's with that peckerwood glaring at us when we pulled into the parking lot?" Reuben stripped off shirt and laid it on the bed before unbuckling his belt. "Little guy looked like he wanted to fight or something."

"That's Gandira. He's in the process of sweet talking the owner into selling to him."

"Gandira who?"

"Just Gandira."

"Like Fabio or Cher, just one name."

"That's all Emily told me," Manny said. "She says he's a real arrogant horse's patoot."

"Well, he better not get in my face." He slipped his swim trunks on. "I'll be enjoying the pool as Emily Mockingbird's guest."

Manny used his pocket knife to carefully cut open the manila envelope the St. Louis PD had sent. "You not going skinny dipping with Emily now?"

"Not skinny dipping." Reuben grinned. "Unless she wants to. What'll you be doing while I'm in the pool?"

"I'm feeling a little gaunt," Manny answered. "Soon's I look these reports over, I'll head to Charly's Steak House—their prime rib is to die for. Want me to wait until you're done with your little romantic interlude with Emily?"

"Don't wait for me," Reuben said as he slipped a bath towel around his neck. "I'm not sure how long I'll be. I'll walk up there when I'm finished… romancing," and he shut the door behind him.

Manny looked after him, hoping Emily knew CPR. At Reuben's age, he'd as likely have the big MI as not if he became too excited.

Manny separated the photocopies of old reports, some dating back to right after World War II when Charlie McKnight started his cab company from money his aunt gave him, the detective found out from his wife, Josephine. She filed the missing person report on Charlie just a week before he turned up in the Fourth of July parade beside his war-time buddy Robbie Bear Paw.

A follow-up interview with Charlie's wife revealed she had been fearful that her husband's drug supplier might have taken him for a swim in the river. "Uppers and downers," she had told the investigating officer, "is what makes him more money than the cab business. All his drivers are in on the action. That's why he don't stiff his supplier." She refused to name the man her husband got his drugs from.

"But you didn't take a swim in the St. Louis River," Manny said to himself as he laid the report aside. "You turned up here handing out a gold sovereign to Freddie Geddes' grandfather at the D&D."

Manny rifled through reports, some little more than notes scribbled by undercover officers keeping a watch on Charlie and his drug business. "The narcs were so close to swooping down on you," Manny said. "Between the police surveilling you and your dealer about to off you, no wonder you got as far away as you could here to South Dakota. But where did you go after that?" Manny flipped pages, turning the barely legible notes to the light. "Did you tap into that benevolent aunt who started you in the cab business… hello!"

Manny turned the floor lamp so he could read a note one of

the narcotics officers filed. That note mentioned a background check the officer had conducted on Charlie a year into the surveillance, a background check that showed he was raised in an orphanage. "There was no auntie setting you up in business," Manny said as he stood and grabbed his coat. "This is starting to make sense," he said, and headed out to his car and that perfect prime rib at Charly's Steak House.

Chapter 28

Manny entered the packed steakhouse at supper time. He asked to be seated in a corner away from Miles and Jake Duddy at a table on the far side of the room. They hadn't seen Manny come in and they sat across from one another talking in low tones.

Manny ordered the medium prime rib with sweet potato knowing that, whenever Reuben finished with his romantic swim with Emily, he'd walk up here and order the largest steak the house offered. Manny often marveled at his brother—no matter how much he ate or what he ate, he still remained in good shape for a seventy-plus-year-old man.

As Manny finished his supper, he became aware that many of the diners had finished and left the restaurant. About the same time that Miles Bear Paw looked across the room and spotted Manny.

Miles stood and staggered his way past tables, stumbling into a chair and knocking it over before he came to stand over Manny with Jake Duddy tugging at his arm. "Let's just go," Duddy said.

Miles jerked his arm free and nearly fell. He caught his balance and said, "And not let this piece of shit know where I stand?"

"Where do you stand?" Manny asked as he let the piece of gooey pecan pie slide slowly down his throat.

"You stole my grandfather's vase," Miles sputtered. "The one he brought back after the war."

Manny sliced into another piece of the pie, ignoring Miles when he bent and picked up another fork and helped himself to Manny's pie before tossing the fork on the table.

"Miles," the waitress said, "leave this man alone before I call the cops."

Miles chuckled. "By all means call them. By the time they arrive, I just might have stomped Mr. Agent Man here into the carpeting."

The waitress hustled off.

Once again Duddy tried pulling Miles away, and once more he jerked free.

Manny looked at the fork with a pecan on the end that Miles had just used to eat his pie, and he felt his face and neck warm. His jaw muscles tightening. As drunk as Miles was, Manny had no doubt he could take the kid. But did he want to? *You bet* he thought to himself. "Did you get this angry at your father?"

Miles stepped back. "Whatcha mean by that?"

"I'd wager your relationship with your father was... rocky. The way he treated your mom... you can see where this is going."

"I don't."

"Miles, Miles," Manny taunted. "It would not be a stretch to imagine you luring your dad away from wherever he was staying after your mom kicked him out and killing him. He stuck around town when he had that affair with the banker's wife, so you were bound to know where he lived. Did you put that scuba diving hobby to good use back then and drag him into the river? Down to American Island where you shot him and roped him to a cabin thinking no one would find him? A big, strapping youngster could do that?"

Manny didn't believe anything he had just said, but it elicited the response he predicted. Miles jerked his hand violently away from Duddy and started around the table. Spittle flew when Miles blurred out, "Sure, I hated my dad for running around on my mom. But I didn't off him and stuff him into the river. I've never even dived that part of the Missouri."

"I find that hard to believe," Manny said, moving his foot to trip Miles if he came closer. "There would be all sorts of treasures and artifacts that got buried when the Corps of Engineers flooded the river. Prime diving I'd say."

Manny clutched his hand around his pie plate and told himself if Miles made one more pass at it, he would beat the kid right here. "Tell me one thing, how many times did you visit your grandfather?"

"Whenever I could once he went into the retirement home."

"Recently?"

"Sure, I drove out to his grave now and again."

"Leave flowers? Maybe a single orchid?"

"What of it?" Miles demanded.

Manny shrugged. "Is it safe to say you worshiped him?"

"Of course," Miles said. "He was a hero and a warrior."

"Did it piss you off when your dad teased your grandfather, keeping his dog tags just out of reach. Calling him names?"

"I usually don't get pissed."

"But I'm betting it pissed you off when your mom asked the sheriff to send someone to go over the company books. I'm betting you were angry that Sam was there intruding into your company records," Manny said, hoping Miles would spring. Some people—Manny reasoned—just needed their ass beat senseless. Miles was one of them.

"How's that?"

"You might have been the last one to see Sam Christian alive," Manny lied, gauging the response, "when he had to go over your company books. Maybe you thought Sam deserved to be beat 'cause he was too deep into the Bear Paw record books. Maybe you beat him just a little with that tire billy you usually carry—"

"I never beat him with anything—"

"And maybe it got out of hand. Maybe you just didn't mean to kill him."

Miles swept his arm across the table, knocking plates and glasses to the floor. And Manny's beloved piece of pecan pie. He stood and faced Miles, keeping a chair between them, dinner plate in hand, picking out a spot on Miles head to smash it.

Miles took off his watch and stepped closer when Jake Duddy pulled hard on Miles' arm.

He nearly tumbled him to the floor but Miles yanked his arm free. "Leave me the hell alone. Me and Mr. Agent Man gotta dance. "

"Son," Manny said, "Life is like a jar of Jalapeno peppers—what you do today might burn your ass tomorrow."

"What's that supposed to mean?"

"Just a fair warning. If you assault a federal officer, your ass is in deep trouble when the cavalry arrives."

"He's right, damn it," Jake Duddy said. "Miles I don't need this! All this FBI agent has to do is drop a report to my PO and I'm back doing the commissary books in the big house."

Miles' face flushed red, his fists clenching and unclenching.

"Take some breaths," Duddy said.

Miles breathed in deeply, the anger diminishing as he stepped back. "One day, Mr. Agent Man, you and me are going to tangle and there won't be no witnesses around—"

"Let's just go," Duddy said and ushered Miles out the door of the restaurant.

Patrons looked over at the mess surrounding Manny's table and at the waitress who bent picking glasses and plates and the saltshaker up off the floor. "I am so sorry for this."

Manny held up his hand. "Not your fault. Figured the law would be here by now."

The waitress chuckled and looked up at Manny. "Guess I shouldn't have told them it was Miles Bear Paw causing trouble—

they're just a little intimidated by him. I figure they'll show up about a half-hour from now when they know Miles is long gone. Can I get you anything—it's on the house."

If Clara were here, she would give Manny the evil eye for eating even that one piece of pie. But then, she wasn't here. "Another piece of pecan pie. Make it la mode this time, please."

* * * * *

Manny nursed the pie and ice cream much like a drunk nurses his last drink of the night. Manny thought back to Miles' reactions to his taunts. Until Miles had confronted him, Manny hadn't much thought about Miles and his relationship with his father. He'd only kicked the notion around that Miles could do just what Manny suggested. Later, when he grew older, Miles could have killed his own father as an act of revenge for Buck stepping out on Annie and for him to have constantly teased and taunted Robbie when Miles' father still lived in the house. Perhaps, Manny reasoned, Buck hadn't eventually left town with Jaz Halverson. Perhaps he had been a victim of a young man's wrath.

And Sam. He and Miles had a history dating back to their high school days where Sam would beat him in fights. A history of Sam arresting Miles for bar fights. Would Miles' dislike for the deputy increase after Annie requested an embezzlement investigation?

Manny checked his watch. He had waited for Reuben to finish with his romantic swim with Emily, and the steakhouse would soon be closing. Another twenty minutes and he would talk himself into another piece of pie. He stood abruptly and brushed crumbs off his shirt front, courtesy of Miles Bear Paw.

When he went to pay with the Bureau credit card, the waitress waved it off. "For what you went through with Miles, it's on the house."

"With all the taxes the business probably pays," Manny said, "I am sure the house could use the extra bucks. But thanks anyway." The last thing he needed was for folks to think he was taking gratuities.

When he left the restaurant, he picked his way through cars in the dark parking lot, looking up at the security light that had illuminated everything so well the last time he was here. He had just realized that the light had been shattered by something, shards of glass littering the lot, as a fist caught him on the chin and he started to go down. Strong hands held him up while more fists flew his way. He tried fighting back, but whoever held him was too strong, finally letting Manny drop to the asphalt.

He cracked one eye, which was already swelling shut. A cowboy—distinctive fancy white stitching on his shirt—cocked his fist again as Reuben, yelling like an old bull, threw himself on the attackers.

He straddled one figure, pummeling the man with fists to his head, when his partner cocked his foot back and kicked Reuben deep in the belly.

Reuben rolled off, clutching his gut and struggling to stand when the pair ran off in the darkness.

Reuben crawled to Manny and held his head up off the pavement. "The chef came out and yelled that he called the cops."

Manny nodded, hearing approaching sirens, seeing the dark parking lot get even darker as he lost consciousness.

Chapter 29

Manny awoke to bright lights overhead and a doting nurse telling him not to fight the oxygen mask. "I think I can breathe just fine," he said, feeling one tooth missing, another loose, compliments of the pair who jumped him in Charly's parking lot.

"Might as well do just what she says."

Manny looked over at Reuben lying on a hospital bed next to him. "They ran a CT scan—I have two cracked ribs from when that peckerwood kicked me."

Manny looked about the room through one eye, the other swollen shut. It would have been worse, he reasoned, if that guy had connected with his boot. *Thank Reuben for saving my butt.* "Did you recognize said peckerwood?"

"I did not," Reuben answered. He used the bed railing to sit up. "Too dark. But he'll have some serious damage from that beating I gave him before his pard kicked me in the gullet."

Sheriff Bain entered the emergency room and said to the nurse fussing over Manny and Reuben, "Can I have a moment with them?"

The RN—a lady in her sixties and who'd surely seen most everything in her career—glared at Bain for a moment before heading out of the room. "Might as well, neither of those two pay me any mind. I'll be back after I have a cup of joe."

After the door closed, Bain took out his pipe and clammed

it between his teeth. He said to Manny, "City police took the initial report. Reuben was awake to tell them his version of what happened. They'll want you to stop at the cop shop to tell them what you remember about your attackers."

"What did happen?" Manny asked as he gingerly felt stitches holding one cheek together. "All's I recall is stepping into the parking lot and realizing the security light had been busted out."

"You were roughed up by two guys," Reuben said. "That's about all I know. But you didn't recognize them either?"

Manny's shrug sent pain shooting up one side of his neck and shoulder. "Like you said, it was too dark. But I had some words earlier with Miles Jamieson in the steakhouse right before Jake Duddy dragged him out the door."

"Surely they wouldn't be so dumb as to jump you right after you had a run-in with them?" Sheriff Bain said.

"They'd be at the top of the suspect list," Manny said.

"Too pat." Reuben swung his legs around and his hand massaged his ribs. "From what you tell me of Jake Duddy, he's pretty smart. Being an ex-con like... some of them I've met, they would be too cagey to try beating you so soon after arguing with you inside the restaurant. Might give it a day or two then get beered-up again and catch you someplace unawares." He massaged his ribs again. "As hard as I hit that one bastard, he's sure to have wound up in the ER. Did you check?"

Sheriff Bain chewed on his pipe stem as if he were annoyed. "City police did right off, but nothing here. They even called as far as the hospital in Mitchell seventy miles away in case they went that far to get treated but no luck."

A doctor many years older than Reuben shuffled into the ER. He donned a pair of reading glasses over the pair he already wore as he bent and looked at Manny's head. "Crap."

"Crap what, Doc," Manny said. "That didn't sound good."

The doctor took off one pair of readers and shook his head.

"The good news is the stitches can come out in four days. The bad news is it appears as if I might have tied the sutures backwards."

"Which means?"

"Which means," the doctor said, "it'll hurt like the dickens dragging the tiny knots through the skin."

* * * * *

The next morning Manny felt as if a horse had kicked him in the head. And everywhere else. He rolled over and popped two more Tylenol before lying back on the pillow. Reuben's bed had not been slept in. Manny wondered where he was after he drove Manny to the motel room last night when the door opened. Reuben stepped in and hung a damp bath towel over the chair. His jeans—faded and threadbare as always—remained dry and Manny said, "Don't tell me you've been down swimming in the pool again?"

Reuben nodded. "That Emily Mockingbird guilt tripped me into taking a dip with her."

"But your trunks aren't even wet."

Reuben grinned sheepishly. "I know."

"So, you did go skinny dipping in the motel pool?"

Reuben shrugged.

"Not all night I hope?"

"Not all night," Reuben said. "After I drove you back here—"

"You don't have a license—"

"And put you to bed, I met her in the pool. Then… well. One little thing led to another thing, and I spent the night in her room."

Manny sat up in bed and his hand went instinctively to the stitches in his cheek. "If you haven't noticed, *kola*, Emily Mockingbird is young enough to be your daughter if you had one."

"So now you're going to give me hell that it don't look good for an FBI trainee to be snagging some young babe?"

"And that trainee act is another thing we're going to have to discuss—"

"No time for that," Reuben said as he fished a note out of his back pocket. "The agent in charge of the forensic audit of Bear Paw Trucking left word at the front desk for you to meet him."

Reuben took off his jeans and crawled into bed. "If you don't mind, this trainee will sit this one out. This old body's not used to an all-nighter anymore."

Manny carefully shaved around the stitches in his cheek before putting on the new pair of jeans he'd bought two days ago.

When he walked outside to his car, Emily sat on the curb, smoking a cigarette. "That lazy brother of yours getting up?"

Manny stopped and stared down at her. Except for a smudge of mascara at the corner of one eye, she looked as if she could do another "all-nighter" with Reuben. "He just got to bed no more than an hour ago. The man needs rest."

Emily chuckled. "After last night, I'd imagine so."

"You know," Manny said, "Reuben's no spring chicken anymore. Maybe you ought to let him rest."

Emily flicked her butt into the gutter. "Believe me—he's not dead yet. Besides, didn't you ever hear men get better as they age?"

Manny dismissed the Reuben *getting better with age* concept immediately as he climbed into his car and headed for his meeting with Agent Sorreno.

When Manny pulled into the marina, trucks packed the parking lot while the lagoon was packed with fisherman who had just launched their boats for a day's fishing on the Missouri. Manny wished he could go along, hang his pole in the waters and catch enough walleye to feed him and Reuben both. But, like most assignments he was handed, there was no time for leisure, and he entered the café.

Agent Sorreno waved Manny over from a corner table.

"You almost look like you're fixing to go on the river for the day," Manny told him as he sat opposite the FBI auditor.

"Matter of fact, I have finagled the best fighting guide around to take me out—and on the Bureau's dime."

"How did you manage to get free time?" Manny asked. "I'd love to go but I'm too tied up."

Sorreno's swarthy face exaggerated a sad frown. "Ah, the bane of being the agent in charge of a case." Across the room a man watched him. "Gotta make this quick—that feller over there's my fishing guide and he's ready to go. Whyn't I give you the headline version and send you the detail report when I get back off the lake."

"Might as well," Manny said, waiting for the waitress to place a cup in front of him. "I'd hate to cut into your guided fishing tour."

If Agent Sorreno detected Manny's sarcasm, he gave no indication as he opened a folder on the tabletop. He lowered his voice and he said, "the audit of Bear Paw Trucking was quite fascinating. I've done Audits that dated back a long ways, but never back to the Second World War. Fascinating."

Manny often marveled how the Bureau accountants could spend days with their heads buried in nothing but figures and think doing so was *fascinating*. Sorreno ran his hand down a page and stopped at an entry. "This is when Robert Bear Paw started his business—with cash. And not a month later, he withdrew half from his bank account and had the bank cut a check for another man," he turned to the back of his report, "Amos Willow Bent."

Manny whistled.

"Know him?"

Manny nodded. "Please continue."

"Okay, so here's where it gets *really* interesting," Sorreno continued. "It appears as if money accrued, and money paid out to cover company expenses were all normal transactions through the years. Until three years into the business at which time Robert Bear Paw started sending monthly checks to one Josephine Wents. Ring a bell?"

"Like Quasimodo, at least that first name does. I'll do some checking into it," Manny said, not committing to telling the auditor unless he was certain. *Josephine* was just odd enough that Manny had an idea who received the checks. "What else you find?"

Sorreno sat back eying the guy at the other table anxiously watching the auditor. "We were going to stop when the payments stopped a year later... mid-1952. But Roberts, you know him, the Bureau just hired him from Goldman Sachs—"

"You were saying the payments stopped," Manny pressed.

Sorreno nodded and finished his coffee. "Sure. Anyways, Roberts wanted to trace the company until the present time for shits and giggles and so we did. It was Roberts himself who came across the discrepancy."

"Discrepancy as in embezzlement?" Manny asked.

Sorreno grinned and closed his folder. "Rather amateurish it was. One of the employees was skimming money from the company for the last two years. Hiding it on the surface but anyone with a basic accounting degree could have caught it."

Manny exhaled audibly and Sorreno asked, "Does it tie in with the forensic audit?"

"Can't say," Manny said. "But a murdered deputy sheriff here was looking into an embezzlement at Bear Paw Trucking."

Sorreno got up to leave when Manny said, "Tell me you have a name of the embezzler?"

"It'd be a state case. Not federal jurisdiction—"

"A name?"

"Miles Bear Paw," Sorreno said, and he and the fishing guide walked out of the café.

Chapter 30

Manny and Sheriff Bain caught a lucky break—Miles was out of the office when they entered. Annie looked up from her desk and frowned at Manny. "Here to take another vase away?"

"No," Bain said, "we're here to take your son away."

Annie stiffened. "How's that?"

"Maybe you should sit for this—"

"I said why are you arresting Miles? Don't tell me he got into another fight and violated his bond. Or that he," she jerked her thumb at Manny, "pressed charges for confronting him at Charly's the other night? He told me about that, and I already gave him what-for."

"Neither," Sheriff Bain said. "We're here to arrest him for embezzlement."

Annie, her arms folded, sat at the edge of her desk. "You're serious?"

"As a heart attack," Bain answered.

"Who was Miles supposed to embezzle money from?"

"Your business."

Sheriff Bain began explaining when she held up her hand. "Wait until Miles is here so he can explain it just the once." She touched a button on an intercom and said, "send Miles into the office and tell him don't worry about washing up." She turned to the sheriff. "He's in the shop. He'll be here in a moment."

Miles burst through the door and stood toe-to-toe with Manny. "I saw the sheriff's truck out there but didn't figure you'd be riding with him. What the hell is it this time? You pissed at me and Jake Duddy 'cause I got a little beered-up the other night—"

"They say you've been skimming off the books here," Annie said.

Miles backed away and his face lost color even as he denied it.

"Maybe you'd better sit while they explain it," Annie said.

Miles used the edge of the desk to ease himself into the chair and sat, his legs shaking.

Annie remained cross-armed sitting on the edge of the desk. "Alright, Sheriff, let's hear it."

Sheriff Bain turned to Manny. "Would you—"

Manny took out his notebook. "Ours auditors found that someone has been trickling money out of the business. Not a lot at a time, but a few hundred here and there nearly every week. But it added up to more than $14,000 bucks in the last year."

Miles began trembling as if he already knew the answer when he said, "They can't trace that to me?"

Manny flipped a page and showed Miles where he had jotted down what the auditor told him. "They can because they all have your authorization notations. There are only two people on the bank records permitted to withdraw from the weekly mechanical account—you and your mother. The bank president doubted—as do I—that it was her."

Miles sat silent looking down at the nautical maps of rivers spread out on his desk as if he hadn't heard Manny.

Annie came off her desk and stood over Miles. "Is that so? You've been skimming the books?"

Without looking up he nodded.

"Look at me!"

Miles looked up. "If you needed money why not just come to

me and ask?"

Miles guffawed. "And say what: 'Mom, I need some money to play blackjack in Deadwood or the Prairie Wind Casino when I stop by grandpa's grave?' I doubt you'd give me a dime."

"You're right there," Annie said. "I wouldn't give you a dime to lose your money at the tables."

Manny pocketed his notebook and faced Miles. "The auditors said it was pretty amateurish a job hiding the withdrawal. If they spotted it right off, I'd wager so did Sam Christian."

"So now you're thinking I had a reason to kill Sam?"

"Staying out of prison is as good a reason as I can think of," Manny said. "I can see you confronting him. Telling him to back off. To not report what he found in his audit. And when he refused—"

"That's assuming my mom presses charges," Miles said as he looked at Annie.

Annie seemed to be mulling that over when she said, "I ought to, but I can't hardly send my only kid to the state pen."

Miles stood and finally grinned. "Of course she wouldn't want me charged, and I knew that at the time. I didn't know that Sam caught me skimming. He was here looking at the books is all Mom said. Even if I did, I knew Mom would never want me prosecuted. So—Agent Man—there goes my motive for killing him. Now you both can turn around and walk outta here."

"Not before I hear what the forensic audit found," Annie said. "You did say they were finished?"

"Finished and following up on their findings," Manny said. He faced Annie—he needed to gauge her reaction when he said, "your father started this business with cash. I believe he got his money from selling loot pillaged during World War II."

"Bullshit!" Miles came around his desk and stood within striking range of Manny. "There wasn't an ounce of criminal in Grandpa."

Sheriff Bain stepped between them and said, "Sit back down, son, and let Agent Tanno explain."

"Yes," Annie said. "I'd like to hear what they found out in the company books."

Manny waited until Miles sat back behind his desk before taking his notebook out and flipping to notes he'd made talking with Agent Sorreno. He explained that Robbie started his business with cash and had a bank draft cut for Amos Willow Bent shortly thereafter.

"Don't mean he used stolen money to start the business," Annie said.

"Then where did your father get the money to start his trucking business and to give Amos a sizable amount? I looked into it and your grandfather never owned any trust land on the reservation, so there wouldn't be money from a big sale there. Where would he have gotten the money? If you have any other explanation, tell me—I have no desire to drag a Code Talker's name through the mud."

"My great-grandfather, Emanual, gave my granddad money to start this business," Miles said, "and felt obligated to give Amos enough to start a bison ranch."

"He's right," Annie said.

"That's what your father claimed?" Manny said.

Annie turned around, red faced, the veins in her forehead throbbing. "Claimed nothing. That is what happened."

"Tell me," Manny asked her, already knowing the answer from his visit to Robbie's grave with Reuben a few days ago, "did you ever meet your grandpa?"

Annie looked away before turning and staring out the window at the trucking yard. "I really don't remember. Dad said I used to bounce on the old man's lap before he died when I was an infant. But I never remembered that."

"That's because your grandfather—Emanual Bear Paw—died

when your *father* was an infant."

"That's not possible."

"What kind of horseshit you trying to pull?" Miles knocked over his chair and he started around the desk when Sheriff Bain drew his Taser. "I only used this the one time, but lordy did it make the guy do the chicken. If you don't want a jolt of this, I suggest you sit back down and listen to Agent Tanno."

"Miles is right," Annie said, "asking what you are trying to pull. If what you say is fact, Dad's whole life was a lie."

"Just the part where he and Charles McKnight returned from that war crimes trials with a couple duffel bags of stolen antiquities and gold."

Annie teetered and Sheriff Bain eased her into a chair. She looked up at Manny, her eyes red and tears trickled down her cheeks. "What now? Do I lose my business?"

"We'll have to wait until the forensic audit is read by the U.S. Attorney. Then I'll have to wrap up my investigation and send him the report."

"When will this be final?" Annie asked.

"Take a few days for me to put together my report to the Bureau and from there to the Antiquities Department. I would retain my own council if I were you."

"We'll get Eillis on it," Miles said when Annie interrupted him. "Old Eillis is okay for arranging bail when you get tossed in for fighting, but I suspect we'll need someone sharper than him." She looked up at Manny. "How much time do we have?"

"Like I said, I have to compile my report. But there's something else I'd like to ask you—"

"Don't say a damn word," Miles said, his hand resting on a glass paperweight.

Annie asked, "if I'm a suspect in this scheme of my father's, don't you have to read me my rights?"

"Only if you're a suspect," Manny said, noticing Sheriff Bain still clutched his Taser in his hand as he eyed Miles and the paperweight. "For right now, there's nothing to indicate you knew a thing about how the business started."

Annie sighed deeply and sat back in her chair. "What is it you want to know, then?"

"Does the name Josephine Wents mean anything to you?"

"Can't recall. Why?"

"Robbie sent money every month to her beginning three years after he started his trucking business, and it stopped abruptly, the auditors learned."

Annie rubbed her forehead. "Sorry I don't know the name. But why would Dad be sending this Josephine Wents money every month?"

"Soon's I know," Manny said, "I might be able to piece together who killed Sam Christian. And who that floater in the river was."

Chapter 31

"We should have taken two outfits," Reuben said, scrunched up in the back seat of Sheriff Bain's patrol truck.

"Your trainee always so cheery?" Bain handed Manny the binos. "They're just going into the bar now."

When Sheriff Bain called Manny at his hotel room and said he'd received word the Horris brothers were in town and he needed help arresting them, Reuben was more than happy to come along. "This place has been getting a little boring," he had told Manny as they started out the door. "Except for Emily—"

"I don't even want to hear what lurid things my brother and a woman half his age do."

Manny handed the binoculars back to Bain. "It's your play."

"We'll give them a little bit to get schnockered-up. Give us a little more edge." The sheriff turned in the seat to face Manny. "You're convinced Miles knew all about where his grandpa got the money to start the trucking company?"

"I do," Manny answered. "I've been interviewing people all my life and I can tell you Miles just feigned indignation when I told Annie the business was started with stolen loot."

"Surely his grandfather never told Miles any of that?" Bain said. "The kid would have been just a youngster when Robbie died."

"I just can't say," Manny said. "He learned it from someone."

"Annie then?"

"Be the most likely except *she* was genuinely startled to learn how Robbie financed his business." Manny grabbed the binos again. Sheriff Bain had parked so they could have a clear view of the Silver Dollar's front doors and the binos showed the Horris boys had lost no time getting hoary-eyed drunk.

"And Annie declining to prosecute Miles... he was right," Bain said. "She wouldn't prosecute her own kid. There goes his motive for killing Sam." Bain rolled his window down and tapped his cold ashes against the side of the truck before pocketing his pipe. "All the more reason to elevate those two peckerwoods for Sam's murder." He checked his watch. "This has been enough time for them to get a snootful. Might as well do this."

Sheriff Bain pulled the truck to the curb in front of the D&D Bar and they all bailed out. "Where's your trainee headed," Bain said just as Reuben disappeared around back of the bar.

"Attacking from the rear be my guess," Manny said. He slipped a pair of lead weighted sap gloves from his pocket and put them on. Sheriff Bain said, "Been a long time since I saw a pair of those. They even legal anymore?"

"Can't say," Manny answered, "but I sure know they're not within Bureau policy. That's if anyone reports me."

"Don't worry about me," Bain said. "I'll be happy with any assistance arresting those bruisers that doesn't involve me getting any broken bones." He paused at the door and breathed deep. "Ready?"

Manny nodded and Bain entered the bar first.

The Horris boys sat in a corner booth. Empty beer bottles littered their table, and they looked up at Manny and Sheriff Bain approaching them. He reached into his back pocket and laid the copy of the arrest warrant on the table. "You boys are under arrest."

Wayne grabbed the paper and looked at it before handing it

to Earl across the booth. He held the warrant to the light as he skimmed it with one good eye, the other sporting surgical tape holding a patch and bandage over it. He tore it up and tossed it on the floor. "You're not arresting us for no cock-a-mamie rustling today or any day. So whyn't you take that federal cop out of here before you two get hurt."

Sheriff Bain drew his Taser and stepped back, aiming it at Earl.

Earl stood a moment before Wayne did. "You can taze one of us, but then the other will stomp you. Or," he snatched a bottle and broke it on the edge of the table. He held the ragged edge before him like a rapier, "I can carve you up a little—"

A big fist crashed down on Wayne's hand holding the broken bottle a moment before Reuben drove a fist into his gut. The air *wooshed* out of Wayne and he doubled over.

Earl stepped into Reuben rearing back for another blow.

Manny cocked his fist and hit Earl in the chest. He staggered for a moment before sagging to the floor even as Reuben hit Wayne in the ribs going down.

Sheriff Bain quickly grabbed two sets of handcuffs and slapped them on the Horris brothers.

He stepped back, breathing hard despite not actually getting into the fray. He looked down at both men moaning in pain. "Now how the hell do we get these two big bastards back to the county jail?"

Reuben smiled. "You got a truck, don't you? What better place to haul these boobs. And I'll ride in the bed with them, just in case they try to get froggy and jump out."

* * * * *

"Your ribs ok?" Manny asked.

Reuben nodded. "I'll live. But that Wayne will have a couple broken to live with as well."

Manny peeked through the window of the Emergency Room where Earl had his bandages changed and Wayne was getting stitched up. Sheriff Bain stood off to one side watching them, pipe in his mouth, Taser in hand. "You're pretty sure it was Earl that night in Charly's parking lot that you hit?"

"By the damages on his face, I am certain of it," Reuben answered. "I connected pretty hard before his brother put the boots to me. I'd recognize that fancy stitching on his boots anywhere."

Manny thought back to the parking lot, the boots being the only thing he knew about his attackers. Not enough for a warrant, though. "I'd love to see them sent up for assault on a federal officer."

Bain walked out of the room. "You guys want coffee? I'm headed to the break room."

Neither Manny nor Reuben was interested in coffee after fighting with the Horris boys, and they remained outside the ER door watching the brothers.

"I'd like to see them go down for attacking you outside the steakhouse, too," Reuben said. "But a felon on the witness stand has little credibility, especially one who served time for murder. Second, the bureau would not look kindly on you for even associating with me. And third, at least you have the goods on them for rustling cattle and they'll go up the river for quite a while for that."

"But there's more to those two," Manny said. "If Sam had the goods on them as well… you saw how they reacted to being served the arrest warrant. Sam, tough as he was, wouldn't be a match if those two tag-teamed him. If I can just get them to talk."

"Good luck with that with their attorney in there even as we speak. They invoked the Fifth and you won't get a peep out of them."

Sheriff Bain returned just as the Horris' were finished getting patched up. He handed Manny his cup and held the door open. The brothers and their attorney stepped into the hallway outside the ER. Wayne stared at Reuben and said to the suit walking beside him, "That's the one who broke my ribs."

The small man said, "We'll get to the bottom of this. Just don't make it harder for yourselves. Go with the sheriff and I'll see about bail."

The attorney handed Manny a business card indicating that his law office—Spencer Kalb—was located in Lake Andes, an hour and a half away. He watched as Sheriff Bain loaded them into his truck before he turned to Manny. "This brute with you?"

Reuben feigned hurt. "Brute? Why, I was just a good citizen helping out the law when those two *brutes* resisted arrest."

"We'll deal with you later." Kalb faced Manny and said, "As for your request to interview them, I cannot allow it. But you could give me the headline version of what prompted you to accuse them of rustling."

"I have video evidence. Airtight."

"Where?" Kalb said. "I would love to see it and the chain of custody."

"Spencer… I can call you Spencer?" Manny said. "You know well enough that you will see the video when you file a motion for discovery. Until then, I cannot let you view it. Unless you'll allow me to question those two in the death of Deputy Christian."

"That's outrageous!"

"Isn't it," Manny smiled. "Let me know if they agree to talk."

As they watched Spencer Kalb storm out of the hospital, Reuben said, "My guess is he still won't allow the Horris' to sit for an interview."

"And you'd be right," Manny said. "Especially after he files a motion for discovery and sees what evidence we have on the tape."

Chapter 32

Reuben offered to go with Manny to talk with Doctor Darden, but it was little more than a half-hearted offer.

"I'll be all right," Manny said. "By now Sheriff Bain and the brand inspector from Sioux Falls have recovered the stolen heifers while the Horris brothers are safely awaiting lights out at the county jail. And," he winked, "I suspect Emily is waiting somewhere by the pool."

"She is," Reuben said. "Might be one of the last times she can use it, too. That Gandira character is so close to buying the motel and kicking her out, she's packed her things just waiting until the sale is final. I might just have a little tete-a-tete with that *Indian*."

"Don't get yourself into any trouble, like stuffing the guy in a trash can headfirst or anything like that."

"*Moi*?" Reuben exaggerated. "I'll be on my best… better behavior. Sure you don't want me to come along?"

"No," Manny said. "I'll go alone and work while you have fun."

Before Reuben could respond, Manny left the motel room and headed for the funeral home.

When he arrived at Hickey's, he wasn't sure if Doctor Darden had left and locked up or not when the door opened. Darden stuck his head out the door and motioned Manny inside. "That little guy you met the other day running the place went home for the night. Told me to lock up when we're done."

Manny followed the pathologist—staggering with the effect of too many beers, Manny was certain—and walked through the casket viewing room. "Why is this place so dark?"

"They want to save on electric bills I suppose," Darden said. "And to anticipate your next question, why not meet someplace besides a funeral home."

"I was wondering just that."

Darden grinned. "Where else would a doctor of death be comfortable?"

He led Manny into the back room where he performed autopsies when in Chamberlain and bent to the fridge. "Want a brewski?"

Manny patted his belly. "Trying to quit."

Manny set his Stetson on a porcelain table, now cleaned and shined and awaiting the next victim, whoever that may be. "Trying to wrap up this floater-thing so's I can head back home in the morning."

Manny sat on a stool beside the table. "Have you narrowed the timeline down on that floater?"

Darden finished off the beer and lobbed it into the trash can. He missed and looked at the can rolling on the floor. Thankfully, he didn't stoop to pick it up as Manny had no desire to help the doctor up after he fell to the floor. "My colleague," he burped loudly, "double checked the figures I gave him and is adamant the victim was between six-foot and six-foot-five. I sent him a tissue sample from one of the long bones, but he could not determine how long it had been in the water, either. But," Darden turned to his briefcase and Manny prepared to catch him, "I sent another specialist I've used a clipping from that thick strand of rope around the victim's neck."

Manny felt his excitement when he asked, "Can the rope be used to age the victim?"

Doctor Darden opened his notebook on the table and snatched

another beer from the fridge in one motion. Practiced. "The rope is hemp often used in the construction business. And ranching. And used for just about everything else for the last hundred years here in the west."

Manny felt his elation wane. "So, it didn't help any?"

"Not necessarily. When Sam and his diver initially brought me the rope, it bothered me that I could tell nothing about it. But when I reexamined the knot closer, I saw it was tied to the victim's wrist."

"That's something," Manny said. "We thought he might have floated down from upstream and gotten caught in the rope somehow."

"And that's good news for you. The victim was tied up just where those kids found him sticking up out of the water." Darden slapped Manny on the back. "Now it's someone else's homicide to worry about. And now I can go to my motel room."

"Want a lift?"

Darden looked pie-eyed when he said, "I'm sure I can make it." He looked at his briefcase. "I hate it when my work interferes with my drinking."

Manny left before he was a witness to an accident whenever Doctor Darden found his car keys.

Outside, a strong breeze kicking up leaves blown by the streetlight cast eerie shadows in the darkness. "Who the hell are you?" Manny said aloud, but he had no more answer as to who the victim was found lashed to an old cabin at American Island than he had before.

As he stepped down the sidewalk and walked to his car, a glint of light in the night caught his eye. A glint coming from somewhere down the block and he dropped to his haunches just as a rifle shot erupted in the night, a bullet striking the side of the funeral home.

He duck-walked as quickly as he could toward the cover of

his car when another shot, another bullet that hit the side of the funeral home.

Doctor Darden threw open the door and Manny yelled, "get the hell back inside and call the cops!"

A third shot dug a furrow in the pavement inches from his legs and Manny dove behind the car, feeling his cell phone crunch against the pavement.

The shooter had his range as the fourth shot hit the side of Manny's government car where he sought cover.

Manny fished his snub nosed .38 from his pocket, thinking that the pint-sized gun was not enough to go against a rifleman. And that he would die clutching a weapon the Bureau didn't authorize.

His breaths came in gasps, yet he breathed deeply, calming himself, peering around the trunk of his car, thinking what Reuben told him after that sweat: that he needed to get right with Clara. And more importantly, that he needed to get right with *Wakan Tanka* and with God, who he expected to meet at any moment.

Manny laid on the ground, using the tire to hide behind as he looked in the direction that he'd seen the muzzle blasts.

Silence, except for a dog barking somewhere down the street.

Was the shooter working his way around to get a fix on Manny?

He quickly peeked around the wheel and immediately another shot, another bullet, crashed into his tire and careened off the rim.

And then, sirens.

Manny never had cared for the loud, angry sound of sirens, but this time he felt like falling onto the ground and kissing it as he thanked the Creator.

A Chamberlain cruiser skidded around the corner, tires chirping, lights strobing off the funeral home, sirens becoming louder as another sped from the opposite direction: Sheriff Bain's patrol truck.

The Sheriff laid on his brakes and nearly collided with Manny's Bureau car even as the city policeman bailed out of his cruiser with his own rifle. "Jump in the back!" Bain yelled.

Manny sprang from his lying position and sprinted across the street. He dove into the bed of the sheriff's truck and Bain quickly backed away from the scene.

When he had backed up a block, Sheriff Bain stopped and stuck his head out the window. "Jump up in here and we'll help that city cop find your shooter."

Manny hopped into the cab and rolled his window down, listening. Silence once again. Until suddenly, tires squealed, the odor of burnt rubber on pavement pungent as—two blocks up—taillights came on. The truck fishtailed as it sped away and Bain said, "Better buckle up for this," and floored the sheriff's truck.

By the time they had reached the interstate, the other truck's taillights had disappeared far up the hill nearly to the rest area when Sheriff Bain turned his lights off and gave up the chase. "Might as well head back to see what Officer Krebs found out."

Bain turned the truck around and headed back to Hickey's Funeral Home. Officer Krebs stood leaning against his patrol car when the sheriff's truck stopped beside him. "What'd you find out Johnny?"

"Shooter used a hunting rifle," Manny volunteered, and Krebs nodded. "I found these cases behind a bush over yonder," he chin-pointed. ".30-06. But how'd you know? The sound?"

"That," Manny answered, "and because the shooter fired four rounds and they weren't in rapid succession like you'd figure if he was using something like an AR-15. Took him a while to reload for that fifth round."

"All I can say is you're luckier 'n hell," Krebs said. "That round into that tire could have penetrated and nailed you but the steel rim deflected it." He looked about. "Doctor Darden staggered out of the funeral home, but he wasn't any help except to tell me a couple bullets struck the side of Hickey's. With any luck we might be able to recover a bullet in case we find a suspect. Any theories?"

Manny, still trembling, stepped out of the sheriff's truck and looked down at his flat tire and at the rim bent from the bullet's impact. He fished into his pocket for the trunk keys, but Krebs took them from him and opened the trunk. "I need to change the tire—"

"Relax," Krebs said. "You've been through enough tonight. I'll do it." He started moving items around to get to the spare and said over his shoulder, "Any idea as to your shooter?"

Manny leaned against the hood, wishing he had a cigarette to calm himself. *I miss my old friend Chesterfield at a time like this.* "Whoever knows something about that floater Sam fished out of the river would be at the top of my list. And who killed Sam as well. I must be getting close to solving the murders but just don't know it." He moved upwind from Sheriff Bain's pipe smoke. "Those Horris brothers would be good for it if they weren't safely in the county lockup."

Bain chewed on the end of his pipe. "They made bail."

"*What?*"

Bain nodded. "At four o'clock this afternoon. More than enough time to find their favorite G-Man and ambush him."

Chapter 33

Manny pulled the blinds tight and shut the door of the sheriff's office as he waited for Sheriff Bain to light his pipe. "Their attorney would only allow them to deny that one or both was your shooter last night."

"And when you asked to examine their rifles in their back window of their truck?"

Bain struck a kitchen match on the edge of his desk. "The attorney said no, but Wayne Horris told me to go ahead. Says everyone carries hunting rifles in these parts for the coyotes and bobcats." Bain blew out his match and sat back. "There were two bolt actions rifles—one a .243 and the other an .06 like the cases Officer Krebs found. Lordy, was Wayne pissed when I seized the gun, especially when I told him it might take a while for the state crime lab to compare the cases Krebs found by the bushes and Wayne's rifle."

"So, for right now we're still at a dead end as far as IDing the shooter? There was no Perry Mason moment when Wayne confessed to winging rounds my way?"

"That's about the size of it unless you can come up with something else or another suspect."

Manny grabbed Sheriff Bain's day-planner filling up the width of the desk and turned it over as he grabbed a Sharpie sticking out of an old car distributor acting as a pen repository. After drawing intersecting lines and labeling them in three columns—

one for Sam's murder, one for the floater in the river, the last one for Manny's assaults—he began as if he were presenting to a jury. "These are the possibilities," Manny began. "At the top of the suspect list in both my beating at Charly's and for the shooting last night are the Horris Brothers. Since I am the only viable witness to their cattle rustling the other night—"

"Don't forget your trainee," Bain said.

Manny winced. "I'm afraid he'll have other duties if this gets to court. What I'm saying is the video evidence I took that night will send them up the river for years. That's if I can live long enough to testify in court."

Bain agreed. "And if they'll try killing a federal officer, they sure wouldn't hesitate to kill Sam for that same reason—that he could have proven they were big-time rustlers. But why is Miles Jamieson so close to them as suspects?"

"I am not convinced that Buck Jamieson just ran off with that banker's wife," Manny began, "That Jaz Halverson. If you could have seen Miles that night in Charly's, seen his temperament change from hostile to damn right dangerous when I asked about his father, you'd see why he's a strong suspect. He hated his father for the way he treated his grandfather, and the way he ran around with other women."

"But Miles was only a kid when Annie kicked Buck outta the house."

"But I can see him holding a grudge all those years. I can see him looking his old man up when he got to be a strapping teen and killing him. Dragging the corpse down into the river where he'd never be found. That is, until the drought lowered the water enough that two kids fishing spotted the body sticking out of the water."

"But I see you still list Miles as a possible suspect in Sam's murder," Sheriff Bain said, "albeit down the list."

Manny tapped the sketch with the Sharpie. "Only because I

can't say if Miles knew for certain that Annie wouldn't prosecute him for the embezzlement. If he thought she would, perhaps he did confront Sam one of those nights he was pouring over the books at the trucking company."

Bain blew smoke upwards before tapping the cold ashes into the round file beside his desk. "I don't see why you even put that hit and run driver on the list for Sam's death."

"If you're looking at a stint in the state penitentiary like the hit-and-run driver was, murder would be a motive to get rid of the only officer who'd worked up a case against you—"

"But the guy offed himself in Sioux Falls before Sam—and I—could even get a chance to interview him," Bain said. "You know that."

Manny stood and paced in front of the desk. "I put him on the list because he might have felt remorse for hitting that biker and killing her, but he might have tried to cover himself. Maybe Sam did talk with him. Maybe the guy wanted to get Sam out of the way. And maybe—just maybe—that driver's conscience finally caught up with him that day you were to interview him and he killed himself."

"More likely," Bain said, "he knew the gig was up when a Brule County Sheriff was coming all the way to Sioux Falls to interview him and possibly arrest him for the accident."

"As for Duddy, no one had a better motive than he did—Sam killing his brother in that botched robbery. Sam being murdered not a week after Duddy was released on parole is more than a little coincidental and I don't believe in coincidences."

"But for heaven's sake, why even put Annie on your suspect list? And for both Sam's death and the floater?"

Manny breathed deeply, calming himself. Last night when he was winding down after nearly getting ventilated by the shooter outside the funeral home, he had thought of everything as he was lying awake trying to get to sleep, his thoughts returning to Annie. What if that floater in the river *was* her husband, and what if Annie could no longer stomach his philandering and abuse of her and her son and her father. Even after she kicked Buck out of the house she may have felt *a woman scorned*, kept popping into his mind, and Manny probably wouldn't blame her for killing Buck. But squaring killing Sam took a bit more thought. What if she actually knew Miles was the embezzler? And what if she feared that Sam would drag Bear Paw Trucking through the muck when it became known Miles skimmed thousands from the company. Would that be enough for her to kill Sam?

* * * * *

Reuben was leaning over the balcony looking down on the parking lot when Manny pulled to a spot at the motel. Emily was loading clothes into her Prius before disappearing back into her apartment.

Manny looked up and shielded his hand from the sun. "Looks like you're standing guard. Hope it's not because of the shooting last night?"

"Partly," Reuben said. "Your shooter or shooters are still out there somewhere. But I'm also waiting for Gandira. He gave Emily her walking papers this morning."

Manny walked up the stairs and leaned across the balcony beside Reuben. "So he finalized the sale of the motel?"

"That's just it," Reuben said. "Emily said the only thing needed to complete the sale is for the contract to be sent to Gandira so he and his attorney can go over it."

"Then why's she moving out?"

"I said, Gandira gave her the bum's rush—"

"He doesn't have the authority to evict her," Manny said. "He doesn't own the motel yet."

"But it's just a matter of time before he does."

"But he doesn't yet," Manny reiterated. "Were it me—and were I a vindictive soul—I'd make the *potential* new owner's life as miserable as possible as badly as Gandira has treated her. I would wait until the sale is absolutely finalized, then I might even fight eviction through the courts."

"She'll lose," Reuben said.

"Eventually." Manny grinned. "But in the meantime, it would take up a lot of Gandira's oxygen to go through the motions. Might even take a few months to evict Emily."

Reuben straightened and a wide smile crossed his leathered face. "Do all cops think like you?"

Manny shrugged. "Just ones who have dealt with jerks like Gandira."

"I think I just might tell that to Emily," Reuben said. He started toward the stairwell when he stopped and said over his shoulder, "Willie left a message for you to call. Sounded urgent. Said you weren't answering your cell phone and he was getting worried."

Manny recalled last night when he had scrambled into Sheriff Bain's truck his cell phone had been in pieces and he'd have to get another one. "I'll call him."

Manny went into his room and called Willie's cell on the room phone. "I can't leave you alone for even a few days. Getting shot at. Don't you beat all."

"Not like I had anything to say about it." Manny gave Willie the headline version and ended by explaining his cell phone had been smashed when he dove for cover. "That's why I didn't pick up."

Manny kicked off his shoes and propped a pillow behind his back. "Reuben said it was urgent, unless the only reason for calling is you're concerned about my welfare."

"I am that, too. But I need you to come back to Rapid City if you can manage it."

"Problems?"

"The worst kind. Clara's been calling Doreen nonstop concerned that you're going to back out of the wedding again," Willie seemed to moan over the phone. "Especially since the *other woman* showed up on your doorstep."

"What other woman?" Manny asked.

"Some Abigail Winehart," Willie said. "Claimed you worked with her for years and had promised to be her personal tour guide around the Black Hills. She convinced Clara you two were old friends, emphasis on the *friends*."

Manny groaned. He explained that Abigail was a records clerk that he often had to sweet-talk into going above and beyond in research he had tasked her to do. "She is not the *other woman*," Manny said. "There is no other woman."

"Tell that to Clara in person," Willie said. "Between calls to Doreen and entertaining this woman."

"Explain entertaining?"

"That Abigail guilt tripped Clara into putting her up in that guest room of yours."

"How could she do that?"

"You know Clara," Willie said. "Growing up on the Rosebud, everyone was hospitable. Especially when *old friends* came to town."

Manny swung his legs over the bed and slipped into his boots. "I better call Clara."

"When you do, talk with this Abigail—she claims to have important information for you that you requested. That'll get Doreen off my case. And while you're here, you can go with me to talk with Amos."

"Can't you talk with Amos by your lonesome?"

"I can," Willie said, "but I know he won't open like he did before. He will to you though, especially if you bring Reuben along. He trusts Reuben."

"Just what," Manny asked, "does Amos need to open up about?"

"Henrietta's Pinto wagon."

Manny started packing his clothes in his suitcase. "I've been away from the rez long enough that I don't follow you."

"Philbilly got called to the Cohen Home to repair a cell phone. Amos' cell phone."

"Is this going somewhere?"

"I hope," Willie said, "'cause Philbilly recognized Amos—he was the driver of Henrietta's stolen car a few weeks ago."

Chapter 34

"You think there's a future with Emily?" Manny asked.

Reuben laughed. "A future at my age would be making sure my name's not in the obituaries every morning. Rest assured, *misun*, Emily knows I'm just a… fling is what they called it in my day. But that's all right. We had fun."

"I saw she was unpacking her car as we were leaving."

"She took your advice," Reuben said. "She's going to make that Gandira go through all the hoops to evict her. She checked with the public defender who advised her Gandira might be able to fire her when the motel sale is final, but it'll be harder for him to kick her out of her apartment." He peeled the wrapper back on a Moon Pie and tried scooting away from the dash to get comfortable. "This Abigail sounds like trouble at home."

"Tell me about it," Manny said as he pulled off the Murdo exit for gas. "She's been hitting on me ever since I was assigned to the Academy."

"You must have given her some encouragement for her to come all the way out west expecting to spend some time with you."

Manny pulled to a pump and quickly got out to fill the car.

Reuben got out and stretched. Leaning on the top of the car he said, "You never answered—you must have led her on."

"So I did just a wee bit," Manny said, "to coax her into digging into whatever records I wanted her to research."

"And now you're sparking two women—her and Clara."

Manny snatched the receipt and waited until Reuben had folded himself back into the car before saying, "I'm not sparking anyone beside Clara. In case you've forgotten, we do have a wedding date set."

"You set a date twice before and chickened out."

"Not this time."

"Better convince Clara of that. By the sounds of Willie, she is convinced you and Abigail have a thing going."

"Don't hardly have time for a relationship with one woman…" Manny trailed off. "You know, you might just help out a little here. I could introduce you to Abigail. Maybe you could be her guide to all things around the Black Hills."

"Me and Emily did part ways with no strings to the other," Reuben said, "so I am available. What's Abigail like? Is she pretty?"

"She is the best records clerk the Bureau has—"

"But is she attractive?"

"She used to come into the office with the tastiest casseroles—"

"You're avoiding the question." Reuben uncapped a Thermos bottle and began pouring a cup. "Which can only mean she's nothing to look at."

"*Kola*," Manny said as he accepted the cup of coffee Reuben had poured. "Just 'cause she a little… chunky—"

"How chunky?"

Manny shrugged his shoulders. "Last I saw Abigail she was… portly. But, she has a nice personality. Besides, she could have lost some weight for all I know. Been a few years since I saw her."

"And you want me to wine and dine her to get her out of your hair?"

"Could you, *kola*?"

"Being a *kola* doesn't mean subjecting yourself to someone you're not attracted to."

"You're superficial?"

"I'm human," Reuben said.

"Just this once keep her occupied," Manny pleaded. "Just until after the wedding or until her vacation time runs out. Look on the bright side, she's youthful. She's about thirty years younger than you—that ought to count for something."

Reuben sat quietly sipping his coffee for long moments before he said, "Just this once. When we get to Rapid City, you can spring for a motel room to get her out of your house and she and I will go from there."

"What's a *kola* for?" Manny said.

As they listened to Sirius radio's old time radio programs; the Lone Ranger had just rescued a ranch family from a band of outlaws when Manny turned off the stereo.

"You're just mad 'cause Tonto played a bigger role than the Masked Man in helping those folks," Reuben said.

"No," Manny said. "I turned the radio off so I could bounce some things off you."

"Great. The last time you bounced something off me I agreed to keep your Abigail Winehart company."

Manny ignored it and braked for a semi-truck turning at the first Wall exit. "What I'm wondering is—"

"That's why I call you Wonder Boy—"

"…what about Amos? If Philbilly's right, Amos was the driver of Henrietta's stolen Pinto."

"Phil's a hillbilly but he's not stupid. I'm sure he can ID Amos as the driver now that he's seen him at the home."

"But driving in his mid-nineties? Why would he even need to take Henrietta's car?"

"From the times I've been at the home during Bingo night, Amos was about the most vocal of the residents. You saw him playing cards—the man's got a gambling obsession. You ask my opinion, Amos took Henrietta's car so he could drive to Deadwood and hit the slots or the tables."

Manny motioned to a McDonald's sign near an off-ramp at Rapid City. "Least I can do is buy lunch at Micky D's."

"You just want to postpone the inevitable with your stalker Abigail."

Reuben was probably right, Manny thought. "I'll call Clara when we're done and plead with her to put Abigail up in a motel room where she can meet her Stainless Steel Savior."

"Don't push it," Reuben said, "or I'll rethink helping you out of this jam. By the way, how am I getting up to Rapid to meet her? Only thing I can do is find a car—"

"Don't you dare! Lumpy already thinks every time a car is joyrode on the rez that you're the likely culprit. I'll lay over tonight at your place and tomorrow when I go up to the office, I'll drop you off at whatever motel she's staying in."

Manny pulled into the McDonald's lot and sat for a moment with the car off. "I suppose at some point I'm going to have to meet Abigail face-to-face. She told Clara she has important information for me," Manny said. "Why do I get the feeling that she's holding that over my head to make sure I meet up with her?"

"I suppose you're just so irresistible, tiger," Reuben said and struggled to get out of the car.

* * * * *

Between bites of his second Big Mac, Reuben kept looking out the window. Searching.

"You expecting someone?" Manny asked.

"I am and you ought to be too." Reuben finished his shake and wiped a dribble of milk off his chin. "Or have you forgotten there's still one or more shooters out there somewhere that'd love to get you in their crosshairs?"

"You think they'd tail me all the way from Chamberlain?"

"I would have back in my AIM days," Reuben answered. "Not giving away any buried secrets, but if there was someone I was ordered to put the muscle on, I followed him to hell until the first chance I got. Just because we're two hundred miles from Chamberlain doesn't mean you're in the clear."

"Now you're getting me paranoid."

Reuben smiled. "That was my intention. I want you on this side of the grass longer."

They finished their meal, but Manny made no move to leave.

"We need to go visit with Amos before he craps out for his early evening nap," Reuben said.

"In a minute," Manny said, "soon's I do that bouncing-off-my-brother thing."

"Bounce away."

Manny leaned his elbows on the table and tented his fingers. "Willie said Henrietta was more upset that time her car was taken by the lack amount of gasoline the suspect—Amos—left in the tank."

"It was dry enough that I am sure it crapped out just as he was pulling into the parking lot of the Cohen Home," Reuben answered.

"See, that's what's been bothering me," Manny said. "If Amos took it to go gambling in Deadwood, it shouldn't have run out of gas if it was full when he took it like she said. Deadwood's about a hundred miles away. What kind of mileage does an old Pinto get?"

Reuben took out his new smartphone but couldn't get the calculator to come up so he grabbed a pen from Manny's shirt pocket and figured it out on a napkin. "Thing's only got a fourteen-gallon tank. When it was new, it got about twenty-five miles a gallon but—looking at that old beater when I put some gas in it—it's probably down to twenty-one or two miles a gallon." Reuben slid the napkin across the table. "Be able to drive right around three hundred miles be my guess."

"That's what I thought. So if all Amos did was head up to play the slots or the card tables, he shouldn't have run out of gas."

"Unless he drove around for any length of time," Reuben said.

"And what?" Manny slid out of the booth. "Drove around picking up chicks?"

"I will be at his age," Reuben answered. "Guess that's the million-dollar question we'll ask him. If we ever get there while he's still awake."

Chapter 35

When Reuben and Manny parked at the Cohen Home, Willie sat in his SUV with the KILI radio playing drum music. He shut it off and climbed out of his patrol unit to stand beside Manny's door. "I peeked inside. Amos is taking some of the residents for a ride at cards. I figure he'll be happy as hell about his winnings and that'll get him off his guard when I interview him. Or rather, when *you* interview him."

Manny stretched and asked, "Philbilly was certain that it was Amos who gave him a ride that night in Henrietta's old Pinto?"

"He was when he recognized the flip phone. He figures it must be the last one on the planet that is still operable."

Willie led them into the home and towards a table where Amos sat dealing to three other residents. Before him was the product of his poker skills: two tubes of Polident, one Aspercreme, and an entire box of Ex-Lax partially open as if someone had already chewed one. Amos looked up from the table and smiled at Reuben. "If you have got some loot to lose, there's another chair."

Reuben turned the chair around and sat with his arms draped over the chair back. He nodded at the items Amos had won and said, "'Fraid I have all my own teeth so I don't need the Polident. And any aches and pains my *initipi* sweats out. As for the Ex-Lax, I'm regular as a baby."

Out of his eye, Manny saw Willie flinch, no doubt recalling his own baby's *regularity*. "We'd like to visit with you, *Tunkasila*,"

Reuben said, using the term of respect for *Grandfather*.

"This sounds serious."

"You gonna raise me that jar of Metamucil?" one of the duffers said.

Amos said, "call" and with his one good hand spread his flush out on the table. "Looks like these fellers want to visit, boys. I will come back and gather my lucre after we are done. Except this," he said as he grabbed the tube of Polident. "This I need now."

He motioned for Manny and Reuben and Willie to follow him through the sliding doors into the back pad where a murder of crows spat angry insults from the safety of the cottonwood trees. Amos chin-pointed to them as he sat in a lawn chair. "Those crows are perched there to give us Lakota what-for. Like every other damn Crow I have ever met."

"Still the animosity?" Manny asked.

"Of course," Amos answered. "Any reason not to hate Crows?"

"Maybe 'cause it's been decades since we Lakota have been enemies with them," Manny answered.

Amos uncapped a bottle of water and stared at the birds. "You fellers did not come here to rehash old tribal feuds."

Reuben scooted his chair so that he faced Amos. "My brother and this tribal investigator are here because of your cell phone."

"Cell phone?" Amos grabbed the phone from his shirt pocket. "I did not steal it—"

"Unlike the old Ford Pinto you took from the parking lot last week," Willie blurted out.

Amos glared at him. "What has that got to do with my cell phone?"

"That guy you called to fix it—"

"Phil Ostert—"

"He recognized your phone from the night you gave him a lift walking back from Rapid City."

Amos looked away. "That is nonsense. I never saw that kid in my life before he came here to repair my phone."

Manny said, leaning closer, "surely you recall Phil telling you about his cousin with the triple mastectomy?"

Amos sucked in a breath before turning and smearing Polident on his dentures. He replaced them and pushed them upwards with his thumb. "That was Phil Ostert?"

"It was."

Amos sighed deeply. "You caught me, boys. It was dark that night and I was too busy trying to keep that beater on the road. Between it about ready to fall apart and my bad night vision… well, you got to know I did not pay him much attention."

Reuben laid his hand on Amos' arm. "Officer With Horn is investigating the theft."

"I brought the car back. No harm done."

"Except you ran it out of gas," Reuben said.

Amos shrugged. "I was going to slip Henrietta some lucky bucks the first of the month when my social security check comes in."

From what Willie said, Amos had more than enough money stashed away. When he sold his buffalo ranch, he didn't give it *all* to the college in Kyle, but Manny let that pass. "Where did you need to go that you had to take Henrietta's car?"

"Around," Amos answered, reseating his teeth with his thumb.

"You had to drive more than just *around*," Willie said, "to have run it out of gas."

"All right," Amos held up his hand. "All right. I went up to Deadwood."

"*Tunkasila*," Reuben said. "You put a whole lot of miles more than just driving to Deadwood and back."

Amos picked up a stone and threw it at the crows nesting in the trees, but it fell yards short and they remained perched squawking angry things at Amos. "I drove back to Chamberlain. Went up to Ft. Thompson."

"Chamberlain?" Manny said. "What on earth for?"

"See old friends on Crow Creek."

"You don't have any friends on Crow Creek," Manny said, taking a chance that—if there ever were friends on that reservation—they would be long dead by now.

Amos's head drooped and Manny bent closer to him. "The only connection to Chamberlain you might have now is Robbie's daughter and grandson. Is that who you went back to see?"

Amos remained silent.

"We know Miles Jamieson comes here to the rez often to visit his grandfather's grave. I would wager if I checked the visitor logs it'd show he stops here to visit with you whenever he does," Manny added.

Amos nodded again. "It will not be long before I walk the *Wanagi Tacanku*, and I just felt compelled to pass along knowledge of Robbie. To tell Miles and Annie what a good man he was. Talk about the war." He looked up at Manny with a tear welling the old man's eyes. "I do not often talk about the war… too hard. I had to gather courage to talk to Miles about it. I felt he needed to know things about his grandfather and only I knew. I just felt like it was something I had to do before I walked on."

Manny motioned to Willie. They stepped back through the sliding door while Reuben remained close to Amos. "Need some advice."

"Always," Willie answered.

"Consider not going to the judge and ask for an arrest warrant for auto theft?"

"You a mind reader?" Willie asked.

"No," Manny answered. "But I've been in your shoes a time or two."

"So what should I do? Last thing I want is for one of the last Lakota Code Talkers to land in jail."

Manny shrugged his shoulder as he looked through the glass

doors at Amos sitting, sobbing while Reuben's hand rested on the old warrior's back. "I can't really tell you what to do."

"What would you do?"

Manny thought for a moment as he dug a pack of Juicy Fruit from his pocket. What he wouldn't give for a nice, fresh Chesterfield. "Were it me—but that's just me pissing off Lumpy—I'd talk with Henrietta and ask her to drop the charges. Then I'd give her money out of my own pocket to pay for the gas Amos drove off."

"Why you say it'd piss off the police chief?"

"Henrietta's stolen car case would be one more case that isn't solved. It'd look bad when Lumpy went before the tribal council."

A wide grin crossed Willie's face. "You're right—it would piss him off."

Chapter 36

Manny sat across from Clara as they ate their supper, neither saying anything to the other until Clara broke the silence. "If you're waiting for me to apologize for being jealous, I'm not."

Manny picked at his meatloaf before putting his fork down. "I just never figured you for the jealous kind. You know I love you."

"That's my point. You basically led a lovely woman to our house—"

"I did no such thing."

"Well, you didn't discourage her, what with your promises of taking her to dinner in exchange for information on one of your cases. Supposedly."

Manny pushed his plate away and dabbed at the corner of his mouth with the napkin. "For one, I guess your opinion of what constitutes *lovely* is far different than mine." Manny thought back to Abigail sitting at her desk, potato chip bags strewn about fighting for room on her desktop with donut wrappers. "But she does have vital information on one of my cases. At least she claims to."

Manny laid his hand on Clara's as he scooted his chair closer. "Look, I don't know what you think is going on between Abigail and me, but it is strictly professional. At least on my part. If I did anything wrong… it was to… lead her on, thinking there might be more. Certainly not enough to warrant her coming halfway across the country just to see me and give me the information."

Clara's hand relaxed and Manny pressed home his point. "Besides, Reuben's going to take her around the Hills in the next few days. She'll get the point."

"You'll still have to meet up with her," Clara said, "so she can pass that information on to you."

"But Reuben will be there. By this time tomorrow, he will have romanced her into forgetting all about me," Manny said, not looking forward to facing Reuben. After having to spend a day with Abigail, Manny was positive that his brother would be none too pleased. Maybe even reverting to the *old* Reuben. Which Manny was not looking forward to.

* * * * *

Manny remained in the parking lot of the Holiday Inn gathering his courage to face Abigail. And more importantly, facing his brother after guilt-tripping him into spending time with her. The only thing Manny had going for him was that he wasn't lying when he had told Reuben she was a nice lady. But he knew that Reuben would feel put-upon about having to spend the whole day with her just because he was trying to deflect her attentions.

Yesterday after Manny called her, Clara had led Abigail over to the hotel in her rental car and had paid in advance for two nights. First floor. The luxury suite. Using Manny's credit card. As if Clara wanted to punish Manny for encouraging Abigail to come visit him.

He took off his hat as he stopped in front of Abigail's door. Reuben's was the adjoining suite and Manny would be brave facing him as soon as he learned what information Abigail thought was so important to his case. He breathed deeply and rapped on the door. When he got no answer, he knocked louder. Reuben threw open the door. He stood taking up the frame of the doorway in only his tighty-whities and said, "You could have called ahead of time so I could throw on some clothes."

Manny looked at the adjacent door and said, "Guess I got your room and Abigail's mixed up."

"No, you didn't. It's just that me and her figured no sense getting another room's bed messed up." He stepped aside. "Come on in while I put my jeans on."

Manny peeked inside the room.

"She's in the shower," Reuben said. "Ought to be out in a minute."

"So, you're not mad at me?"

Reuben shut the door and motioned to two trays with plates that had been cleaned of breakfast. "Mad? Setting me up in a fancy motel like this with room service? And," he jerked his thumb to the bathroom where the shower had stopped running, "introducing me to a babe like Abigail."

Manny wondered what had finally overtaken Reuben when the bathroom door opened and Abigail stepped out. A terry cloth robe was draped loosely around her shoulders as she tousled her hair with a room towel. She stepped to Manny and kissed him lightly on the cheek. "You look like you don't know me."

Manny looked Abigail up and down, wondering what was beneath the robe. She had dropped fifty pounds and, even with her wet, curly hair, she looked as if she were about to do some photo shoot for a fashion magazine. "You're... different."

She tilted her head back and laughed. "The Bureau began a health program, and I took advantage of it. I cut out the snacks and hit the gym five days a week. Then when I dropped weight, I rewarded myself by having a hair and facial makeover. Do you approve?"

"All that matters is if *I* approve, right?" Reuben said. He had dressed and moved to stand with his arm wrapped around her thin waist.

Abigail stood on tiptoes and planted a wet one on Reuben's mouth. "Absolutely."

She turned to Manny. "But you didn't come here to watch me and your brother do the wild thing. I am betting you are curious as to what I found out concerning that floater case you've been working on." She slipped away from Reuben. "I'll get dressed and we'll grab lunch and discuss it."

* * * * *

Manny tried looking away from Abigail but he was too stunned by her transformation. She definitely was not the same Abigail Winehart he was used to. Sitting behind her desk while Manny marveled at the strength of the chair in which she sat…

"I guilt tripped one of our Anchorage agents into checking out this lead on Jasmine Halverson." Abigail opened up a notebook and took out a field report, which she handed to Manny. "But he thanked me afterward—he loved that twelve-hour train ride to Fairbanks to hunt up Jaz."

Manny squinted and Reuben reached into his shirt pocket. "Here, use my glasses."

Manny accepted them and spread the field report open that had been penned by Special Agent Donner.

"He located Jaz after I reissued that BOLO," Abigail said. "You can thank me now if you wish."

Manny turned to the field notes scribbled on the report and barely read where Agent Donner had interviewed Jaz Halverson at a nursing home in Fairbanks. "She and Buck Jamieson skipped around the country losing money in assorted ventures," Manny said aloud as he read the field notes. "The last one being a convenience store just outside Fairbanks city limits." Manny turned the field notes over. "Donner found Jaz but he doesn't say he interviewed Buck Jamieson."

"'Cause he didn't." Abigail took a letter-sized envelope from her purse and waved it under Manny's nose. "I was going to use this as my ace-in-the-hole when we met. Some assurance that we'd get close. But," she nudged Reuben, "now I got someone I can get *really* close to. Here."

Manny took the envelope and slipped the last page of the field note out.

"Interesting reading?" Reuben asked.

Manny read and reread the field report before putting it with Donner's other notes. "Looks like Buck Jamieson made it to Fairbanks where he ran a stop-and-rob with his common-law wife," Manny said. "Died six years ago when he froze to death walking home from the bar one night."

"Why that hound-dog look?" Reuben asked. "You finally found out what happened to Buck."

"I was so sure that Miles Jamieson had hunted his father up when he got older," Manny said. "So sure Miles killed him and used that expensive scuba gear to drag him down into the river to tie him up to that abandoned cabin."

Abigail laid her hand on Manny's forearm and exaggerated a frown. "Don't be so down—at least you know that floater of yours isn't Buck Jamieson."

"But it does tell me who the victim at American Island was and who murdered him. And why."

Manny stood and headed for the door. When Reuben called after him, "Wait, *misun*. Where are you headed?"

"I need to go back to Chamberlain."

"Give me a few days to show Abigail around the Black Hills and I'll go with you," Reuben said.

"Can't, *kola*. This is one job I wouldn't want anyone to have. Even you."

Chapter 37

Manny sat watching Bear Paw Trucking under the shelter of a maple tree a block away. After he had arrived in Chamberlain earlier, he had stopped and talked at length with Sheriff Bain. Manny explained who had killed Deputy Sam Christian and why, and that he dreaded talking with Annie about the floater in the river.

"Miles isn't around the trucking yard?"

The sheriff tamped the ashes from his pipe into the round file beside his desk. "After you called from Rapid, I made a pretense visit to Bear Paw telling Annie a trooper had stopped by the office wanting to schedule inspections for all their trucks and talk with Miles about the inspections. She said he would be back tomorrow as he and a diving partner went to Angostura Reservoir by Rapid City to do some treasure diving. She'll be at the office alone."

When Manny stood to leave, Sheriff Bain said, "Want that I should come with you? Give you moral support?"

Manny forced a smile. "I believe this is one time that I need to do this alone. This is one time when I will feel as badly passing on sad news as the one receiving it. I need to talk with Annie alone."

"Then afterward—"

"Afterward there'll be time enough to take care of our business," Manny said.

Manny sat watching the Bear Paw Trucking yard. Just as he drained his Thermos, the last of the truckers and mechanics left the yard. Suddenly, the coffee tasted too bitter, and he tossed the rest out the window before driving to the trailer the trucking company used for an office.

Annie's Cadillac sat parked in her reserved spot, the lights in the office cutting the darkness when Manny stepped out of his car. He eased the door closed as if slamming it would interrupt the stillness of the night. A stillness that would soon be broken, he was certain, by her sobs. And her anger.

When he walked into the office, Annie was bent over digging something from her desk drawer. "Make sure you clock out—"

"It's me, Annie."

She looked up and shut the drawer. "I've been expecting you. Coffee?"

He shook his head. "Just finished a pot. All coffeed out."

"Miles isn't here if that's who you want to talk with."

"I don't," Manny said, hanging his hat on a deer-horn hat rack beside the door. "I came to talk with you."

"Don't mind if I have a cup, then," she said and poured from a carafe before sitting at her desk. "Your voice sounds serious."

Manny sat in a captain's chair in front of her desk. He kneaded his palms that had become sweaty with anticipation of telling her the news. "In my law enforcement duties, I've given death notices more times than I like. They're never easy—I never could figure a way to give someone such bad news—"

"Is it Miles?" Anne said, her hand shaking so that she had to put her cup down. "Did he have a diving accident—"

"It's not Miles," Manny answered.

"Then spit it out. Tell why you stopped by."

"All right, then," Manny blurted out. "We found what happened to Buck."

"Buck?" Annie said. "I haven't seen him in so long I just figured some jealous husband caught him and he ended up worm food. Why do you think I care what happened to him?"

"I think you know." Manny grabbed his notebook from his back pocket and flipped pages, not to read from, but as a prop while he gauged Annie's reactions. "I think that you figured that floater those kids found was your husband." He explained that Buck had been just one more victim of a cold, Alaska winter. "And that would be bad news for you."

"Wouldn't bother me if he froze to death."

"You sure?"

Annie shrugged and sipped her coffee lightly. Stalling. "Of course. But for the record, who was that victim those kids found?"

Now it was Manny's turn to stall. To gauge how anxious Annie was to hear his explanation. "I think I will take that cup of coffee," he said.

She nodded to the carafe and Manny stood and poured himself half a cup. "Your father was a thief and a murderer," he said abruptly.

Annie locked eyes with Manny and leaned her forearms on the table.

"My father was a war hero."

"As were all Code Talkers," Manny said.

"Then you'd better explain yourself or you're going to find yourself in a messy lawsuit. Defaming my father like that."

"You already know what the FBI forensic audit team found this last week."

"You claim he started the business with money he'd gotten from stolen antiquities he brought back after the war. But I know that's absurd. I know for a fact that returning servicemen were carefully checked to make sure they had no souvenirs. And even if he did slip through the inspectors with one or two items—like that vase of mine you took—that wouldn't be enough to finance starting a trucking business."

"You're forgetting he and Charlie McKnight were sent back over *after* the war to testify in the war crimes trials. I have to do more investigating, but I would wager they or their luggage were never checked at all coming back after their testimony. We know they took a few weeks after the trials to allegedly go sightseeing. But like my brother Reuben pointed out, who returns to a war zone to sightsee? No, I believe your father could recall the spot where he saw those Japanese soldiers take trucks loads of stolen, antiquities and later returned with Charlie McKnight."

Annie guffawed. "If that were the case, the amount of Yamashita's Gold would be sufficient my father wouldn't have had to start a business. He could just live off the sale of collectibles."

"But they had only two weeks to dig the tunnel out where they could get to the loot. I am convinced they took what they could, gold sovereigns and bars and, yes, even that exquisite vase he gave you when you got older. I believe they took all they could carry without drawing anyone's suspicion."

Annie stood and walked around the desk. She stood glaring at Manny when she asked, "A moment ago you accused my father of being a murderer. This I gotta hear."

"Your father hated your husband Buck—"

"But you just said Buck died of natural causes."

"I think he hated Charlie McKnight more than your husband. Your father and McKnight served in the Philippines during the war and they traveled back for the trials a year after being discharged. You would think they were pards. Until you look at that photo of the 4th of July Parade. Your father was none too happy in that photo."

"So at some point they had a falling out. Big deal."

Manny stepped around Annie and walked to the coffee cart for a refill. "I think it was more than a falling out. Knowing what people told me about Robbie, he was an honorable man. One who wouldn't steal *any* antiquities. Unless somebody pressured him. Like Charlie. I am of the belief that when the Army ordered them to go back to testify that Charlie pressured Robbie to show him just where he'd seen the Japanese soldiers stash the loot."

"How would this Charlie McKnight know about that?"

"He was the officer transcribing what Amos relayed back to Robbie that day. He knew the Japanese had hid loot in a cave but only knew that your father could find it again."

He faced Annie. "I would like to think that McKnight pressured your father into showing him where the cave with the antiquities was. I would like to think McKnight forced him to dig it up. Either way, they returned to the states with a considerable amount."

"You almost sound like you're exonerating my father."

"The gut feeling I have is that Robbie had no desire to steal the antiquities, and he had no desire to keep them but that when he got it back stateside… well, greed might have overtaken him like it might any man in that position. What I do know is that the money he gave Amos to start his buffalo ranch was given with a good heart."

"You know my father couldn't be a murderer. He loved life. Loved everybody—"

"Except Charlie McKnight when he came to town that July. I don't know why but I feel as if your father and Charlie got into an argument over something. Probably because Charlie was shaking him down for money."

"Dad never told me anything like that," Annie said.

"The Bureau auditors found Robbie had paid Josephine Wents money every month but that it stopped abruptly in 1952. Josephine Wents was the common-law wife of Charlie McKnight in St. Louis. I believe Charlie was blackmailing your father."

Manny leaned on the edge of the desk. "Charlie had already squandered his own share of the antiquities theft to drugs down in St. Louis. Whatever their difference, it must have escalated to where your father had no other choice than to lure him out to American Island where he shot Charlie. And while he was unconscious, tied him to that last abandoned cabin to await the flooding Robbie knew was coming."

"Nonsense. Anyone could have killed McKnight."

"Not just anyone could have gotten Robbie's dog tags and wrapped the chain around Charlie's neck before he fled the area. You said your father treasured his tags. He wouldn't have given them up easily."

"You're saying Dad killed Charlie and in the struggle Dad's dog tags would up around Charlie's neck?"

"Somehow," Manny said. "I'll have to do some more thinking about that."

Annie sat behind her desk and grabbed a pencil that she began chewing on. "You can't prove any of this."

"I can't prove it for a court of law, but then I don't need to. I only need to prove it to the point where this case can be closed. Whether he was a scoundrel or not, Charlie McKnight's death needs closure."

Annie swirled coffee in her cup. When she looked back up, tears had filled her eyes. "When your report is final, will it be made public?"

"It is the Bureau's policy to do so."

"But... but folks hereabouts will know my father murdered another man. And as bad, that he started his trucking business with stolen loot. I am pleading with you to bury the report. Not for my sake, but for Miles. He worshipped his grandfather. He would be devastated."

Manny knew Annie spoke to truth. Miles would be devastated. But would he kill again?

Chapter 38

Manny sat silent, giving Annie her time to grieve. Her father had been everything that was right with returning war heroes—being successful in life after they'd experienced the anguish and horror of the battlefield. And it was not easy to tell her, "I need to speak with Miles."

"Haven't you done enough? You'll go public with McKnight's murder, and no one will be more ravaged by the news than Miles. So, you don't really need to talk with him."

"I do."

"About what?"

"Sam Christian's death," Manny said. "And about ambushing me the other night outside the funeral home."

"Ask me yourself." Miles entered the office and shut the door. "Amos said you'd be coming back to Chamberlain to talk with mom."

"When did you see Amos?"

"I stopped by the Cohen Home to see him after the Angostura dive was a bust. He said he figured you had things figured out. He warned me, in his own way, God bless the old dude. Now ask away."

Manny set his cup down and slipped his hand in his pocket where the grip of the snubbie .38 felt reassuring. "You're not the best shot in the world. When I came out of the funeral home a few nights ago, you missed every time."

"What makes you think it was me?"

"Bullets," Manny answered. "Officer Krebs dug one intact slug out of the side of Hickey's—a one-hundred-thirty grainer. Same as you load in your rifle."

"Word around town is that you figured the Horris brothers for that."

Manny moved ever so slightly, and he spotted the bulge under Miles' coat. "Much as I'd have liked to pin it on them, Sheriff Bain checked their rifles. The .30-06 belonging to Wayne Horris was loaded with 180-grain bullets. Sheriff Bain figures Wayne needs something heavier for all the suspected poaching of deer he does. But the way I figure it, you like the lighter bullets for coyote hunting. I'll have to seize your rifle and send it in for a ballistics comparison."

Annie stepped closer and asked Miles, "Is any of this true? Did you try killing Agent Tanno?" When Miles said nothing, Annie's tears flowed, and she used the edge of the desk to steady herself. "You have gone too far this time. All those times I bailed you out of jail… Miles, how could you have done this?"

Miles stepped back as his hand inched toward the inside of his coat. "Did you not hear what he just told you about Grandfather? Did you not hear that his name will be dragged through the mud of public opinion when Agent Tanno's report is made public? Grandfather might have killed Charlie McKnight, but he deserved it."

"But you could have killed a federal agent."

"Wouldn't be the first time Miles killed someone," Manny said, eying Miles' hand inside his coat pocket. Could Manny draw his .38 out of his pocket before Miles drew his? He wasn't too confident that he could beat Miles to the draw.

Annie's head jerked up. She swiped a hand across her eyes. "Miles killed no one. You said Buck was found up in Alaska—"

"I am talking about Sam Christian," Manny said.

Miles' hand trembled. He put his back against the door as if to prevent Manny from leaving. "Me and Sam fought now and again, but that was it. I'd have no reason to kill him."

"Even after he poured over your books looking for the embezzler?"

"Miles is right," Annie said, her arms crossed, ready to defend her only child. "I already told you I would not be pressing charges for that. How could I see my own son in prison."

Manny's hand clutched his revolver, wishing he had something heavier, fearing a gunfight at any moment. "Sam was pretty sharp with accounting. He spent a few days digging into the company books—"

"We've already admitted he found that I was skimming a few bucks every month."

"But he found so much more, didn't he?"

"And what do you think he found," Annie said, "that would cause Miles to kill him?"

Manny squared up to face Miles when he said, "Sam found just what my Bureau auditors found—that your grandfather started the business using money he'd gotten from stolen, antiquities."

"Bull shit."

"It's not bull shit," Manny said. "When the lead auditor gave me his findings, he said it was an amateurish job of cooking the books. He said any first-year accounting student could have found what they did. And Sheriff Bain said that Sam was hell-on-wheels in the accounting department."

Miles forced a nervous laugh. "Sam was one double-tough son-of-a-bitch. Every time we fought in high school, he kicked my butt. Every time he went to arrest me for fighting, he kicked my butt. There's no way I could have gotten the best of him."

"Unless you had an equalizer."

"Equalizer?" Annie said. "Deputy Christian was beat, not shot."

"An equalizer that's round. Hard. Like that tire billy Miles always carries to check truck's tires."

Miles hand instinctively went to his back pocket where the handle of the short, wooden club stuck out. "I'll need to take that for evidence, too. I wager we'll find enough blood on it that our techs can match it to Sam's."

Mile's hand came out from under his coat pocket with the Colt .45 revolver in it. "You got things all figured out except any motive I might have had for killing him. So he found out I embezzled company funds and that I knew Mom wouldn't want to press charges for if she ever found out. And it was a shame he learned how Grandfather financed the start of his business, but surely not enough reason to silence him."

"No?" Manny tried focusing on something other than the gaping hole of the Colt barrel, looking about for something to use as a distraction. Manny figured Miles would get off one shot before Manny could draw his own gun. He only hoped some distraction would put Miles' shot off just enough. "You idolized your grandfather—"

"Who wouldn't? Not many Lakota Code Talkers left alive after the war."

Manny backed up slightly and his hand rested on a stapler. Could he lob it, drop out of the way while he drew his own gun? "Your grandfather and you were inseparable when you were younger. I can see him teaching you of the old ways. Teaching you to walk the Red Road, the *Chunka Duta* every righteous Lakota walks."

Miles' face softened. "Grandfather taught me the four Lakota virtues and I was happy to learn them."

"But then he died," Annie said. "And there was no example for Miles to follow. I did my best but running a trucking company took time. Too much time, and I realized I should have sold it and devoted time to my son."

"Now it is too late for any of that. I suspect you have a gun in your pocket. Skin it and toss it aside," Miles said while he motioned to the door. "Come on, Agent Man—we'll take a ride down by Bijou Hills, you and me."

"No!" Annie stepped closer to Miles. "It stops here."

"Mom, I cannot—I will not—allow Grandfather's name to be dragged through the mud. What he did during the war... he was the consummate war hero and that is how people remember him. Now stay out of this."

Manny slowly took his gun from his pocket and tossed it on the desk, clutching the stapler, knowing it would be a feeble attempt to spoil Miles' shot when it came when Annie stepped close to Miles. She laid her hand on the revolver, but the barrel never left Manny's chest. "Give me the gun."

"I can't—"

"The gun." She stepped between Manny and Miles and took hold of the pistol.

"Mom—"

"The gun!"

Miles released his grip on the revolver and Annie grabbed it.

Miles hung his head, a deep sadness crossing his face. "If you allow him to file his report... you know what people would say about Grandfather."

"It is too late for that now."

Manny walked around the desk toward his own revolver when Annie said, "leave it."

Manny turned and saw that Annie leveled the gun at him. "Now you're going to take me for a ride instead of your son?"

"First," she said, "step away from the gun and have a seat where I can watch you."

When Manny did, Annie looked at Miles out of the corner of her eye and said, "Go. You have one chance to run as far and as fast as you can. Just never come back here or you'll be arrested."

When Miles balked, Annie caressed his cheek. "Now go. Far."

After Miles left the office, Annie sat in another chair facing Manny.

"Looks like you got yourself into a hell of a dilemma," he said. "You're either going to have to kill me or eventually let me go. Either choice and you'll be in serious trouble for holding a federal agent against his will."

"Believe me, I didn't want it this way. But after it is made public that my father was a crook and a murderer, it'll make little difference. Besides, I'll take my chances in court. What jury would convict a mother for helping her son." She leaned over and grabbed the carafe of coffee. "Way I figure it is—by the time we polish off this coffee—Miles will be safely away."

"We'll find him eventually."

Annie shrugged. "Maybe. But who would blame a mother for giving him the chance?"

Chapter 39

"Who was that doll hanging on your arm at Big Bat's yesterday?" Willie asked while he waited outside his patrol SUV for Manny and Reuben to climb out of theirs. "She your daughter or something?"

Reuben grabbed his bad leg and extricated himself from Manny's car. "That doll, as you refer to her, is Manny's research source at the FBI. She headed home but she's planning on coming back next summer for another *marathon* visit."

"Did you two actually go anywhere in the Hills?" Manny asked.

Reuben shrugged. "We went to a couple eateries close between... time in the motel. I look forward to her coming back next summer."

"And you plan to escort her?"

"I do," Reuben answered.

"Maybe you better plan month-to-month," Willie said. "At your age, I wouldn't plan as far ahead as next summer."

"Reuben's as fit as any seventy-year-old, aren't you?" Manny said while he gathered his notebook.

"Thanks," Reuben said. "I think."

They all waited, staring at the entrance to the Cohen Home, none wanting to make the first move to go inside. "We're going to have to talk with him eventually," Manny said. "Might as well be now."

"It's just not quite right accusing an old Code Talker of conspiring with Miles Jamieson."

"Maybe he didn't actually conspire," Willie said, ready to give him the benefit of the doubt.

"Then let's give Amos that chance," Manny said and led them into the home.

They walked to the receptionist's desk and interrupted Henrietta nose-deep in a *Cosmopolitan* magazine. "We need to talk with Amos," Willie said.

Henrietta looked over her half-glasses and set the magazine down. "If you're here to arrest him for stealing my car I told you I'm not pressing charges. He already gave me gas money so we're square, him and me."

"We're not here to arrest him. We just need to visit with him is all."

Henrietta jerked her thumb toward the back patio. "He's farting around with those birds like he always does. Like he's the bird-man of the Cohen Home or something."

Willie led them through the dining hall bustling with people playing checkers and dominoes and a side game of cribbage. Amos sat lobbing kernels of popcorn at crows begging for more at his feet. They scattered when Manny and Willie and Reuben walked onto the patio and pulled up chairs to talk with the old man. "You're not taking residents for a ride in poker today?" Manny said.

Amos glanced over at him, a sad look on his weathered face. "A birdy told me you fellers were coming to talk serious business."

"A birdy," Reuben said, "as in a meadowlark?"

Amos finally grinned. "The meadowlark does speak Lakota. But then you knew that. And you knew just where to find me."

"We need to ask you questions about Miles Jamieson."

"Agent Tanno," Amos said. "Surely you know we *Injuns* need small talk before serious, war business."

Manny thought the old man was stalling. Putting off the inevitable of answering questions, but Manny went along. "You're right, *Tunkasila*. I should ask how you are getting along here."

"Fine. Just fine. But not as fine as Reuben, what with that babe hanging on his arm."

"A meadowlark told you that, too?" Manny asked.

Amos lobbed another piece of popcorn at a group of thirty crows on the patio. "No, Reuben did. Yesterday."

Manny looked at his brother. "You didn't tell me you'd already talked with Amos."

"Not important that you knew as it wasn't anything you are involved in. I stopped and we spoke at length about injustices we Indians go through. We talked about Emily getting the bum's rush from the motel in Chamberlain when that *Eastern Indian* buys the place."

Amos patted Reuben's knee. "Her job is safe now."

"How's that?" Manny asked.

"After Reuben and me talked, I got the urge to invest in a motel somewhere. What better place than Chamberlain? So I called my attorney and instructed him to raise whatever bid that Gandira character put in and I got it." He looked at Reuben with a twinkle in his eye. "I will need a manager."

Reuben held up his hands as if in surrender. "Not me. But I would bet that Emily Mockingbird would make a great one as long as she's worked there."

"You just want free access to the pool whenever you get back thataway," Amos said with a smile. "Or free access to Emily."

"Except for next summer when Abigail comes to visit again," Reuben answered.

Amos uncapped a bottle of water and took a long pull. "If you are not careful, you will be walking down the aisle like Manny… next weekend, is it?"

"Next weekend," Manny confirmed. "You're free to come."

"I will think about it." Amos tore open the sack of popcorn and tossed the rest to the crows. "Now you wish to ask me things."

Manny opened his notebook. "Miles came here a few days ago to see you."

"He often stopped by whenever he came to visit Robbie's grave."

"And you drove to see him last week."

"I already admitted that?"

"And when you drove back to Chamberlain to meet with Miles, what exactly did you tell him?"

"Things about his grandfather."

"How Robbie and Charlie brought enough stolen loot back to start his and your business?"

Amos nodded. "I felt he should know. By the way, have you located him yet?"

"There's been sightings of him up by Ft. Thompson. We'll eventually arrest him." After Annie had kept Manny at the Bear Paw Trucking office for the better part of an hour three days ago, she handed the gun over to Manny. "He's safe by now," she told him. The closest place Manny could think that Miles could find sanctuary was on Crow Creek. "Back to your meeting, why did you go back there to meet up with Miles?"

"Honor," Amos said. "The honor of an old man looking out for the grandson of another Code Talker. I suspected Miles was knee-deep in that deputy's murder and drove back there to talk him into giving himself up before he was confronted by cops and killed."

"That's how you racked up so many miles on Henrietta's old Pinto," Willie said.

"If I just had not picked up that goofball Phil Ostert no one would have been the wiser."

"Tell me about when Miles stopped to talk with you a few

days ago," Manny said.

"He said he was fixin' to hang around this part of the state for some diving when I told him I had heard you were headed back to Chamberlain to talk with Annie. I told Miles once again he ought to go back and turn himself in rather than implicate his mother in all that. By the way, I heard you have not arrested her yet."

"I'm mulling over whether or not I want to pursue her holding me at gunpoint."

"No harm done, was there?" Amos asked.

"Except Miles walked free and now we're hunting him."

They sat in silence for long moments when Reuben said, "Amos, tell Manny and Willie about Robbie's last days here at the home."

When Amos just stared at the crows in the cottonwood at the edge of the patio, Reuben said, "You already told me. No harm telling them."

"You got a piece of that Juicy Fruit?" Amos asked.

Manny took the pack from his shirt pocket and handed Amos a piece. "Damned gum will just stick to my dentures, but that is what I have Tidy Bowl for—to clean crap off them."

Amos began chewing on the gum, his eyes closed, either savoring the flavor or gathering his thoughts. "Robbie learned he had pancreatic cancer six months before he died. That's when he told me the story of Charlie McKnight. *Lieutenant* Charlie McKnight. See, ol' Charlie was the transcriber at the other end of the line that day I radioed back that the Japanese were stashing something in a cave. Lt. McKnight ordered me to forget it and move to locate the main Japanese force so Sergeant Kimbre, my security man, and I continued."

"But Robbie knew the exact location and they returned to the Philippines after the war?"

"They did. Here." Amos held out his arm and Reuben helped

him stand before grabbing his cane and walking out a cramp. "Robbie wanted nothing to do with it. But Lt. McKnight… now there was a greedy S.O.B. He told Robbie to either help him recover some of the antiquities McKnight was certain were buried in that cave, or he would concoct some cock-a-mamie story that it was *Robbie* wanting to steal what was already stole by the Japanese."

"Why didn't Robbie report Lt. McKnight?"

Amos shooed crows away with his cane and they retreated to the tree. "He didn't figure the Army brass would believe an Indian over a *wasicu*. After all, things were different back then."

Amos stopped and reached over to grab his empty shirt sleeve and tuck it into his shirt pocket. "After they returned, Robbie still had that powerful guilt because it was me who took that booby trap hit rather than him. He figured he would start me in my buffalo ranch claiming it was his father who gave him the money. And the money to start his trucking company. Only when he told me all this at the end of his life did I learn how I really got my seed money."

Manny leaned closer and looked the old man in the eyes. "What did he tell you about killing McKnight?"

Amos looked at Reuben who said, "You told me yesterday. Might as well get it all out now."

"End of life confession?"

"Something like that," Reuben said, "except you're going to live for many more years so I suppose it's not an end-of-life confession after all."

Amos smiled knowingly and turned to face Manny. "Who is to say I want to live much longer?"

Amos sat gathering his thought when he finally nodded his head. "The summer of '52, Lt. McKnight came to see Robbie in Chamberlain. Day before the 4th of July Parade. McKnight had wasted all his money on drugs and was fixin' to lose his cab business. 'All I need is a few of those gold sovereigns,' he said to Robbie. 'Just a few and I'll be moving on.' McKnight had bled Robbie for three years—demanding money every month to keep his mouth shut as to how Robbie came into the money to start his business."

"Sent to Josephine Wents?"

Amos nodded. "McKnight's… wife. Sent to her so no one could connect McKnight to any blackmail scheme. But that July he was broke and demanding more."

"And Robbie gave him some I would wager," Manny said.

"He did. He gave him a few sovereigns just to get him to move on. But McKnight was not going to move on. He intended on staying in Chamberlain and mooching off Robbie until he bled Robbie dry. If he had given McKnight all he wanted, it would have ruined him. Robbie would have had to sell his trucking business just to pay for the blackmail. The thing that Robbie feared most—as a lot of us Lakota do—is being locked up. Robbie would not have lasted long in prison."

"Tell Manny and Willie about the day Robbie killed McKnight," Reuben said.

Amos took the gum out of his mouth and stuck it under the chair. "Taste never lasts long."

"That day," Reuben pressed.

"Sure," Amos said. "That day. Robbie told McKnight he had more gold coins and some other antiquities stashed on American Island where Robbie had just moved a bunch of cabins prior to the Corps of Engineers flooding the river to create the reservoir. Robbie had an old ratty .22—he never was much for guns—and he shot McKnight in the chest. Big as he was, about all it did was punch a hole in his chest and knock him unconscious. Robbie was going to shoot him again when he thought it more fitting to tie McKnight to that abandoned cabin so that the last thing the scoundrel saw was a wall of water coming his way."

"At some point," Manny said, "there must have been a struggle for Robbie to lose his dog tags."

Amos shook his head. "After Robbie had tied McKnight to that cabin with rope, he draped his dog tags around his neck. Robbie—above else—was a Lakota warrior and he wanted people to know years afterward just who had killed McKnight."

Amos looked longingly at the sliding glass doors. "Now if you fellers will join me, they are serving Salisbury steak, followed by a night of Bingo. I hope to win more Polident."

Epilogue

**The resort of American Island,
off the shores of Chamberlain, South Dakota
along the banks of the Missouri River, 1952.**

He awoke, the pain in his chest feeling like a cow sitting on him. He felt the blood weeping out of his chest, his breathing labored. Raspy. His lungs filling with fluid, he was sure, for this wasn't the first time he had been shot.

He tried standing. Fell back down, screaming in agony. What the hell? He felt thick ropes encircling his legs, shackles like the MPs were wont to put on a feller if he got rowdy,

But this wasn't the stockade and this wasn't the Army. This—he realized—was the small island in the middle of the slow-flowing Missouri River, and he was roped to something. He tried reaching the rope around his ankles but the rope around his wrists prevented movement.

His vision blurred, his coordination lost as he fidgeted with the rope before pain shot through him once again and he leaned back against... he craned his neck around. He was chained to the corner of the last log cabin on the resort island, its roof collapsed, the only cabin no one wanted hauled out of here before...

Was this the day? The day the Corps of Engineers were to flood the river and the island he was a prisoner on?

He sucked in painful breaths, feeling the sticky, half-coagulated blood on his chest. Someone had shot him. He struggled to remember what had brought him here or who he'd been with but all he could think was this was *the* day.

He grabbed onto the corner of the log cabin to try standing, but the pain in his chest sliced through him once more. He fell back onto the ground when his hand fell on a chain around his neck. A thin chain. A chain threaded through the hole in the dog tag and memories returned. Of the fight with… he closed his eyes, fighting to remember how he had gotten here to the island. He was remembering who had shot him when the roar of water—for there was no sound like the sound of millions of gallons of water rushing at a man—reached his ears.

Closer.

He strained against the ropes and grunted with all his might, but they were like steel and he was but flesh and blood.

Closer the water came.

Louder.

Mixing with his screams.

Threatening to explode in his ears, the sound so intense. So malevolent.

He screamed anew as the first rush of water washed over his body.

Soon, he screamed no more.

Acknowledgments

My thanks to Doug Greenway, director of the Corn Palace (Mitchell, SD), Mitchell Library director Kevin Kenkel, and long-time resident of the Mitchell area Dennis Geidel for their knowledge of that area and the world's biggest bird feeder, the World's Only Corn Palace.

To the Cozard Memorial Library for their research material about American Island Resort.

To the Army Corps of Engineers for their material about Lake Francis Case and American Island.

To my wife, Heather, who—once again—stood by me as I pulled my hair out, fleshing out this story, *Death Under the Deluge*, while playing footloose and free with particular times involving the flooding of Lake Francis Case.

About the Author

C. M. Wendelboe entered the law enforcement profession when he was discharged from the Marines as the Vietnam War was winding down.

In the 1970s, he worked in South Dakota. He later moved to Gillette, Wyoming, and found his niche, where he remained a sheriff's deputy for over twenty-five years. In addition, he was a longtime firearms instructor at the local college and within the community.

During his thirty-eight-year career in law enforcement, he served successful stints as police chief, policy adviser, and other supervisory roles for several agencies. Yet, he has always been most proud of "working the street" in the Wild West. He was a patrol supervisor when he retired to pursue his true vocation as a fiction writer.

Wendelboe is a prolific author of murder mysteries with a Western flair and traditional Westerns. He writes the Spirit Road Mysteries, the Bitter Wind Mystery series, as well as the Nelson Lane Frontier Mysteries, and the Tucker Ashley Western series. Wendelboe now lives and writes in Cheyenne, Wyoming.

If you enjoyed this book,
please consider writing a review
and sharing it with other readers.

Many of our authors are happy to participate in
Book Club and Reader Group discussions.
For more information, contact us at info@encirclepub.com.

Thank you,
Encircle Publications

For news about more exciting new fiction, join us at:

Facebook: www.facebook.com/encirclepub

Instagram: www.instagram.com/encirclepublications

Sign up for the Encircle Publications newsletter:
eepurl.com/cs8taP

Printed in the USA
CPSIA information can be obtained
at www.ICGtesting.com
JSHW080922060923
47891JS00001B/31